D1486378

WAY OF THE WORLD

WAY OF THE WORLD

The Forgotten Years: 1995-6

AUBERON WAUGH

Century · London

This edition published by Century Books Limited 1997

1 3 5 7 9 10 8 6 4 2

Copyright © 1997 **The Daily Telegraph** and Auberon Waugh

All rights reserved

Auberon Waugh has asserted his right under the Copyright,
Designs and Patents Act, 1988, to be identified as
the author of this work.

Century
Random House UK Ltd,
20 Vauxhall Bridge Road, London SW1V 2SA

Arrow Books Ltd
Random House UK Ltd,
20 Vauxhall Bridge Road, London SW1V 2SA

Random House Australia (Pty) Limited
20 Alfred Street, Milsons Point, Sydney,
New South Wales 2061, Australia

Random House New Zealand Limited
18 Poland Road, Glenfield
Auckland 10, New Zealand

Random House South Africa (Pty) Limited
Endulini, 5a Jubilee Road,
Parktown 2193, South Africa

Random House UK Limited Reg No 954009

A CIP catalogue record for this book
is available from the British Library

Papers used by Random House UK Limited are natural,
recyclable products made from wood grown in sustainable
forests. The manufacturing processes conform to the
environmental regulations of the country of origin.

ISBN 0 7126 7893 X

Typeset by SX Composing DTP, Rayleigh, Essex
Printed and bound in the United Kingdom by
Mackays of Chatham plc, Chatham, Kent

INTRODUCTION
by Auberon Waugh

The first **Way of the World** collection under my authorship covered five years, 1990-1995. This second volume covers only two. Tumultuous public demand may provide part of the reason for this unseemly haste, but the chief reason is to be found in the tragic and untimely death of William Rushton at the age of 59 on December 11, 1996. Willie had illustrated every **Way of the World** column I wrote, three times a week, seldom fewer than 50 weeks a year, never missing a deadline. His inspired drawings used to wing their way from Australia or strange northern cities where he would go from time to time to entertain the masses, bringing a taste of his warmth and geniality from the dourest and sootiest of them.

The last picture he drew – showing the author as an Agony Uncle, is also the one which has been chosen for the cover of this book. He prepared it in advance, reckoning that he might not feel up to drawing anything immediately after the heart operation from which, in fact, he was not to recover. It appeared five days after his death, and remained at the top of the column thereafter.

It seemed obvious to end this second volume at that moment, although, as I say, the column has continued to limp along without him. The immense time which modern methods and new technology demand for the printing and publication of a new book – in sales conferences, briefings, e-mail consultations, and the imponderable rituals of the booksellers' buying departments – adds a certain poignancy to my chosen title *The Forgotten Years*. If it had appeared weeks or days after that nice Mr Major's disappearance from the political scene on May 1st 1997, the assumption that these would prove to be the forgotten years of Britain's post-war history might have been seen as mildly playful, even cheeky. However, since the book trade could not possibly put copies into the shops before the autumn, in preparation for the Christmas market, the prophecy will, I imagine, have become glum fact. Few people under the age of 17 will have the faintest idea who Mr Major was.

Did anything, in fact, happen in those two years, apart from the death of William Rushton at the very end of them? Willie's death caused enormous grief all over the country, as I discovered, in the months after the event. But even that is forgotten after a time. Journalists and entertainers cannot hope to be remembered for long. It is not part of the deal, and some will judge it presumptuous even to put collected journalism into a book, as if it were aspiring to be literature. The best journalism is often so topical as to be incomprehensible within a matter of months – or so I consoled myself, as I leafed through the **Way of the World** files.

If nothing happened in those two years, the best possible monument to them must be a volume of similarly un-remembered, largely incomprehensible journalism. But there is a deeper significance in the word 'forgotten' than is to be found in the idea of something which is merely unremembered. The first suggests an activity of the intellect – if not of the will – the second an absence of activity. What will be forgotten about these unremembered years, I would suggest, is how extraordinarily happy they were. Towards the end of my introduction to the first volume, I wrote: 'I would guess, in fact, that we are living in the happiest, most prosperous and carefree society in the history of Britain.' The purpose of this book is not to remind us of these years, but to celebrate the fact that they will have been completely forgotten by the time anyone gets round to reading it.

Cynics will say that a further purpose of the book is to make some money, have a second bite at the apple. On this occasion, they will be wrong. I have published numerous volumes of my collected journalism – from the *Evening Standard* (**Country Topics** 1974); from *Private Eye* (**Four Crowded Years** 1976, **A Turbulent Decade** 1986); from the *New Statesman* (**In the Lion's Den** 1978) and from the *Spectator* (**Another Voice** 1986) – not to mention assorted other publications (**Waugh on Wine**, 1986) but the *Telegraph* is the only employer which insisted on taking a huge slice of the royalties. This must be seen as part of the exciting new age of accountancy power, whereby the relationship between employer and employee, far from being governed by the affection and loyalty of two people working together for a common purpose, is seen as an ongoing confrontation between opposed interests, each determined to screw the maximum advantage from the other.

No doubt this system brings many benefits, but it is alien to the more genial tradition of my trade, and rather puts a blight on the idea of voluntary effort. When they told me they wanted a 1,500-word Introduction to the present volume, I groaned. What is there to say about a book which should be able to speak for itself? A similar, unworthy thought may have inspired my decision to have no part in choosing the extracts for inclusion, taken from some 285,000 words published in the two-year period, although I conscientiously persuaded myself that an author is the worst judge of his own work, and the task would be better undertaken by someone else.

In the event, it was selflessly undertaken by Mr Mark Booth, of Century publishers. It was a monumental task, and I wince, sometimes, when I think of all the rubbish he had to read as he conscientiously ploughed his way through those 285,000 words, some written in a state of exaltation, others in dejected sobriety. I do not suppose for a moment that Century paid him a farthing extra for the weekend he spent burning the midnight oil in his country home. To that extent, at least, the present volume should be seen as a labour of love. I hope he will accept my heartfelt thanks for his unquenchable enthusiasm, his energy and the fine result he has achieved.

Further thanks are due to the Editor of the *Daily Telegraph*, Mr Charles Moore, who took over from Max Hastings in 1995. I first worked for Charles when he became Editor of *Spectator* as a young lad in his twenties – a magazine for which I had been writing regular weekly columns for some 17 years. He never treated me with anything but kindness and generosity – there is no doubt whose side he takes in the perpetual war between journalists and accountants.

These are the things which happened. Everything else is make-believe, distortion, special pleading and untruth, worthy only to be forgotten. In welcoming readers to this celebration of the forgotten years, I feel I should repeat an earlier warning, that the density and richness of material in this book make it unsuitable for prolonged reading. Copies should be kept in every room, as well as at your place of work, as solace in moments of affliction, an inexpensive way of impressing your colleagues. I hope everyone who buys it has a happy Christmas.

Combe Florey
March 1997

Wednesday, May 17, 1995

Animal fun

IS IT because we have despaired of the human race that so much of the news nowadays is devoted to animals? In Newmarket, they have discovered a pony which gives a ringing sound out of its ears. Scientists at St George's Hospital, in South London, claim that a bacterium carried by certain of Britain's seven million cats kills 6,000 people a year from peptic ulcers and stomach cancer. This is far more than the total killed on the roads, let alone by drunk drivers.

In New York there is a scare about killer mice whose droppings cause a pulmonary syndrome which has a 54 per cent chance of proving fatal. At least two people are thought to have died. Knowing how sensitive the Americans are about death, the Health Commission has set up a 'mouse hotline' which has been inundated with calls. In Los Angeles an increasing number of joggers complain that they have been mauled to death and eaten by mountain lions, called cougars, as they go about their lawful business. As many as eight are believed to have suffered this gruesome fate in the past 10 years. Now cougars have been seen prowling near schools, and there is talk of closing the schools.

Giant mice are being bred which may prove an important food source in the Third World; sexless pigs and bullocks, which do not need castrating; almost featherless chickens are already

1

available – they grow faster and do not need plucking. Next we shall see featherless four-legged chickens, in acknowledgement that most people prefer the legs.

The ultimate improvement will be a beef steak which grows by itself on a plate, without any of the other parts – hooves and horns, neck, shanks and lights – which Americans do not wish to eat.

But perhaps the only real reason we pretend to be interested in animals is that humans have become so boring.

Saturday, May 20, 1995

Secret society

TREMENDOUS over-excitement has been caused in the secretive ranks of Vespa, the Venerable Society for the Protection of Adulterers, over the Bishop of Edinburgh's announcement that adultery is not a sin, that it is caused by genetic inheritance and should not be frowned upon.

It has been suggested that the Bishop should be asked to become the society's chaplain, but I am not entirely sure that we need one. Our purpose is not to encourage adultery, merely to balance the crazed hacks of the Murdoch empire who seek to spread misery by exposing it.

The Bishop does not have an elegant turn of phrase. Complaining that he had been misrepresented, he told reporters he had been 'stitched up' by the media because he liked to 'shoot from the lip', adding: 'I wish you guys had a good war to cover somewhere.'

This sort of sentiment does not come well from a bishop. Although it is true that vocations for the ministry increase in wartime, it is not often suggested that the church should start a war for that reason.

When asked about his own experience of the matter in question, he replied: 'If you expect me to get personal, get lost.'

No, I don't think he strikes quite the right tone to make a successful chaplain. In fact, I might veto his membership. So far the Venerable Society has only one official member, its president. All the rest are secret.

2

A man of talents

PERHAPS we should rejoice that a John Cleese anti-smoking television commercial has been banned from appearing with children's programmes on the grounds that it was unacceptably offensive. But I would be sorry if Mr Cleese disappeared entirely from the advertising scene.

His advertisements for the Liberal Democrats – or was it the now defunct Social Democrats? – must have helped to convince many voters that these allegedly middle-of-the-road parties are, if anything, even more bossy, self-important and odious than the two great parties whose position they seek to usurp.

His disgusting advertisements in support of the police terror on the roads must have made many realise there are worse crimes than driving home after luncheon or dinner, that police efforts to concentrate on the minor incidence of road mortality hide a sinister attempt to distract attention from the collapse of law and order. Next, he should be asked to advertise the benefits of McDonald's hamburgers, Pepsi Cola and brightly coloured kagouls in place of ordinary clothes.

Wednesday, June 7, 1995

The new angle

IT IS easy to criticise President Yeltsin's refusal to participate in a ceremony to mark Stalin's murder of thousands of Polish officers at Katyn during the war, but we must remember that it was Yeltsin who, in 1992, gave the Poles documents signed by Stalin ordering the murders. There can be no question of a further cover-up.

The Russian leader, who sent a deputy in his place, agreed on the need for general reconciliation and atonement. What deterred him from the grand gesture on this occasion was that the Poles have suddenly started demanding compensation for all those people killed 55 years ago.

Russia is a poor country, and if it has to start paying compensation for everyone murdered by Stalin it will never get out of the woods. But the spectre of compensation must hang over every initiative, nowadays.

When we read that Mr Major is bravely sending another 5,000 British troops to add to the general participation in Bosnia's civil war, our first reaction is to cheer and wave Union flags. Then, if we are tax-payers, we will have to start thinking of all the compensation we must pay to any of our boys who stubs his toe, or has a disagreeable experience which later causes bad dreams. Perhaps we should not look at things in this way: it does rather take the glamour out of the news.

Saturday, June 10, 1995

An unmixed blessing

THE Government is expected to commission research – no doubt costing hundreds of thousands of pounds – into whether the National Lottery causes addictive or excessive gambling, especially among the poor. I suppose this is typical of our new style of government. The National Lottery is probably the best idea it ever had, certainly the cleverest. Inevitably, as with anything new, there is opposition to it. So the opposition must be appeased by spending large sums of money to make some obvious points which any of us could have guessed without spending money on research.

It is not true that the lottery has created an obsessive gambling culture, but it has certainly created a settled optimism in society which is no less welcome for being unfounded.

In our heart of hearts, none of us seriously doubts that we will win the jackpot, although our reason tells us otherwise. Our knowledge is a secret one, seldom communicated to others, but it adds a certain consciousness of our own superiority as we go about our daily tasks. We no longer look with hatred and envy at our neighbour's superior house or car; we secretly plan something much better.

We cheerfully spend what money we have, reckoning that it cannot be very long before the lottery transports us to an entirely different plane of consumption. We debate which of our friends and relatives will benefit, which of them won't.

4

Wednesday, June 14, 1995

A boy for ever?

WHEN I joined the All Hallows troop of the Boy Scouts I swore on my honour to do my best to do my duty to God and the King, to help other people at all times and to obey the Scout Law. The Scoutmaster who took my oath, the late Jocelyn Trappes-Lomax, believed this promise held for life. Nervously reflecting on this, I sometimes wonder whose life is involved. Not only has Mr Trappes-Lomax died since that awesome ceremony, but so, of course, has King George VI.

The Scout Law is no light matter. As I remember, it required me to be at all times:

Trusty, Loyal, Helpful
Brotherly, Courteous, Kind,
Obedient, Smiling, Thrifty,
Pure of Body and Mind.

I sometimes wonder whether anybody with all these qualities

would be able to earn a living in journalism. Surely, at 55, I am too old to be bound by a promise made when I was 11, below the age of legal responsibility?

Of one thing I am absolutely sure. If the present Chief Scout, reputed to be called Garth Morrison (in my day it was always a peer, or at very least a baronet), succeeds in removing the oath of loyalty to the monarchy, replacing it with some sort of exclamation in approval of the community and the environment, I shall regard myself as absolved from any loyalty to Scouting.

If any Scout comes to my door demanding a Bob a Job or whatever is the modern equivalent, I shall make lewd suggestions to him until he goes away.

Saturday, June 17, 1995

Give them space

RECENTLY I met a very nice Labour candidate for a constituency in north Somerset. He seemed thoroughly sound on every point, like all these New Labour people. But when I asked him how he would vote on the great hunting issue which threatens to turn our once-proud country into a nation of cringing slaves tyrannised by urban animal sentimentalists who can't tell a deer from a sheep, he demurred.

Although his natural instinct was to allow freedom of choice, he said he would have to vote for a ban on hunting; otherwise his children would make his life unsupportable.

It is in this context that we should consider the new information, supplied by an NOP survey, that the average British father spends an average of five minutes a day with his children. Five minutes is obviously too long if we are to avoid contamination from all the ignorant Left-wing rubbish about animal rights and global warming that has been put into their heads by idle, halfwitted teachers.

There is a rumour that Mr Blair intends to pass a law requiring all fathers to spend at least an hour a day with their children, talking about rainforests, pop groups and suchlike drivel. It is at such moments that we welcome the news of a collapse in male fertility – brought about, apparently, by DDT, the miraculous chemical which has all but removed the curse of malaria from the world.

In sensible countries such as Australia, with a population of 5.7 to the square mile compared to England's 950, they spray all visitors with DDT on arrival to stop them breeding. On the other hand, when the last kangaroo has gone blind and died, Australia may be rather a lonely place to live.

Reconciliation time

'WE HAVE been trying for years to get some form of reconciliation from the Japanese government,' said Mr Titherington when told that the Archbishop of Canterbury had appealed for reconciliation between the two countries. 'What we want from the Japanese government is £14,000 compensation and an apology for each of the people they ill-treated.'

It is plainly true that many Japanese behaved abominably in the war. Although I was too young and in the wrong place to have any direct experience, I saw the film *Bridge on the River Kwai* in the Fifties and it gave me an idea.

It has always been difficult to reconcile the cheerful, well mannered, intelligent, attentive people we meet in Japan today with the screaming monsters in the film. John Keegan, this newspaper's defence editor, believes that Japanese troops were so maltreated by their officers that their characters deteriorated. This may go some way to explaining their disgraceful behaviour, but watching the film nearly 40 years ago another possible explanation occurred to me.

If you remember, Colonel Alec Guinness, assisted by William Holden and Jack Hawkins, all British PoWs, are building a bridge as part of the Burma railway, to help the Japanese advance. Guinness decides, for reasons of morale, to build the best damned bridge the Japanese have ever seen. All the Brits throw themselves into the task with fanatical energy.

It occurs to me that this was Japan's first experience of British working habits. What appeared to us as demented over-enthusiasm probably appeared to them as deliberate slacking. Hence their furious demeanour. Not having been there at the time, I cannot be sure I am right, but any idea which might help towards a reconciliation without costing too much money is surely to be encouraged.

7

Recipe for disaster

NOT many of us, I imagine, spent much time reading the Government White Paper called *Our Future Housing*. We tend to rely on others to read it for us and provide an accurate summary. My heart sank to read last Wednesday's heading: 'Gummer pledge of decent home for every family.'

Have they learnt nothing, these wretched Conservatives? Why on earth should every family have a decent home? How does Mr Gummer dare make such a promise which can only raise expectations within a dependency culture which saps the morals of the young and has already destroyed the economic vitality of the nation?

The existence of slums and near-slums is essential not only to the work-ethic but also to give the Left-wing conscience an opportunity to exercise itself and Anglican clergymen something to preach about.

On Tuesday the Archbishop of Canterbury demanded that greater subsidies be given to housing the poor at the expense of tax-relief for home owners. Personally I do not propose to pay the slightest attention to anything Dr Carey has to say on faith and morals until he wears a nose ring. But one can see the poor man has to have some anchor for his platitudes.

Think of all those rich Left-wing housewives in Islington who would have nothing to feel guilty about. It is their *concern* about these things which gives them the moral superiority so essential to their self-respect. Think of all the BBC social documentary programme-makers who need slums as horseflies need manure. They would all be out of a job, just like everyone else.

O gentle sleep

WHETHER or not nice Mr Major was wise to resign from what we humorously describe as the leadership of the Conservative Party, we can't possibly deny that he has added immeasurably to the gaiety of the nation in these past few days.

It is held against Michael Heseltine that he has already had one heart attack and might easily die in office, if he becomes Prime Minister on the second ballot. I do not see that this should count against him. A few old ladies might cry, but we are not, as

8

a nation, particularly attached to our political leaders and most of us could survive the shock. Then at the very least we would have all the fun of watching another one being chosen.

Heseltine may not cut such a good figure as Lord Howe, but at 62 he is the only candidate of respectable age. It would be madness to elect a young, male Briton knowing what we now know about them. Look what happened to Baring's bank when it decided to recruit young British talent.

Redwood, at 44, and Portillo, at 42, have just got their O-levels behind them. They haven't even had time to ruin a merchant bank since leaving school. They have no experience of anything. How can they hope to be allowed to preside over the ruin of our once-great country? Nice Mr Major, at the more respectable age of 52, has still to convince us that he has finished preparing for his A-levels.

Heseltine is reasonably sound on Europe, lacking the suicidal urge to expose this indolent, easy-going nation to competition from the United States and Pacific Rim. But he is not at all sound on welfare, the insidious force which is slowly turning us into a nation of whingeing unemployables.

We may doubt that either Portillo (who was supposed to be cutting state expenditure as Financial Secretary) or Redwood (who now threatens to increase expenditure on health) will do anything useful against welfare when in power, but Heseltine won't even make the right noises.

Perhaps the best thing would be for him to win the second ballot, introduce a single European currency (based on the *denarius* or silver penny), and then expire.

This might provide the historic opportunity for the nation to decide it didn't really want another Prime Minister; that we can all manage perfectly well without any new laws, or elections, or political thinkers to bore us all.

The states of Heseltine on the empty plinth beside Nelson's column, Crusader-like in armour, will be known as The Sleeping Prime Minister, and everyone will walk past on tiptoe.

Monday, July 3, 1995

Reconciliation later

I RATHER like the look of Barry Leach's twin sculpture, called

Reconciliation, to be put in the ruins of Coventry Cathedral next month, although one can never tell until one has seen the thing, and one is generally right to be suspicious. An identical pair is to be put in Hiroshima to commemorate the 50th anniversary of the dropping of the atom bomb. Richard Branson, who is paying for the sculptures, believes they will be 'symbols of friendship between the two peoples'.

This has not gone down at all well with the anti-reconciliation lobby among the nation's oldies. In the new spirit of vindictiveness, those who suffered at Japanese hands 50 years ago have grown more and more bitter with the passing of the years. Atom bombs on Hiroshima and Nagasaki were not enough for them. They want an apology and compensation before there can be any talk of reconciliation.

I begin to have the feeling that the time has come for another war. We have done the Germans and Japanese, but Swedes are particularly annoying people. They have no body hair and never stop grumbling about all the acid rain and atmospheric pollution we send them. Their behaviour in the last war was not distinguished, and now they have started a fashion for arresting any of their citizens guilty of sexual impropriety abroad.

Needless to say, the British government proposes to copy them, but I feel that Hugh Grant has suffered enough. It is time to stamp out these Swedish practices once and for all.

There are obvious attractions in the idea of a short, sharp war with Sweden. After it, the Swedes will be required to apologise, pay compensation and put abstract sculptures on the theme of Reconciliation in all their public places.

Teach them to sing and dance

GREAT anger has been reported throughout Britain at a rumour that nearly £80 million of National Lottery money may be spent on the Royal Opera House in Covent Garden. Our old friend Terry Dicks, MP, the much-loved Tory Member for Hayes and Harlington, has been asked for another of his scintillating observations.

'It's a scandal that lottery money, paid for by ordinary folk, isn't going to medical research but being squandered on the rich who go to the opera.'

The idea that ordinary working folk are more in need of medical research than they are in need of the spiritual and aesthetic benefits of opera strikes me as deeply insulting. It may be part of the new Conservative ethos to insult ordinary working folk, since most people now think of themselves as middle class, but to suggest that they need special research into their medical problems is as untrue as it is rude.

It was always a great mistake to apportion money from the National Lottery to specific causes. It should have been lumped in with the general fund of government revenue, and been spent like other government revenue, on servicing the loans from previous overspending.

Otherwise the matter of spending the lottery money will be left to Mr Murdoch's stinking, lower-class newspapers and their imitators to decide. The effect of this is to reduce our cultural level nationwide to that of such proletarian centres as Coventry, Rochdale, Salford and Barnsley, now recognised as the four most unpleasant places to live in the whole of Britain. If only someone would teach the inhabitants of Barnsley about opera and ballet, they might have something to look forward to do while waiting to win the lottery.

Monday, July 10, 1995

Let them eat worms

IT WAS inevitable that as soon as we had enjoyed a few days of reasonable summer weather, the country would suffer an acute water shortage. It can rain for 100 days, but if the sun shines on the 101st there will be hosepipe restrictions on the 102nd.

More than a million homes were described as being hit by a water crisis last week, with householders forbidden to water their gardens. Another headline assured us that water supplied to more than 10 million homes contained so much lead that it threatened the intelligence of small children.

Perhaps this explains the extraordinary poor performance of so many 14-year-olds asked to write their appreciation of a *Romeo and Juliet* video: 'Juliet is sposter marry parris . . . Romeo user have is head in the cloweds . . .' etc.

If our water really has this deleterious effect on young people, we should rejoice whenever there is a water shortage and pour what little water remains all over the carrot patch. But of course

11

it is nonsense. There is less lead in the water now than there has ever been in the past 100 years. British water has reached its highest standards of purity since records began. As children, we all drank infinitely more lead than the present crowd, yet we were writing literate, articulate essays by the time we were 10.

It is no good blaming lead in the water, and not much use blaming the teachers, because nothing can change them now. Those who care about their children's education should send them to France or Kenya – anywhere except the local comprehensive. But the truth is that not many of us care all that much. The great thing is to take a more positive attitude. Our children do not shine at reading, writing or arithmetic but they may excel in more 'creative fields'. Nothing can alter the fact that British kids are the best in the world when it comes to modelling Plasticine worms.

At the root of it

THERE IS always a tendency to look for root causes of riots, muggings and the other things that vex us about the modern age. Are they the result of poverty, racial tension, poor education, insufficient policemen or health organisers? In what direction should the politicians throw our money?

One might suggest that evil is the root cause of all these things, just as it is the root cause of Lockerbie and poisonous gas released into the Tokyo underground railway, but that is too theological a concept for the present age. It might be more acceptable to suggest masculinity as the root cause. The important thing about muggers and burglars is not that they are black or white but that they are 80 per cent male.

This is not the same as saying that 80 per cent of males are violent criminals, of course. Some are very well behaved. Their problems may be summarised in a Danish report that records a marked drop in the sexual urge of Western man. 'About a third of our patients shun sex. This is far and away the biggest sexual problem of our hemisphere,' says Dr Bo Mohn, professor of sexology at the Rigshospitalet. 'We place greater demands on each other and this gives an angst of not being able to live up to requirements.'

It is all very well giving women the right to kill any men who harass or abuse them. Soon it may be necessary to give them the right to kill any man who doesn't. Even this fudges the issue of whether males are really fit candidates to be released into the community, or whether they should be kept in secure hospitals, supervised by women.

Wednesday, July 12, 1995

Bring out the good

A HATRED of flower beds seemed to be chief motivation behind scenes of violence which broke out in the village of Tickhill, South Yorkshire, where teenage thugs allegedly beat the 60-year-old mayor senseless after he remonstrated with them for vandalising one.

Teenagers had destroyed the flower bed before, so it might be said that the flower-fanciers had been warned. The mayor and a group of friends had built the beds themselves and tended them lovingly, but perhaps they did not ask the young community whether flower beds were acceptable in the first place. All of which must underline the importance of *consultation*. The great thing about teenagers is to find out what they want, and give it to them.

If they can't think of anything they want, you have to think of it for them. Tickhill provided them with a youth club, but they didn't use it. It seems to me that if these victims of the playschool education theories are to be saved, they must be found some voluntary 'work' which they will take a pride in.

Bat conservation seems the obvious answer, but bats fly

13

around rather a lot and are quite hard to look after. On Sunday, I read of proposals to make our native black rat – the *rattus rattus* – a protected species. This rat, carrier of all the plagues of the Middle Ages and most of modern times, is in danger of being driven out by the brown or Norway rat (which arrived from South East Asia during the 18th century).

If every British male teenager, after his first conviction, was given a black rat to look after, I honestly think it might save a lot of them.

Is this humorous?

MY OWN theory about the death of Vincent Foster – that he was caught smoking in the White House and shot out of hand by a member of the First Lady's Secret Service bodyguard – does not rely on an elaborate conspiracy. Both the *Washington Post* and *Newsweek* have answered criticism of the American media's gigantic cover-up by suggesting that the criticism relies on a conspiracy theory, which they then mock and repudiate.

The scandal of Foster's death is not that someone should have shot an Arkansas hillbilly – any of us could do that. It might even have been an accident. No, the scandal concerns the attitude of the 'responsible' press to these strange events.

What is particularly shocking about the cover-up is not that there was any conspiracy or connivance in it (they might have been patriotically concerned about the national interest) but that there wasn't any connivance at all. Not a single telephone call was made. It was an instant, gut reaction on the part of all three of America's 'quality' newspapers to ignore any of the more lurid explanations and settle for whichever was dullest and most respectable. Perhaps loyalty to the Clintons and to their briefly held socialist ideas was a factor, but I should explain that the American journalist operates on a set of ethical principles entirely different to those of his British counterpart. The American journalist will not print anything as fact unless it has been confirmed by an official source. To do anything else would be sensation-seeking and irresponsible.

On the other hand, the American journalist is happy to have information supplied and commentary on it controlled by advertisers and pressure groups. An English journalist distrusts official sources of information, finding them tendentious and unreliable, and would regard any newspaper or magazine with the greatest contempt if it deferred to advertisers or pressure groups.

The sad truth is that although we and Americans talk the same language, our attitudes to life are so different that we can scarcely communicate with each other.

Intelligent, respectable Americans are quite genuinely *not interested* in what happened to Vincent Foster. They will not be able to understand one word of this column.

Saturday, July 15, 1995

Too many apologies

IN THE course of his long apology to womankind throughout the ages, the Pope deplored the way women 'sometimes continue to be valued more for their physical appearance than for their skill, their professionalism, their intellectual abilities . . .'

I hope that his Holiness is not suggesting we should ignore feminine beauty, or fail to value it. Some women are beautiful and some less so, it is true, but that does not make it any more unfair to value feminine beauty than to value feminine skill, feminine professionalism, feminine intellectual abilities . . . all these gifts are unevenly bestowed. Who is to say which is more important?

At a time when everybody seems to be apologising, the Pope has got off lightly. Jonathan Aitken faces moronic resignation demands from the Rev Don Witts, communications officer for Canterbury diocese, after a woman – how intellectual, skilled and professional I do not know – told the *Sunday Mirror* she had sexual intercourse with him (Aitken, not Witts) 15 years ago.

Poor Hugh Grant, struggling to maintain his affability after three weeks of relentless hounding by the world's media, has seen his beautiful friend Miss Hurley reduced to sphinx-like misery. Typically, the world's media blame it on Grant's ludicrously trivial offence rather than their own behaviour.

I think the Pope has got off too lightly. He is wrong to make these gestures to Women's Lib, whose driving force is largely destructive, evil and embittered. Perhaps the Church was wrong to burn the ugliest and nastiest of the sisterhood as witches all those years ago, but it seemed a good idea at the time and nothing is to be gained by apologising now. The Pope was not responsible, nor was I, and the only result of apologising must be to give comfort to the new generation of witches about their evil purposes.

Another American mystery

I WAS relieved to learn that police investigating the death of Glen Pelmear, 33, in a public lavatory at Ryde, on the Isle of Wight, now treat it as an accident.

Pelmear died instantly when he electrocuted himself on an all-metal lavatory. It was originally thought that malevolent persons had rigged up a connection with the broken 240-volt light fitting.

No reason was given for such an outrage. Like Lockerbie, it might have been designed to argue some abstruse point in Middle-Eastern or Gulf politics, or some animal activists might have been arguing the case against vivisection or factory farming or hunting. Or it might just have been mischief for mischief's sake. But, fortunately, it appears to have been an accident. But one mystery remains.

If a 33-year-old builder can be killed instantly on a metal lavatory made 'live' because of a broken light fitting, why do the Americans, when they wish to electrocute each other, require an infernal contraption using tens of thousands of volts which causes the eyes to pop out, the blood to boil, and takes 20 minutes to kill the victim? American thoroughness and American preference, perhaps.

We should think of that little electric lavatory seat every time we hear an American call for air strikes in the Bosnian civil war. They will cause a lot of damage, and Americans will enjoy them very much, but I doubt they will achieve anything.

Monday, July 17, 1995

A moral dilemma

PERHAPS there are some floating voters who will be persuaded to vote Conservative by Mr Major's decision to make school games compulsory, spending £300 million a year of National Lottery money on sports facilities. If I were a floating voter, that would not be my reaction.

16

Every school I attended had compulsory games, and I spent a large part of my time avoiding them. It would appear that in the eternal war between swots and hearties, the hearties, with their moronic, Nazi-style emphasis on physical endurance and team spirit, have officially come out on top.

As further salt in the wound, we are to have a British Academy of Sport as our answer to the French Academy of arts, sciences and letters. I hope every swot in the country will join with me on calling down a curse on Mr Major's head for humiliating us all still further and pointing out to the world what a stupid country we have become. Perhaps it is all we could expect when we chose a PT instructor *manqué* as Prime Minister.

Those of us who detested organised games at school are now left in a moral dilemma: are we justified in supporting a National Lottery that will inflict so much misery and oppression on our kind? If we don't, how are we to secure the £15 million or so necessary for a comfortable, secure old age? Perhaps, on balance, we should let the young suffer.

Monday, July 24, 1995

Highest motives

THERE is something wonderful about the *Sun*'s current campaign to persuade its loutish, grunting readers to give up the National Lottery in protest against the Arts Council's award to the Royal Opera House. We are asked to believe that more than 15,000 have vowed not to buy another ticket until the money is spent differently – medical research seems to be the predominant enthusiasm.

I do not know who gave them the idea that they can lose money gambling and still direct how the money they have lost should be spent. Perhaps it is part of the new 'education' that any concept of losing is unacceptable.

The *Sun*'s motives in whipping up hatred against this imaginary 'élite' of educated and cultivated people are clear enough: 'Up yer arias!' it shouted on Saturday in its diatribe against putting 'rich bums on opera-house seats'.

If ever *Sun* readers lift their snouts from their newspaper's hideous, half-naked women to glimpse the sublime through music, opera, the pictorial and plastic arts or literature, then

17

they will never look at the *Sun* again.

It is the *Sun*'s function to keep its readers ignorant and smug in their own unpleasant, hypocritical, proletarian culture. So they thought they were aiding medical research when they entered for the National Lottery, did they? No doubt they thought the same when they trustingly entered the *Sun*'s £50,000 'Instant Cash Game', also announced on Saturday.

Trying to be fair

CAN it be true what I read in Friday's newspaper, that students at Leeds University can now take a degree in Yorkshire studies? Unless it is a cruel joke, they can become Bachelors of Art through studying a range of Yorkshire subjects from Cricket and Its Heroes or Pigeons and Whippets as Working Class Hobbies to Fish 'n' Chips or Yorkshire Pudding. The head of this course, Yorkshire's own Dr Tony Donajgrodzki, explains: 'It involves a lot of hard work, dealing with the social, economic and cultural history of Yorkshire.'

If true, it may point to a final solution in the great problem of educating Anglo-Saxon males without recourse to corporal punishment. A distressing characteristic of these Anglo-Saxon males is that they don't take kindly to education, needing to be beaten frequently and unjustly before they toe the line.

Now that beating children is frowned upon, not to say forbidden, the best expedient may be to invite them to eat large amounts of Yorkshire pudding and fish 'n' chips, then give them a degree for it. This will appeal to everyone as being the *fairest* solution.

Another possible way out of the education impasse may be found in a summer programme brochure from the University of Bristol's department of continuing education: 'counselling and personal development courses'. About 40 courses are offered, for which fees swing between £35 for a single course on Paradise Island Discs – 'an opportunity to explore your personal history through the resonances of much-loved music'; participants will be encouraged to bring along music which holds 'significance for them and to explore its personal meaning' – to £240 for a four-day workshop which is 'person-centred in style and values and will provide opportunities to extend knowledge, skills and awareness'.

My own choice might be the two-day workshop without words.

18

For £80, counsellors and those in training will be introduced to 'the concept of silence and its potential power in the counselling relationship:

'The use of silence will be an integral part of the course and participants will be encouraged to participate fully in the processing of this. Silence and its effective use as part of a helping relationship will be introduced and explored. Participants will be expected to spend part of the course in silence.'

Between giving degrees in Yorkshire Pudding and teaching the arts of silent counselling, I should think we might have solved the problem of today's young people. But probably not.

Wednesday, July 26, 1995

Recessional

AS Parliament settles into its summer recess – at 89 days, the longest in 15 years – a wonderful spirit of ease and well-being settles on the country. For three months we shall be spared noises and sights which have become particularly unpleasing to us over the years; above all, we shall be spared the constant activity, the production of unnecessary new laws to irritate and oppress us.

The longer the MPs stay away, the more apparent it will become to everybody that we are much better off without them. They should be encouraged to stay away for the rest of their lives, as I urged striking steel workers at Consett all those years ago when we were still threatened by a steel industry.

The best thing would be to spend the next three months refurbishing Charles Barry's magnificent Palace of Westminster as a luxury hotel for Japanese guests and those Britons who happen to find themselves in charge of our privatised monopolies.

The two chambers would make excellent places for publishers to give book launch parties – much better than the library in the Reform Club which, although also designed by Barry, lacks the Pugin decorations and carries with it the danger of meeting Reform Club members in the lavatories.

When the MPs return from their holidays expecting to make speeches about Bosnia and share options, they would be given a glass of sour, warm white wine and introduced to Josephine Hart, lovely author of the year's outstanding popular novel, *Oblivion* (Chatto & Windus).

Those who seek leadership to guide them through this uncertain world will be relieved to learn that the West has at last found a leader of substance, a man who is not only unafraid to lead, but in fact relishes nothing more. His name is Jacques Chirac.

In hoc signo

SOME may have been dismayed to learn that the Cross, 2,000-year-old emblem of Christianity, is less easily identified by the public of the capitalist world than the 'golden arches' logo of the McDonald's fast food empire. In a survey of 7,000 people in Britain, Germany, the US, India, Japan and Australia, 88 per cent were able to identify the McDonald's logo, with only 54 per cent recognising the Cross.

I do not find this surprising or shocking. Christianity nowadays catches the imagination and inspires the loyalty of a fairly small minority. Even among active, evangelical Christians there is a tendency to play down that part of the Bible story which involves the Cross. Young people, we are told, look to religion for an assurance that life is a feast of generous emotions, and do not find it in the Cross.

In former times crusaders wore a cross on their tunic to announce they were soldiers of the Christian God determined to impose His laws on the infidel. Nothing could be more inappropriate for our soldiers to wear in Bosnia, where their purpose, in so far as they have one, is to prevent the Orthodox Serbs dispossessing the Catholic Croats or the Bosnian Muslims in a civil war that would have been settled three years ago if the United Nations had not decided to send 'peace-keepers' to prolong it.

But if Unprofor requires a badge for its tunics, it could do worse than adopt the McDonald's logo. Not only would it be easily recognised by most participants in the struggle, it would also be making a clear statement of the values the UN is fighting for: the global mass culture whose noblest expression is to be found in the jumbo-sized beefburger with cheese and onions, pickled gherkins, and ketchup.

A possible explanation

ON August 28 Channel 4 proposes to show a film which claims to show two extraterrestrial aliens being dissected after their flying saucer crashed in New Mexico in 1947.

The story is that a film was made of their autopsies by a US Air Force cameraman who kept a copy without telling anyone what he had done. The figures would appear to be humanoid, but have six fingers and six toes, very large heads and no trace of an umbilical cord.

All of which might be quite interesting, if by any stretch of the imagination we could possibly decide they were genuine. I would be happy to inspect the corpses, if asked. But who wishes to see them dissected? What on earth gave Michael Grade the idea that this is the sort of thing British people enjoy watching in their homes?

The films will be shown all over the world. Either it is a practical joke, which seems to have been gigantically successful, or the result of a terrible misunderstanding. The two figures not only have no evidence of having had umbilical cords but are sexless, with no sign of breast development and no hair on their heads or bodies.

I have a terrible feeling, having examined a photograph in this week's *Observer*, that they may have been a Swedish couple on holiday in New Mexico in 1947 when their car was involved in a terrible crash which knocked it completely out of shape, and suggested a flying saucer to the credulous Americans who found them.

It may not be well known in New Mexico that many Swedes show no sign of having had an umbilical cord after their third or fourth birthday. Everything else can be explained within the allowable range of human diversity.

Monday, July 31, 1995

Keep us apart

IT IS no wonder that few pubs have applied to have a children's licence when one looks at the conditions imposed by some authorities – regulating the temperature of water in the taps, demanding special low-level lavatories (almost certainly decorated with a Mickey Mouse – no modern child can expect to be able to urinate without the necessary stimulation) and a total ban on smoking.

But I hope an element of common sense interposed itself, too. Other people's children are seldom a source of pleasure. They are liable to be unattractive, noisy, demanding and have disgusting manners. Pubs are not places for kiddy-talk. They are deeply subversive places, where those in authority are made the subject of gross and often obscene libels, where bad language may be used to express our disgust at politicians, do-gooders and the way of the world generally. Children have no business to join such grown-up conversations. It was one of the silliest ideas the Government ever had.

No doubt it was with the same objections in mind that that wise and kind man, Judge Stephen Tumim, Chief Inspector of Prisons, has urged in his latest reports that young offenders should be kept out of adult jail. They would only teach the old lags bad habits.

The boom in juvenile offenders is blamed alternately on Mrs Thatcher, for encouraging a materialist frame of mind in the young, and on Mrs Shirley Williams, for the education reforms which make the young unemployable. But that is no excuse for sending them to annoy the older lags in prison. That would be cruel and unnatural punishment, just as wives who object when their husbands go to a pub must find other ways of registering their disapproval than sending in children to humiliate and embarrass them.

Journalists' talk

IT IS easy for professional columnists to be irritated, not to say jealous, when people like Mrs Clinton are suddenly given a weekly column – not because she has anything of interest to say, or any particular skill in saying it, but because she is Washington's First Lady.

About 100 newspapers carry her column throughout the United States, and one has been found to reprint it even in this country. I have no intention of demanding the right to act as Washington's First Lady for one day every week in exchange, but I feel Mrs Clinton should ponder the idea, if she wishes to be made welcome in journalistic circles.

We columnists must stick together. I was shocked to learn that the novelist Alice Thomas Ellis, who writes a brilliant column in the *Catholic Herald*, was under attack from Cardinal Hume, Archbishop Worlock of Liverpool and a gaggle of lesser bishops who object to her robustly conservative attitudes.

Oddly enough the *Catholic Herald* was where I wrote my first signed column nearly 33 years ago – probably before Cristina Odone, the present editor, who has successfully rejuvenated the newspaper, was born. In those days cardinals had other ways of registering their discontent. My first column appeared, as I remember, in January 1963. Cardinal Godfrey died a week later.

Whenever Cardinal Heenan wished to fire a shot across a columnist's bow, he would ask him to dinner at Archbishop's House and assure him that he secretly agreed with him. It always worked – with me, at any rate. Cardinal Hume lacks the necessary finesse. I think he should resign, and so should Archbishop Worlock.

Monday, August 7, 1995

New view of teenagers

'SADLY, the Home Secretary does not want the death penalty back,' begins a leader in the *Sun* relaunching its campaign to hang child murderers, and using three recent examples as a means of reviving the spectres of Ian Brady and Myra Hindley:

'If the people are to be denied the retribution of the rope, then at least prison should be made less comfortable for lifers . . . How much better it would be if people like them could hang.'

Punishment freaks have long settled on the murder of children as being the most unacceptable form of murder, and so the one most likely to help them in their sadistic fantasies about judicial execution and ways of making prisoners' lives more unpleasant. I wonder how long this attitude will survive the perception that three quarters of all burglaries and muggings are now committed by children in the 12-20 age group. The time is approaching when the law may have to re-think its attitude to young people.

The Leicester hospital consultant who was arrested, charged and convicted after catching a youth in his orchard stealing the apples, offered the police a clear target. Given a criminal and a victim, they are bound to arrest the victim under the present system, especially if the criminal is a youngster.

But the trouble with murder as a crime is that it leaves no victim behind who is able to be arrested. Perhaps that is why police take such a dim view of it. Meanwhile I learn from Swansea of three teenage brothers – they cannot be named for legal reasons – with more than 500 convictions for car crime between them. Police say they are probably responsible for more than 1,000 offences, and if they were safely locked away, car crime would halve. Nothing, of course, will ever justify the ultimate crime of taking the law into our own hands, but I do feel that our view of teenagers as sacred animals might be modified.

Ask your barber

THE nation's hairdressers are combining through their powerful professional body, the Fellowship of Hair Artists of Great Britain, to demand the withdrawal of an advertisement which might be thought to brand them unfairly. It shows a four-wheel drive vehicle being put through its paces on rough terrain, with the caption: 'Hairdressers need not apply.'

Among those hurt by the suggestion was Mr Andrew Collinge,

vice-president of the fellowship. He said:

'I just couldn't believe it. It is just so shocking and offensive . . . We are a major employer of young people and a serious industry.'

Sue Clark, news editor of the *Hairdressers' Journal*, agrees: 'Hairdressers feel they're being branded as limp-wristed or stupid. They are just as capable of being rugged outdoor types as anyone.'

No doubt this is true, but it begs the question of whether people should be permitted to express the contrary opinion. How much freedom of speech should we be allowed? If we are forbidden to express the view that hairdressing is a sissy profession, however hurtful and untrue the opinion might be, the next thing will be that the British Safety Council will be forbidden from showing photographs of the Pope to promote National Condom Week. The poster claimed that the Pope was enunciating an eleventh commandment: 'Thou shalt always wear a condom.'

Simpler Catholics might have taken this commandment at face value, and suffered terrible physical injury as a result. If the message is intended to be universal, it is a recipe for the destruction of the human race. However it was intended, it was insulting to the Pope and to many of the country's five million Catholics. When a spokesman explained that 'the Catholic Church is directly responsible for the spread of sexually transmitted disease, including HIV and Aids', she was revealing the true depths of ignorance which inspires her organisation. If Catholic doctrine on sexuality were followed by everyone, there would be no HIV, no Aids.

But it is one thing to describe the National Safety Council's message as vulgar and misleading, quite another to ban it. Many think National Condom Week is a good cause. Mr John Major is among its supporters. Obviously, he agrees with Mr Jack Tye, director general of the council, that the Pope is being ridiculous in his attitude to condoms. Some of us may muse about Mr Major's interest in them. I have often wondered whether in some earlier incarnation he might not have been a barber.

Great welfare error

IT WOULD be easy to find a parable or a sermon about our great welfare error in the fate of those who scrimped and saved to pay for a holiday at Pontins resort at Christchurch, Dorset, only to find that homeless families were enjoying exactly the same facilities free, having been sent there by Christchurch Council.

'I am bloody angry,' said single mother Sandra Bailey, who was paying for her holiday. Charles Watson pointed out that his wife had been stacking shelves in a supermarket. 'It seems we have to pay for their holidays as well as our own.'

It might make sense if there were a punitive element in housing provided free for the homeless. I have never stayed in a Pontins camp, but I stayed in another one many years ago, with wife and family, to write an article about it. Even after boarding school and Army life, it was one of the most unpleasant weeks I have ever spent.

Some people like these regimes, obviously enough. But with a little refinement along the lines of compulsory PT and cabbage with every meal, they might make a contribution towards solving the problem of the homeless and correcting our great welfare error.

Monday, August 14, 1995

Threat to morals . . . and to health

I AM not sure which government minister is in charge of the nation's morals, but Mrs Bottomley could reasonably claim they were not her responsibility when, as Secretary for National Heritage, she announced a huge increase in television channels. So it was that as Secretary for Health she announced that she had no compunction in knocking down St Bartholomew's Hospital – one of London's most historic and beautiful buildings – to suit some temporary medical convenience because, as she said, she was not Secretary for National Heritage at the time.

But has she forgotten she was once Secretary for Health? On the same day she uttered her reckless threat to bombard us with more American rubbish on television, the *British Medical Journal* printed a report from the Dunn Nutrition Centre in Cambridge which pointed out that, while total food intake in Britain has declined by one fifth in the past 10 years, we have grown much fatter as a nation simply from watching television. Television viewing has doubled from 13 to 26 hours a week.

A terrible example of what this can lead to is provided by the Evans family of Tongham, Surrey. John Evans, 29, who weighs 28 stone, and his sister Joan, 39, who weighs 29 stone, lived together in Tongham with their mother, Mrs Evans, watching television all day, until Mrs Evans died in 1992. She was so fat by then that she had to be lifted from her bedroom by a crane.

John and Joan then turned on their mother's nurse, a 66-year-old widow, and imprisoned her, using considerable violence to make her do all the work while they planned to take her £65 a week housing benefit. Sentencing this gross couple to prison at the Old Bailey last Friday, Judge Henry Pownall said that, although he was aware of the 'horrendous' problems caused by their obesity, it was their appalling behaviour which struck him most forcefully.

Is it to this sort of condition that Mrs Bottomley now hopes to reduce us all?

Taste of heaven

THOSE who argue that the free supply of heroin to elderly addicts in Denmark would help to cut the crime rate – nine out of 10 burglaries in Copenhagen are thought to be drug-related – ignore an important question. How many Copenhagen burglaries are committed by the elderly?

Yet it goes against the grain to give young people heroin. No British government has dared adopt the 1969 Wootton Report on cannabis because of claimed progression from cannabis to hard drugs.

One may doubt whether any government in the world would dare to decriminalise all drugs, even without the colossal American pressure against it. This is because drug enforcement is a major item of government activity, an important justification for the great fat toad of over-government squatting on us all.

I do not know exactly what proportion of British prisoners are held for drug-related offences, but I have been told it is two out of three. If all drugs were legalised, just think how many public employees would be put out of work: the prison staff, the policemen and Customs officers, the liaison officers and intelligence agencies, the lawyers and judges . . . and then the poor people in prison would be thrown on the labour market, too.

Perhaps they could all become counsellors and counsel each other all day. But it would not be much fun for the politicians, reduced to a few regiments of sanitary inspectors and bat protection officers to feed their self-importance.

Saturday, August 19, 1995

Great British victory

WHILE the rest of the country agonised over the Japanese apology to Mr Major for outrages perpetrated either before he was born or in the first two years of his young life, the *Sun* brought its readers exclusive news of a signal British victory in Majorca.

'We boot Germans off their Hunbeds,' read the headline over a colour picture of three British tourists waving Union Jacks.

'Crafty David James stopped the Germans from grabbing all the sunbeds at his hotel in Majorca – by hiding them in his room. He and his pals were fed up after spending most of their week's hol lying on a lumpy lawn because all the loungers had been taken . . .

'David, 31, a British Telecom manager, said: "The following morning we marched proudly out to the pool with our sun-loungers under our arms and with all the other Brits cheering. It was great. Julian draped his with a Union Jack towel to add to the patriotic flavour." '

The quarrel arose because the Germans got up early and reserved the sunbeds by putting towels on them. 'By the time we got to the pool there was nothing left. It was just too much so we

28

decided something had to be done. And I don't regret doing it one little bit,' said David.

One would hope not, but I am surprised the matter is being allowed to rest there. I should have thought that David, his girlfriend, Joanne, 26, and his mates, Julian, 27, and Lee, 25, could expect an apology from the Germans and compensation from the travel firm which arranged their trip – if Mr Major cannot arrange for the German government to pay it. The Germans have enough money, after all.

Monday, August 21, 1995

Two separate issues

I SOMETIMES think that if I win more than £20 million on the National Lottery, I might give £50 to the Roman Catholic Church on condition it never allows women priests. This is not at all the same as the issue of allowing priests to marry, on which the Catholic Bishop of East London, Bishop Victor Guazzelli, has spoken out so bravely.

People constantly urge me to give a lead on the matter of married priests, but I am not sure where I stand. A survey by one of the Catholic newspapers reveals that almost two out of three Catholics fear the whole thing will come unstuck unless priests are allowed to marry.

The matter is complicated, however, by the fact that 80 per

cent of the prominent Catholics questioned said they would lie if asked to put their views on record. How can we be sure they are not lying when they express their views off the record?

The question of women priests is much simpler. It is an insult to womanhood to expect members of the fairer sex to do half the things priests have to do. Many male Catholics, for instance, would be deeply ashamed to ask any woman to hear their Confessions.

There is a further complication that many men, in their anxiety to become women priests, would tell lies about their sex. Priestly garments have always been sexually ambiguous. I can see nothing but endless confusion where two priests sincerely wish to marry each other but cannot be certain about each other's sex.

When I win the Lottery jackpot, it will be proof that my views on this matter are the right ones. Someone Up There will have approved them. But perhaps the promise of a £40 donation to the Church will be enough to do the trick.

Holiday hints

CLAIMS that the viper is disappearing in France are an obvious attempt to encourage tourists who have been frightened away in their tens of thousands by the appalling rate of exchange. My part of France – the Lauragais region of Languedoc – is still crawling with them.

In England it is a criminal offence to harm, frighten, annoy or in any way displease a viper. Holidaymakers are flocking to the West Country with very little knowledge of what awaits them, apart from the occasional panther-like Beasts. In 55 years, I have never seen such a good summer for vipers.

They have been joined by swarms of wasps, driven mad by hunger, who attack tourists almost indiscriminately, paying particular attention to those in sleeveless shirts and short trousers. Anyone planning to visit the West Country would be well advised to wear thick ankle-length skirts and long-sleeved flannel tops, buttoned tightly at the neck – or heavy flannel suits with long trousers and stout shoes, according to taste.

In 1976, the last year when similar conditions prevailed, a man was bitten to death by ladybirds in Minehead. No such tragedy has been reported this year, although there have been accounts of ladybirds swarming and showing aggressive tendencies.

It may just be a question of time, but with a bit of luck people will decide to enjoy the sunshine at home instead of disturbing the ecology of the West Country with their seasonal migrations.

Wednesday, August 23, 1995

Let them dream

THE Cabinet Office, we learn, has been taking part in a conference of experts to decide how Britain would cope with a major calamity. At a Massive Disaster Seminar at the Emergency Planning College in Easingwold, Yorkshire, two were mooted: an earthquake in mid-Wales and a small terrorist nuclear explosion in Coventry.

Both eventualities would require someone to take national command of disaster planning, they agreed. Bureaucracy would need to be swept away. Powers would be needed to requisition accommodation. All this fits into a familiar pattern of power fantasy. The Cabinet Office does not appear to have addressed the delicate question of who should assume supreme power. Nice Mr Major has many qualities but lacks the required decisiveness. People often ask me if I will take over the reins, but I have to reply that I simply don't have time, what with editing *Literary Review* and running the Spectator Wine Club.

The obvious candidate is Joan Collins, the celebrated actress, model, novelist, mother and political thinker. She has sound opinions on many subjects, but I have my doubts about others. 'I think we need more of a police state,' she avers, but has she studied what has happened to the once-proud police under its new generation of chief constables? Eaten up by class resentments and chiefly concerned to protect their overtime, they are in no more of a position to run the country than I am. Supporters of law and order must now look to the nation's milkmen.

Saturday, September 2, 1995

Price of protection

IT WAS foolish of the organisers of the Reading Festival to

31

squabble with Thames Valley Police about the number of officers required to cover the event – unlike the organisers at Glastonbury who seemed to have paid up without a murmur and had a smooth ride.

At Reading, they settled for 100 officers at a cost of about £87,000 or nearly £300 per officer per day. There was bitter criticism from the police of the supplementary private security staff, three of whom were arrested. At Glastonbury, where the police were paid £360,000 there was no such criticism.

No doubt the police do a magnificent job but I think we need to be careful. At present, police can demand a certain level of manning at these ludicrous rates of pay under threat of opposing the licence and preventing the festival.

They can then choose whether or not to make trouble at the event itself, whether to harass young people present for suspected drug offences or whether to adopt what they call the 'kid glove' approach. Finally, as they demonstrated at Royal Ascot a few years ago, they can make things unpleasant by setting up doubtfully legal road blocks to breathalyse parting guests.

I am not, of course, for a moment suggesting that any improper pressure has yet been brought. It is hard to understand why all police at these events are invariably on overtime rates, or how the bill comes to £290 per officer per day. I am never likely to attend a pop festival, but I suppose it would be sad if organisers took them abroad.

The great International Lesbian Jamboree, I observe, is to be held in Peking, where policemen may be rather cheaper.

Monday, September 4, 1995

The serious side

'WE ARE used to stories about priests, cabinet ministers and air marshals hopping into bed with tarts,' exclaimed the *Sun* on Saturday. 'But we never thought we would see the head of one of our most prestigious public schools cited in a sex scandal.'

Why on earth not? What these wretched people describe as 'sex scandals' can be found wherever you look for them. They will be there for as long as the sexual urge survives. The *Sun*'s sermon, under the heading 'Serious', continued: 'Charterhouse's

Peter Hobson has resigned after bedding a call girl. It is all very entertaining, but there is a serious side to this bizarre behaviour. If we can't trust a custodian of vulnerable young people to set an example, who can we trust?'

There is indeed a serious side to this bizarre behaviour of the tabloid press, but it does not concern the standards of our headmasters and headmistresses in the private sector, which are mercifully very high and not in the least bit affected by whatever perfectly legal activities they may get up to in private, outside the circumstances of their work. It concerns the standards of our prostitutes.

Never mind that the prostitute concerned, a 19-year-old with three A-levels, is a refugee from Newcastle University. If she had been bribed enough, she might have continued her studies, since her major interest appears to be money. But we cannot afford to bribe all our teenagers with vast sums in lieu of putative earnings from prostitution. Like it or not, prostitution is going to become a major economic factor and Britain may well be poised to become the prostitution centre of the world. But it is no good saying it is all our young people are good for if they are not much good even at that.

If British prostitutes cannot be trusted to maintain professional discretion – if they shop their clients to the *Sun* and *Daily Mirror* for extra money – they will not have many clients, and foreigners will stay away. One trembles to think how Britain will pay its way. The trade does not require a very high standard of rectitude, but our young people are plainly not up to maintaining even this minimum level.

The only silver lining may be found in reports that the two newspapers which agreed to pay the prostitute are trying to rat on the payments. Perhaps the untrustworthiness of buyers will eventually cancel the untrustworthiness of vendors, but it seems to offer only a tenuous prospect of national survival.

Next in line

ON SATURDAY, I suggested that it might be sad if exorbitant police demands for money to protect pop festivals and rock concerts drove the organisers abroad. This has not been well received. Letters, telephone calls and faxes make the point that it would be an excellent idea if all such events could be held abroad. Rock festivals and nuclear tests are what abroad is *for*.

These people miss my point. I am sorry to have to spell it out. When Thames Valley Police tried to increase their charges at Reading Rock Festival by 258 per cent, the organiser, Mr Benn, suggested they were trying to make up the £7 million cut from their budget by Mr Michael Howard. That money will still be needed, even if they succeed in driving rock and pop fans abroad.

My great fear is that middle-class weddings will be next on the police hit-list. This would be in line with their observable hatred of the traditional middle class. If they start threatening that, unless we have 20 policemen at £300-a-head at every wedding, they will set up road blocks outside and breathalyse all the guests, one of two things may result: either the traditional middle classes will stop marrying altogether and stop breeding, whereupon British society will be reduced to something like that of a criminal lunatic asylum (*vide* Worsthorne *passim*), or middle-class weddings will become teetotal – an even greater national disgrace.

That is why I suggest it might be sad to see all the pop festivals, lesbian jamborees etc, driven abroad.

Wednesday, September 6, 1995

A signal is needed

IT IS hard to think of anything more pointless or money-wasting than the Grand International Lesbians' Jamboree which opens today in Peking. This is particularly so if it is true, as has been claimed, that by no means all the 50,000 women attending are lesbians. Perhaps we should treat this suggestion with caution. It may be part of the drip, drip, drip of hostile propaganda from misogynists and male chauvinists.

Poor Mrs Clinton, who is attending in her role as President of the United States, does not seem to have understood this at all. 'The Deputy Chair of our delegation, Marjorie Margolies-Mezvinsky, is one of America's most devoted mums,' writes Mrs Clinton in her abysmal column. '. . . she and her husband are raising eleven children – two are adopted and three are refugees from Asia – in their home in Pennsylvania. "I don't get involved with things that don't celebrate the family," she said.'

Mrs Clinton goes on: 'Voices of American women must be heard. And they will be heard.' The conference promises to be the most boring event ever held, with 50,000 women all demanding to be heard. Why should the rest of us pay any attention? The only possible way to make it interesting is suggested in reports from Beijing saying the Chinese authorities are terrified that all these women plan to take their clothes off. Thousands of Chinese women have been posted around with small hand towels to cover them up if they do.

One cannot deny that the spectacle of 50,000 women without any clothes would be an interesting and unusual one. Mrs Clinton, whose nude photographs taken by a sex-mad doctor at Yale university are said to have worn well, should give the signal.

Taking our medicine

A QUARTER of a century ago when I wrote a regular column on medical matters for a magazine called *British Medicine*, I was surprised to learn that it was an acknowledged perk for morticians at a post mortem to remove the pituitary gland from its place in the front of the brain and sell it for 4s. (20p) a time to a drug company.

It was used to produce a drug which assisted growth in small children, but the practice was stopped in 1985 when it was discovered that it could also hand on the human version of mad cow disease.

Now that everybody is suing the National Health, we learn that 900,000 bodies had their pituitary glands removed in this way. It all confirms my suspicion that we should watch the medical profession much more closely than we do. A new anti-depressant drug, clomipramine, is said to produce the unexpected side effect in some patients that they experience a sexual climax every time they yawn. If isolated, this side effect could have terrible social consequences. Bores would be in great demand everywhere, and all the normal incentives of courtship and childbearing would be lost.

Breast screening for cancer, we now learn, is not only expensive but also inefficient, producing much anxiety and saving very few lives.

Against this, if everyone took an aspirin a day, at least 7,000 lives would be saved in Britain every year and 100,000 worldwide. Aspirin is an incredibly cheap and cost-efficient medicine. Most doctors discourage it, pointing to side effects on the digestive system. But it is better to suffer a little indigestion than mad cow disease, or experience a sexual climax every time you yawn.

When I come to power the NHS may be reduced to supplying every citizen with one free aspirin every day – if we can still afford even that.

Monday, September 11, 1995

A hero for our times

BRUCE Forsyth, the family entertainer, made a ferocious attack on BBC chiefs last week, saying they attached too little importance to family entertainment. The way the BBC treats its biggest stars, he said, is 'shameful and disgusting'.

'Family entertainment' can mean one of two things. It can either mean entertainment without sexual innuendo or other filth, or it can be a euphemism for entertainment which is devoid of any intelligent content, aimed at backward adults and exceptionally stupid children. Forsyth, presumably, falls into the second category.

The *Sun* endorsed his sentiments, avowing that Forsyth is 'Britain's best-loved family entertainer'. In a leading article the following day, it said: 'When he speaks, only a fool refuses to listen.'

Perhaps he is as well-loved as they say, but he is also hated. I distinctly remember that whenever he appeared on our family

36

television set there were groans, catcalls, and noises of people being sick. On top of the distaste of refined folk for anyone whose performances are so vulgar, stupid and affected, there is the traditional hatred by *Sun* readers of anyone who is successful or makes a lot of money. National Lottery winners complain they are treated like lepers by their neighbours.

So perhaps our Brucie is indeed a national hero, after all. We have been searching high and low for one to put on the empty pedestal in Trafalgar Square. To be a popular entertainer in modern Britain is probably the bravest thing anyone can do. Let us see what the pigeons make of him.

Wednesday, September 13, 1995

A fine prime minister

AS SUPPORT grows for General Colin Powell as the first black president of the United States, I notice a curious thing happening to him. The presidency is a perfectly suitable reward for the fact that America won the war against Iraq, much to everybody's surprise, and I am sure he will make a fine president. But will he be a black president? With every photograph, as we follow him around on his book promotion tour, he seems to grow paler and paler.

Perhaps he is merely losing the tan he acquired in the desert, or it could be a deliberate ploy to reassure old-fashioned white voters in the South. But it will be a cruel blow for many if, when he is elected, he suddenly announces he was a Welshman all along.

So far as Britain is concerned we must wait and see who Mr Murdoch will choose as our next prime minister. Rumour has it he took against Tony Blair on discovering that Blair went to a public school. Present indications are that his choice will fall on Sir Frank Bruno, the well-known footballer or popular singer, or whatever.

Over the weekend, Murdoch newspapers organised a triumphal parade in Bruno's honour down Oxford Street, Regent Street and into Trafalgar Square, where crowds greeted him by singing 'Rule Britannia'. *The Times* quoted him as saying: 'It is unbelievable, know what I mean? It is brilliant . . .'

If these words can be interpreted as accepting the Conservative

37

nomination, then things are looking up. Bruno is easily the most popular person in Britain. It doesn't really matter who we have for prime minister, as everybody knows exactly what needs to be done. It is just a question of finding someone to do it.

Saturday, September 16, 1995

All that is left

IF I WERE a goldfish lover, I do not think I would be reassured by the pictures we saw on Thursday, showing the leaders of all three political parties. Mr Blair, the socialist, Mr 'Paddy' Pantsdown, the Liberal Democrat, and 'nice' Mr Major were all roaring with laughter at the discomfiture of a goldfish.

It appears that a goldfish belonging to Mr Major had shown symptoms of distress in the recent hot weather. The Prime Minister explained to his two rivals in office how he had smothered the unfortunate fish in sunburn cream. All three found it tremendously funny.

These three men hold our future in their hands. Never mind that as individuals they may be deeply second rate, motivationally flawed or unable to keep their trousers up. The fact speaks for itself that the only thing they can find to laugh about together is a suffering goldfish.

Villagers of St Tudy, the small Cornish village near Bodmin, were recently moved to address a petition to Mr Major asking for a referendum on further European involvement. A senior villager, Vice Admiral Sir Louis Le Bailly, 80, one time head of 'intelligence' at the Ministry of Defence, thought the petition would be ignored. He explained:

'I would not be so naïve as to suppose that what St Tudy says today, the Government will do tomorrow. But at least, before we die, we have done the best we can for our grandchildren.'

If that is the best he can do, it is pathetic. So is the entire level of political debate in Britain. There is nothing wrong with resistance to change, in fact it is the only sane position to take. What these people fail to realise is that we have a much better prospect for resisting change within the protection of a selfish, inward looking Europe than we have when exposed to cultural takeover by the United States and economic takeover by the Pacific Rim.

38

Terrified and resentful of the tiny changes required by participation in the European Union, Britons miss nearly every opportunity to shape the union to their own advantage. Instead they mumble their platitudes about British sovereignty, and having fought two major wars to preserve it.

Let them examine the picture of Pantsdown, Blair and 'nice' Mr Major laughing cruelly about a goldfish. They are what is left of British sovereignty.

Monday, September 18, 1995

To be a person

THE elderly patient in Colchester who has occupied a hospital bed for almost five months and refuses to leave it may sum up the dilemma of the National Health Service. Despite everything his doctors say, this man believes he is not well enough to go.

Perhaps it is not the fault of doctors and staff that the NHS has become a gigantic cancer, simultaneously destroying the physical and economic vitality of the nation. Perhaps unrealistic expectations of the public are to blame. But when one sees how the prescription charge is now considerably greater than the cost of the medicine in most cases, one begins to wonder for whose advantage the service exists.

Recently I suggested that it should be reduced to a free supply of aspirins for all those who complain of being ill. In nine cases out of 10, aspirin will alleviate the symptoms until Time the great Healer does his work (or not, as the case may be). But then one reads of the miraculous delivery of Siamese twins in Manchester and one feels there might be some point in it all.

Not everybody agrees with this. Polly Toynbee, the female thinker, feels that the parents should have been 'counselled' into having an abortion. As I understand her argument, she feels that most if not all handicapped children should be aborted before birth, because of the grief they bring into the world; the love a mother feels for her unborn child is a false and sentimental love, because the unborn child is not yet a person as she, Polly Toynbee, is a person.

Toynbee had the good fortune to be born without any grave physical deformity, so far as one can see. Her greatest handicap would appear to have been born without the faintest glimmer of a sense of the ridiculous. The grief to which this handicap can lead is tragic enough, but I fear no ultrasound machinery has yet been invented to detect it in the womb.

Unfair to our dumb chums

A KIND reader, knowing of my interest in the latest theological developments, has sent me a cutting from the *Chipping Sodbury Gazette* which shows on its front page a colour photograph of the Rev Donna Dobson eating from a tin of Pedigree Chum in the Chipping Sodbury Baptist Church.

There might have been many lessons to draw from this spectacle – the need to make sacrifices for the poor of Rwanda, support for the Muslim cause in Bosnia (the dog food was chicken-flavoured) or a general mortification of the flesh. But the Rev Donna's sermon was slightly different.

'I was trying to make the point that Jesus rose from the dead and walked about for everyone to see him. But people would not have believed if they had not seen it with their own eyes . . . A lot of people asked me afterwards if it really was dog food. They didn't really think I would do it, but it definitely was. I just hope it got the message across.'

The message, as I understand it, is that we would not believe that a priest (or priestess) would eat dog food in the pulpit unless we had seen it. But in this case we would have been wrong to disbelieve it, *ergo* we would be wrong to disbelieve in the resurrection of Christ, merely because we had not seen Him walking around, *ergo* Jesus rose from the dead.

This classic example of feminine – or Toynbee – logic should be included in all the textbooks, but what worries me about the new method of preaching is the effect that it might have on any dogs in the congregation.

Far from confirming their belief in the resurrection of Christ, the spectacle might turn them against all religion. I wonder if the Rev Donna Dobson has thought this one through.

Sentencing notes

A YOUNG man walking outside York recently found a dead badger by the roadside and decided its head might look nice on his living-room wall. So he cut off the head, took it home to Danebury Drive, York, and put it in his fridge.

What nobody had told him was that since some drivelling new law passed by the present Government, it is illegal to take a dead badger home with you, or possess part of one. As a result, James Pipes, 21, was sent to prison for three months.

The brief news report does not tell us how York police discovered that Pipes was keeping part of a dead badger in his fridge. Perhaps they possess ultrasound detection equipment in their helicopters, able to pinpoint pieces of dead badger to within inches. Or perhaps it was part of the routine inspection of fridges they have up north, to ensure they are not eating each other.

But we must congratulate York police on bringing this young criminal to book. If it had not been for James Pipes, the dead badger might still be lying intact by the roadside, adding its fragrance to the Yorkshire air. Can we really think three months in prison is enough?

By contrast, a young stonemason in Worcester received an extraordinarily savage sentence. Twenty-year-old Stephen Ball became annoyed with a woman constable when he was passenger in a car which she suspected of being overloaded. So he kicked her in the mouth and bit her male colleague in the arm.

Worcester magistrates sentenced him to attend an anger management course, undergo bereavement counselling and debt counselling *and* attend an alcohol education scheme. If he lives through that programme, I think we may safely reckon he will never overload another vehicle.

Saturday, September 23, 1995

These bossy people

PERHAPS it was their proximity to Sweden that influenced Liberal Democrats to behave so oddly at their conference in Glasgow. On one day, they called for teenage MPs as young as 16; then for a punitive tax on tobacco; then for a national boycott on all French goods in protest at the recent nuclear tests in the South Pacific.

One does not need to approve of the French tests, as I do, to see this last suggestion as absurd. The level of the debate was set by Mr Matthew Taylor, MP for Truro, who declaimed: 'If you buy St Austell beer rather than French wine, make sure you write to the French President and tell him it's not just because of the better flavour of Cornish beer.'

The idea that serious wine drinkers will change their habits of a lifetime to accommodate the anti-nuclear lobby seems to be just about on a par with the suggestion that Cornish beer has a 'better taste' than French wine.

The excuse of a punitive tax on tobacco is that it would pay for free dental and eye check-ups. Might as well have a punitive tax on ice cream to pay for foot inspections. This is bossiness gone mad. Why cannot those who want a dental check-up pay for it, those who want a cigarette pay for that, and those who want neither, keep their money? What on earth has it got to do with these crypto-Scandinavians in Glasgow?

The idea of recruiting teenage MPs may be seen as an easier option than Mr Howard's 'boot camp' solution. Many sincere efforts are being made to employ our young people. I read recently that Belfast City Council had taken on a university-leaver with two degrees, three A-levels and nine O-levels to pick up litter. This was very compassionate of them, although we did not learn whether he was any good at the job.

Teenage MPs would do less harm than incompetent refuse collectors. They could sleep late most days, so long as they got up in time for the vote in the evening. Even if they overslept or voted in the wrong lobby it would not make much difference, as nearly all new legislation is a waste of time, and it is ignored for the most part. My only fear is that the easy money will be bad preparation for the time when they have to get a proper job.

Monday, September 25, 1995

Millennium suggestions

PEOPLE have been understandably derisive of the plan to erect a 40ft bronze bust of Winston Churchill on the South Bank as part of the millennial celebrations financed by our wonderful lottery. It would be seen as too obvious an attempt by London to woo back the American tourists who are now flocking to Newcastle for the promised sight of a Geordie relieving himself.

One may doubt whether it would even work, since by the end of the century very few Americans will have the faintest idea who Churchill was. A statue of the great man relieving himself might attract some attention for a time, but by no means everyone is convinced that London needs more American tourists.

A 40ft statue of John Major is too extreme as a means of keeping them away. The best solution would probably be for a huge bust of Bernie Grant, the popular MP for Tottenham, who has given such a cheerful lead to the country's racial minorities for the past 10 years.

It would give London's blacks a pride and sense of belonging, as well as remind Westminster that there are quite a lot of them living south of the river who might easily come across if they feel forgotten or maltreated. It would be a symbol of racial harmony such as the Americans have never achieved, despite their great advantage in having a capital that is 70 per cent black.

The American response is to retreat in terror. For years I have been giving it as my opinion that the *New York Times* is the worst and most boring newspaper in the western world, but it now appears I should have been watching the *Washington Post*. A brilliant report by Ruth Shalit in *New Republic* reveals how the *Post* has been covering up for corrupt practices by the city's black mayor, spiking stories about black delinquents and generally lowering standards in its anxiety to impose 'racial sensitivity' on its reporters.

We have none of these problems in London. A 40ft bust of Bernie Grant would make the point very well, as well as mark our gratitude to him for his moderate and engaging treatment of these issues.

43

Rambler mystery

MOST sensible people, I imagine, spent Sunday locked indoors while Janet Street-Porter and her 100,000-odd Ramblers celebrated what they called Open Britain Day, demanding the right to swarm over the countryside and spoil what little is left of its serenity.

One of the nastiest stories I have heard from this urban invasion is told by a Tyneside farmer, Mr John Patterson, whose property runs along the Roman wall.

On Sunday morning his two sons, aged 13 and eight, were out rabbiting with ferrets on their father's land. They had done rather well, catching seven, when they were accosted by a furious female who was rambling across their land with her male companion. She demanded to know what they were doing.

On being told that they were catching rabbits, the woman became abusive and informed them their behaviour was barbaric. She then demanded to know why they were not at school and on being told it was Sunday, she allegedly became hysterical and struck the 13-year-old, effectively ordering him off his own land.

I do not know what defence countrymen have against these urban invaders. Rabbits are a major nuisance on many farms, and farmers must be allowed to control their numbers without coming under attack from Street-Porter's urban guerrillas, who

also try to stop them ploughing their land and keeping their animals fenced in.

Obviously it would be a waste of time trying to appeal to the gentler side of these roamers, ramblers or swarmists, urging them to stay at home rather than spread their diseases over the countryside. But it might be useful to stress the risk to ramblers of being bitten by vipers, catching spongiform encephalitis from cows and bovine tuberculosis from badgers. Oddly enough, police and park attendants were never able to trace the two roamers who attacked 13-year-old Robert Patterson. They seem to have vanished from the face of the earth.

Saturday, September 30, 1995

Better than a tonic

DOCTORS are an argumentative lot. After my recent note suggesting that the ever-expanding National Health Service could usefully be reduced to a free supply of aspirins for the poor, I was not at all surprised to see a headline in Thursday's newspaper: 'Kicking is best prescription, doctors told.'

It was typical of doctors to be unable to accept advice from outside the profession, I decided. The new suggestion comes in a British Medical Association guide which advocates the 'bash and dash' principle: inflicting severe pain on the patient and then running away. 'Kick the shinbone as hard as you can,' it says. 'Practise kicking like a rugby player – kick through and hard.'

Reading more carefully, we learn that this advice is intended only for the doctor confronted by a violent patient. This is an increasingly common phenomenon, especially in London, when a patient is kept waiting or finds himself irritated by something in the doctor's manner.

I wonder if the new system might not be applied more generally. Most patients who visit the doctor have nothing wrong with them – the figure is put as high as four out of five. They are just depressed or bored and given to worrying about themselves. A kick may be just what they need to take them out of it. I will write to my guru, Dr Theodore Dalrymple, and ask for his opinion on this matter.

Call to arms

SINCE my brief moment of glory last week when the Princess of Wales came to give away the *Literary Review*'s Grand Poetry prize and help me launch the Literary Review Trust to secure the magazine's future, my colleagues in the press have tended to treat me as the nation's expert on the princess: her health, her heart, her plans for the future.

This is a role I am not entirely qualified to fill, although quite prepared to try for a week or two. But I am also expected to be an expert on the marriage of Will Carling, the popular footballer or whatever – someone I had never heard of until a few weeks ago. Nor do I have any opinions about his wife of 15 months, who suddenly seems to have made herself famous.

'The princess is now in grave danger of being seen as a cynical manipulator of men,' writes a pompous fellow in *The Times*. My colleagues of the press, who are easy-going, jokey people for the most part, have a curious way of assuming clerical bib and tucker when they write about the Royal Family.

The truth is that the monarchy has little chance of surviving the present incumbent if it has to rely on respect. This is not a respectful age. It can survive only on affection. There is little affection (although some) for the Prince of Wales, none at all for princes Andrew or Edward, let alone the disastrously charmless Fergie, very little (although some respect) for the Princess Royal and little of either for Princess Margaret.

The Princess of Wales may have made one or two mistakes. Haven't we all? But she has an extraordinary ability to inspire affection and loyalty that does not derive from what is easily dismissed as 'charm'. It derives from a genuine warmth of nature, a kindness of outlook, a natural friendliness and good manners.

People will say these are the ramblings of a besotted middle-aged man, but there is an underlying truth that must not be denied. It is the princess's job to manipulate, in the sense of delighting and charming those who meet her, and her nature responds to the task. She does it magnificently. If a few men make fools of themselves as a result, that is in the nature of things. By allowing us to watch her progress through life, her thrills and spills, triumphs and near-catastrophes, she adds immeasurably to the gaiety of the nation, even to our sense of nationhood.

It is the essence of gossip to be fun. Nobody knows how much of it is true. Those who affect to be scandalised by it, or to pass ponderous judgments, miss the whole point and make fools of themselves. Why should we allow ourselves to be ruled by these miserable, jealous people? I think I hear a call to arms.

Saturday, October 7, 1995

Much to learn

MANY millions of people must have been as irritated as I was when they switched on the BBC Radio Four news at six o'clock on Wednesday, hoping to hear the O.J. Simpson verdict. Instead, we had to listen to nearly a quarter of an hour of Tony Blair's 'keynote' speech to the Labour conference at Brighton.

Now we learn that this was deliberate. Blair's office had written to the BBC imploring that his speech should be given precedence. This shows an appalling lack of judgment on the part of his advisers. Nobody listened more kindly as a result to those silly squeaky noises about making Britain young again, creating a young country full of traditional moral and family values.

Instead, we felt very angry at having to hear all this tosh while other people, listening and watching on other channels, were learning the main news of the day.

Political speeches have always been a problem. In the course of a strict religious upbringing I found my mind had trained itself to switch off automatically as soon as it identified the sermon sound. When I later became a political reporter the same thing happened as soon as anyone started making a speech.

This might have been a disadvantage for a political reporter, but after a few months I discovered it did not matter. No political speech ever says anything. Even if it did, very few people would wish to hear it. Nobody in Britain outside a tiny circle of misfits and deviants is interested in politics. That may be the single most important truth about British politics. Blair has much to learn.

47

Generation of poodles

ONE could not help smiling at his promise to give every child in the country access to a lapdog computer. This will apparently open up the Information Superhighway through links to every lapdog in the world by Internet and e-mail and other delights. Or so I understand him to boast.

If only these dear young people had anything worthwhile to tell each other. But Blair had obviously not heard of the new virus which is poised to travel down the Information Superhighway like a proverbial dose of salts, leaving not a wrack of information behind. Blair would do better to offer every child a kitten or a budgerigar. Who wants to be left with a row of dead lapdogs?

Another scheme has been introduced by a school in Newcastle upon Tyne which gives each of its 250 seventh-year pupils an alarm clock to help them get out of bed in the morning. This may seem an intelligent use of technology, but the question arises: do we really want them to get out of bed?

Police in Nottinghamshire, which is only halfway to Newcastle, drew attention to a gang of six boys, aged 13 and 14, who, while in council care, are said to have committed 419 offences since the beginning of April this year. Now that borstals no longer exist, these boys can only be remanded back into council care, from which they emerge to steal cars and break into houses at will. Would they not be better left in bed?

Blair is obviously not the sort of person who is capable of leaving well alone. I wonder if he read that Stephen Hawking, Lucasian Professor of Mathematics at Cambridge, has decided it may well be possible to travel backwards through time.

Most of us, on hearing the news, probably decided it was time for Hawking to take an aspirin and check his sums. But Tony Blair is bound to believe this sort of rubbish. Let him promise to send our teenagers back in time to the early Victorian era, when children were expected to make themselves useful down the mines and cleaning chimneys. This would be more popular than giving them digital lapdogs. It depends on how much he wants to win the election.

Monday, October 9, 1995

Say it in spuds

BERTIE Ahern, leader of the Fianna Fail opposition in the Dublin parliament, has had the splendid idea that Britain should apologise for the Irish potato famine of 150 years ago. He does not claim that the English actually started it, although I have heard that opinion expressed. He hints that Britain deliberately withheld aid for Malthusian reasons of its own.

I do not see why Mr Major should confine himself to apologising for the potato famine. He should also apologise for the Black Death of 1347-1351. If that did not reach Ireland (I am not sure) he should apologise for the Ice Age, which lasted two and a half million years, finally ending only 10,000 years ago. It must have caused endless inconvenience in Ireland, if there was anyone there to suffer it.

An even better idea might be for the British Prime Minister to spend his whole time apologising to the rest of the world for every misfortune which has ever visited it, above all for the fact that Britain was ever anything except a nation of whingeing scroungers led by timid, lower-class incompetents.

But on the 150th anniversary of the great Irish potato famine, it seems unlikely we will get away with an apology. Compensation is the order of the day. Since we don't have any money left in Britain – the Government has spent it all – we should pay compensation to the Irish in potatoes.

Potatoes are very easy to grow – once planted they need no attention except occasional spraying with poisonous chemicals to discourage the potato blight. This might be a job for our idealistic young people.

Wednesday, October 11, 1995

Money supply

LAST WEEK we learned that nearly three months earlier, on the morning of July 19, Britain was within a whisker of running out of electricity. The National Grid, in making this admission, blamed the generating companies for failing to produce the power they had promised. National Power, PowerGen and

Nuclear Electric deny responsibility. Now an inquiry has been set up to find out what went wrong.

The fact that we heard nothing of this crisis until three months later makes one wonder what other little dramas are being enacted even now. After the few days of miraculously sunny weather we have just enjoyed, we must suppose we are about to run out of water again. Standpipes may be able to produce a few rancid drops of sewery chemicals, but that is the best we can hope for.

Is the country also about to run out of money, perhaps? It crosses my mind, as Mr Clarke looks gloomier and gloomier every time someone asks him to cut taxes. I wonder if it was his idea to sell surplus blood from the National Blood Authority's stocks to foreign countries.

At least the NBA assures us that we have surplus stocks of this blood plasma, called factor eight, although others point out that we are spending £18 million importing more of it from America. Perhaps the American blood is cheaper. Other countries may be a little nervous of it, for one reason or another.

My own guess is that it is probably more expensive, and the whole thing is just another example of the incompetence which has overtaken every aspect of British life since the collapse of state education.

But it must be nice for blood donors to reflect on how their blood, sold to foreign countries, is helping the government in its money problems. If they produced enough blood, it might allow Mr Clarke to cut taxes in time for the next general election. But they should not injure themselves in the attempt. He will probably find something else to spend the money on.

Saturday, October 14, 1995

Shed a tear

THE main reason for voting Conservative at the present time – apart from a general preference for the devil one knows over the devil one doesn't know – is that Labour promises to make hunting illegal, as do the stinkers who congregate under 'Paddy' Pantsdown's banner. The problem is that hunting people are outnumbered by those who do not hunt, and in the mean spirit of the times anyone who does not do something, wants to stop anyone else from doing it.

The good news is that the nation's anglers have decided to make common cause with the British Field Sports Society in defending countrymen's rights. There are an estimated four million people in this country who go fishing. Unlike the Ramblers, they do not barge around in groups of 40 or 50, declaring that the land belongs to the people and trying to annoy landowners. One can understand any government banning Ramblers, or making them pay for their anti-social pleasures, as the National Trust is very sensibly doing.

But anglers hurt no one, except possibly the fish. A Cambridge professor called Donald Brook claims to have discovered that fish feel pain, just as we do. Labour will have no alternative, when faced with this scientific evidence, but to ban fishing, too.

When all is said and done, there is something rather poignant about the thought of a fish in pain. Of course there is no good reason why fish shouldn't experience pain, as we all do.

Next time we eat one, perhaps we will find it in our hearts to shed a little tear, like the Carpenter, over his oysters.

Monday, October 16, 1995

Thoughts for the day

MR CLINTON will not be in Washington today to receive the

Million Man March with which Louis Farrakhan hopes to promote pride, personal responsibility and moral fortitude among black men. *But only among black men.* Women of any colour or description are excluded. Perhaps it is right that black men should regard their case as particular, since one in three of American black men in their twenties is either in jail, on probation or on parole.

While the March is being held, Mr Clinton will be at Texas University talking about race issues. Race is the burning issue of the day in the wake of the O J Simpson verdict, but the United States has always been prey to nine-day wonders of this sort.

In fact the Simpson verdict is not nearly as interesting as the Karen Roberts verdict in Melbourne, Florida, which I mention occasionally. There, a jury of six whites found a 31-year-old British teacher guilty on the flimsiest evidence of having sexually pleasured four black youths who informed on her.

The Simpson verdict merely illustrated what was already common knowledge in Washington, that a black jury will not exactly disfavour a black defendant. What the Karen Roberts' verdict would seem to reveal is a justice system and a whole United States society paralysed by terror of its own blacks.

This may seem odd, as blacks account for only 12 per cent of the American population. Perhaps white American males are not very brave, having too much to lose. I do not know. If Mr Clinton wishes to remove a major source of grievance among blacks he should end the war on drugs. This has quadrupled the black prison population in five years. But perhaps Mr Clinton is secretly quite happy to keep one in three American black men in their twenties either in jail, or on probation, or on parole.

News from Yorkshire

FOR some weeks now I have been haunted by Prof Elliott Leyton's discovery (in *Men of Blood; Murder in Modern England*, published by Constable tomorrow) that England has one of the lowest murder rates in the world: a man is eight times more likely to be murdered in Scotland.

When one reads of this new 'Status Zero' generation of aimless criminals, unable to read, write or communicate in any way, without loyalties or any sense of the most rudimentary morals, one is amazed that there are not more killings. I hate to raise the question, but might the status zeros think the death penalty still applies?

Perhaps mercifully, since so few of us are naturally equipped to play the part of Mother Teresa, we learn about these worlds only through the newspapers. *The Yorkshire Post* recently led on the story of a 15-year-old schoolgirl, Mandy Zani, found strangled on Harden Moor above Bingley. She was thought to have been dead for three weeks, but neither her school nor her family had reported her missing.

It turned out that the school had warned her mother 40 times about her daughter's persistent truancy, but the mother still failed to escort the girl to school or telephone to ask if she had arrived safely. In fact, the mother had been out of communication with her daughter for 10 weeks. 'I thought everything was fine. Now I know she deceived me,' she told *The Yorkshire Post*.

The chairman of Bradford Council's education committee, while offering the mother his 'deepest sympathies', suggested that the bulk of the responsibility did not lie with the school. The mother, it appears, is training to be a social worker at Bradford College.

Saturday, October 21, 1995

Another dead-end job

JOHN BIRT, 50-year-old director general of the BBC, has apologised to the City of Liverpool, its inhabitants and, above all, its football supporters for a tasteless television trailer advertising the police drama *Backup*. In the course of this trailer, skinheads were seen dressed in the Liverpool FC supporters' uniform. A voice-over said: 'When football hooligans are about to clash . . .'

The inference was obvious: that among Liverpool's football supporters – who are among Liverpool's most respected citizens – there are some who might be, or might have been, or might be about to be noisy or disruptive in their behaviour.

It would be hard to imagine a fouler libel against a city which may have produced a few geniuses in its time – John Lennon, Albert Einstein, even John Birt himself – but has certainly never produced a single football hooligan.

It is this sort of libel which is responsible for the general sense of despair on Merseyside. As we all know, Liverpudlians are the best workers in the world, but the constant drip of snide, satirical comment creates unemployment and explains why comparatively few Liverpudlians ever become seriously rich. Andrew Neil, the Glaswegian 'meritocrat', may not be a Liverpudlian, but he is the sort of person who could easily be one.

John Birt himself is a typical case: Liverpudlian born and bred, he finds himself at the age of 50 stuck in a dead-end job, apologising to these tearful, whingeing, unemployable football hooligans when he could be playing ping-pong for England.

Revere him anyway

NOBODY has ever doubted that Roger Casement was hanged in 1916 for high treason because the Home Office had deliberately destroyed his character by releasing parts of his alleged 'Black Diaries'. These revealed that Casement had for years been addicted to the grossest sodomitical practices.

All that prevents his being recognised as a great hero of the gay movement is the suspicion that these 'Black Diaries' may in fact be forgeries. Whitehall's newest admissions shed no light on this aspect. The present situation is unsatisfactory from every point of view.

If Whitehall is prepared to admit that the diaries are forged, the Irish republicans can continue to revere what they believe to be Casement's bones, dug up a few years ago in Pentonville and reburied in Dublin. If the Diaries are genuine, and Casement was indeed hanged for his sodomitical practices rather than for his high treason, then Dublin will be embarrassed and it will be time for American gays to dig him up again and transport his bones to a new shrine in San Francisco or New York.

Another aspect is that they had difficulty identifying Casement's bones among those of all the prisoners who had died or been hanged at Pentonville. It seems as likely as not that the bones shipped to Dublin were really those of Dr Crippen, the Holloway GP with a wife problem, hanged six years before Casement.

Crippen is not thought to have had any particular views on the Irish problem and, although American by birth, was almost certainly uninterested in the grosser sodomitical practices. But we should not discourage anyone from their own pious observances. It doesn't really matter whose bones they are.

Monday, November 6, 1995

Solving the problem

IT IS the Children Act of 1989 which allows a gang of teenage criminals to hold the town of Mansfield to ransom and a 14-year-old boy, arrested or reported to the police 72 times, to continue his life of crime with complete impunity in Peterlee, Co. Durham, because he is too young to be sent to a young offenders institution. As Peter Kemp, Durham's director of social services, says with all the wisdom of his training: 'Locking children up is not going to solve the problem.'

When another 14-year-old boy who killed an old woman of 83 while in the process of mugging her was finally ordered to be detained for five years last week at the Old Bailey, his girl cousin of 14, who had egged him on, was given a two-year supervision order for stealing the old lady's handbag. This was after her counsel had explained that she suffered from an absence of direction. Her life revolved around junk television and junk food, he said.

Now the Government has launched a massive plan to wean children off junk food. Schools will be given advice on healthy eating. They do not quite dare try to wean children off junk television, of course, in case that annoys Mr Murdoch, but at least we are doing something to solve the problem, are we not? If one lost soul can be saved from hamburgers and redirected towards salad and fresh vegetables, Mr Major will have done something to justify the £300 billion of our money he will spend this year trying to make himself useful.

Meanwhile more and more children will commit offences, each in its deadly cloud of hamburger gas. The great thing is that they must never be identified. Perhaps it would be a good idea to pass a blanket law against the photographing of children in any circumstances. Those of us who retain childhood photographs of ourselves in various sporting postures had better make them unidentifiable, for fear of a midnight knock from the local constabulary.

Monday, November 13, 1995

All we have left

THE slightly ludicrous face of Bill Gates, richest private citizen in the world, who has succeeded in selling his lapdog computers and other devices to practically every man, woman and child in the United States, smirked out of one of the Murdoch newspapers yesterday, assuring us that computers would alter the lives of us all for ever.

So they might, but not, I fancy, in the way Mr Gates has in mind. Many of those who actually operate these machines have a blind loyalty, not to say infatuation, for them which brooks no criticism. But those of us who employ others to use them are painfully aware of how unreliable they are. They are capricious, forgetful, prone to long blackouts, and at the mercy of a growing number of viruses.

They can lose whole novels which have been entrusted to them, and will jumble any information they are given, or reveal it at an inopportune moment, in such a way as to make them a menace to the orderly running of affairs. It is for this reason, apart from the opportunities for embezzlement, that I urge no one to sign a direct debit order.

The great exception to this rule seems to be the National Lottery. It comes as no surprise to learn that five deadly new viruses have found their way into the Internet, being passed from computer to computer by e-mail. Any linked computer is prone to infection, but unless there has been a gigantic cover-up, the entire National Lottery operation appears to have gone without a hitch.

I marvel at its efficiency – how Camelot somehow manages to assimilate bets from 14,000 agencies in such a way as to work out within minutes the numbers of winners there are in each category, and the sums they have won; how it manages in the flutter of an eyelid to exclude fraudulent entries not only from members of the public but also from the tens of thousands of people trained to issue tickets; and how it pays up every time on the nail.

There can be no doubt that the National Lottery is Britain's greatest achievement in the past 16 years, probably since the war. If anything happens to it – if it becomes infected with any of these new viruses – there will be no shortage of those who will say that some sort of divine retribution is involved, as with the Aids virus in America. Perhaps they will be right. It seems to me that if we lose the National Lottery, we shall lose just about the only thing left which holds us together as a nation.

Wednesday, November 15, 1995

Very interesting

PEOPLE often complain that there is little of interest in the Sunday newspapers, but a fascinating correspondence has been running for several weeks in the *Sunday Telegraph* on the subject of aged parents.

Mr R.J. Buckstone of Emmer Green, near Reading, reveals that his paternal grandfather was born in 1802, and wonders if any other reader can claim a grandparent born in the 18th century. William Court's father, who fought in the second Afghan war, was born in 1848.

G. C. Williams, who lives in Winchester, had a grandfather who met a man who saw Bonny Prince Charlie's army cross the border in 1745.

This seems to me far more interesting than all the rubbish about the Beatles, or the new James Bond girl, or Bill Gates the computer king, with which other newspapers fill their pages. I wonder if anybody will be interested to learn that as a boy of five,

I wandered into a bathroom in my grandmother's house and saw my step great-great grandmother with no clothes on.

Granny Grace, as we called her, was the widow of the 10th Earl of Wemyss, who was born in 1818. She survived my sighting of her in the nude by only one year, dying in 1946 at an unknown age. Her husband, my great-great grandfather, who married her at 83 in 1900 as his second wife, and died in 1914, would be 177 years old if he were alive today.

It may be hard to know exactly what record I have established, but I am sure there is one there. There are those who say that the nudity aspect is irrelevant, but this sort of thing makes a profound impression on a young boy. It may explain why, at the age of 55, I still smoke cigarettes from time to time.

Saturday, November 18, 1995

A profound effect

THE *Sun* has been celebrating the 25th anniversary of its series of photographs of topless young women with a trip down what it calls Memory Lane. It has invited us to return to 1983, when 16-year-old Sam Fox bared her breasts for the first time. In the same year, seat belts became compulsory; the £1 coin came into circulation; the first heart and lung transplant in Britain was reported; Cecil Parkinson admitted an affair with his former secretary, Sara Keays.

None of these, I would guess, has had as much effect on contemporary Britain. It would be easy to measure the effect of these titillating 'page three lovelies' in the statistics for sexual assault and rape. Less easy to measure is the psychological effect on a male population which has been bemused, stultified, enraged and ultimately, perhaps, driven mad by the 'virtual reality' of these apparently naked young women who may be looked at but not touched, lusted after but never possessed.

The parade of page three 'lovelies' provides an alternative history of our times. When one thinks of the numbers involved – six 'lovelies' a week for 25 years – we have a fairly substantial minority of British womanhood prepared to take the Murdoch shilling and bare its breasts to the panting millions.

Another result has been to cheapen the female breast to the point where men can no longer revere it as belonging to the realm of art, or to the more intimate moments of their personal experience. It has become a saucy appendage to the female form, something to be joked about in public and shared with other male friends. This must be most disagreeable for women.

I wonder if the new demand for women-only carriages in trains marks a genuine desire to escape from the sexual assault which, they claim, awaits them in mixed carriages. I doubt this. They are likely to be assaulted only when they are alone, in which case they can be assaulted just as easily in a women's carriage. More likely, I feel, they prefer the company of other women in case they decide to sit topless, so that nobody will laugh at them.

Monday, November 20, 1995

Question of survival

A FORMER mayor of Barnsley who said he suffered from severe depression which prevented him from walking, so that he had to be pushed around in a wheelchair, has been charged with dishonest receipt of £653 disability living allowance after he was secretly filmed walking around Barnsley at the head of a Yorkshire Day procession, running up stairs at the Town Hall, digging up potatoes in his garden and picking up an overturned bench.

I always thought that everyone in Barnsley was on disability living allowance, mobility allowance, and all the 57 other varieties of welfare payment which attach to most Barnsley folk as of right. Social Security officials in Yorkshire should concern themselves with those citizens who are too preoccupied to claim all the benefits which are available, not the tiny majority who might claim too many.

The Mayor of Barnsley surely has set an example. No wonder Clive Cawthrow has received hundreds of letters of support, and a fighting fund has been set up to pay his legal expenses. The point at issue is nothing less than Barnsley's survival as the social and cultural centre of northern England.

Saturday, November 25, 1995

Too much Falstaff

NICE Mr Major was quite right in his instinct that the whole country is suffering from a dangerous level of Soames fatigue. Nicholas Soames, Minister for the Armed Forces, is a genial soul, affectionately known as 'Fatty' among his intimates. One would be as happy to buy a second car from him as one would from any other old Etonian who had come down in the world, but I am afraid that as leader of the Prince of Wales's heavy mob, he lacks the honeyed eloquence to convince us of the justice of his cause.

Many people in Britain, understandably suspicious of anything they see on television, and on their guard against being manipulated, were deeply shocked to hear the clear voice of undiluted truth when the Princess of Wales spoke about her recent history, her hopes and fears for the future.

It was unacceptable, they felt, for anyone to bare her soul (or, as they preferred, to wash her linen) in public. Never mind that much human communication is taken up with presenting a case, otherwise known as persuasion. We expect people to lie to us, to have a hidden agenda on television. Jane Austen's *Persuasion* should be re-named *Manipulation* for the modern reader, and served up as a textbook for our stupid, suspicious age to be on its guard.

Then Fatty Soames appeared on the screen – he has scarcely left it since – and restored the status quo. It was evidence of 'the advanced stages of paranoia' of the Princess of Wales that she believed there was a heavy mob waging a campaign against her. He found her performance 'toe-curlingly dreadful'. She must either work inside the system – Fatty Soames is the system – or she must shut up and go away.

I do not think that the Prince is well served by his heavy mob, nor does it reflect well on his judgment that they should rely on the misogynist rhetoric of ex-public schoolboys to explain his marriage difficulties. Before he comes to the Throne, he must emulate Prince Hal in *Henry IV, Part Two* and send Falstaff packing. The sight of a Prince cowering behind these overweight minders is not an inspiring one.

Wednesday, November 29, 1995

A tiresome old man

THERE is nothing surprising about Alan Clark's wish to return to the House of Commons, but I would hesitate to encourage any constituency to adopt him. It is all very well to say that he is a 'character', and I suppose we will need a replacement for Terry Dicks, but we should still ask ourselves what sort of character he is.

To be anti-hunting and pro-hanging may seem to be an amusing paradox, until one reflects that it is one he shares with nearly all the New Conservatives who, by their dismal terror of Europe, are even now destroying this country's last hopes of a dignified and reasonably prosperous future.

There is nothing wrong with being an overgrown schoolboy and a show-off, so long as you don't also try to stop other people

having their own fun, too. But his desire to put a rope around our necks and hang those of his fellow countrymen and countrywomen who displease him is something different.

Never mind that about half of them will almost certainly be innocent. It is the desire to do it which is unamiable. At 67 he might be thought beyond doing much harm, but it is the effect he has on the young which is most harmful. He should find other ways of spending his money. Why can't he buy Express newspapers, like everyone else?

Saturday, December 2, 1995

Quite normal

AFTER reading William Safire in the *New York Times* on Oliver Stone's new film, *Nixon*, I feel more excited than ever by the idea of it. With Anthony Hopkins playing Nixon and another Briton, Bob Hoskins, playing J. Edgar Hoover, director of the FBI, we may even be able to understand what they are saying.

Safire, who was once President Nixon's chief speech writer, describes the film (which neither of us, I fancy, has yet seen) as a violation of the truth about what really happened. He describes Stone as part of a 'new breed of cinematic pseudo-historians who hype conflict and twist facts to suit dramatic requirements or political ends . . . Stone's purpose is not to illuminate history, but to spread distrust about American institutions.'

According to Safire, the film tries to implicate Richard Nixon in murders during the Eisenhower era. I find this charge very hard to believe. Among American institutions, the presidency is the most sacred, but I see Stone's motive as altogether more noble. He is trying to protect the presidency from the recent terrible calumnies.

If he can convince the world that it is perfectly normal for US presidents to murder people in their spare time, then Mr and Mrs Clinton would not even have to go to the trouble of refuting speculation about the mysterious death of Vincent Foster, the former White House aide, whose suicide note was recently exposed as a forgery. And if it turns out, as I suspect, that Foster was a secret smoker, then at least half the nation will positively applaud.

Monday, December 4, 1995

Britannia indisposed

FEW will be surprised to learn that beefburgers have been identified as a possible cause of Creutzfeldt-Jakob Disease (CJD), being the human form of the incurable mad cow disease, bovine spongiform encephalopathy (BSE). It would appear there are few ills which may not be explained by the hamburger habit.

In Amble, Northumberland, recently, an unemployed man, Philip James, who was warned by police to leave the Tavern pub in Queen Street, was fined £150 plus £40 costs for throwing his burger at a police car. This final debacle was plainly caused by the hamburger, but we must ask ourselves whether its fumes might not have been responsible for his earlier unruly behaviour. Need he, even, have been unemployed if he had not fallen prey to this noxious addiction?

Even now, when we can see its appalling effect on our manners

63

and morals, we seldom ask ourselves the right questions. Last week, two highly respectable Englishwomen were each jailed for five years after being extradited to the United States to face a charge that 10 years ago they discussed plans to bump off a local official among their branch of the Oregon Bhagwan Shree Rajneesh cult. Some Britons protested at their being extradited in this way. We none of us asked if, in their earlier life in America, they had been subjected to hamburgers, whether by primary or secondary, 'passive' ingestion. Many newspapers were fiercely critical of Nicholas Soames, the normally genial Army minister, after his intemperate attack on our lovely Princess of Wales, but only one reproduced the old photograph of him, as Food Minister, forcing himself to eat a hamburger in the line of duty. History may yet judge him a martyr.

Of all the evidence which points to our national decline, most can be laid at the door of the hamburger and its associated gases. The tragedy is that nobody can see it.

Wednesday, December 6, 1995

Are we human?

THE Cabinet is deeply divided, we learn, on whether we will lose more face if we withdraw from the European Court of Human Rights or if we continue our membership and allow it to go on finding us guilty of flouting the convention on human rights which it enshrines.

The Court has nothing to do with the European Union, about which so many Britons have such interesting opinions. It was set up after the excesses of the last war to establish simple rules of common decency among the sovereign states of Europe. It is particularly necessary for Britain, which has no Bill of rights and no formal constitution to protect its citizens against an all-powerful legislature, but our leaders have become upset by the sheer number of cases brought against them.

In the past 20 years, Britain has had to answer for its behaviour to its own citizens 50 times; in 30 cases, it was found to have violated basic rights, and in 10 cases British law has had to be changed.

This is thought to violate the rights of our politicians. They reckon that public opinion was behind the SAS killing of three unarmed suspects in Gibraltar, for which the Court criticised us, and they may be relying on a cretinous saloon-bar jingoism against anything European for support in taking away the only remaining guarantees we have. Do they really think we trust them?

Politicians are now even less trusted in this country than estate agents or journalists. I am not sure where lawyers come, but Mori reckons politicians come bottom, and in another sample of public opinion, the annual British Social Attitudes Survey, whose respondents were asked whether they trusted politicians of any party to tell the truth in a tight corner, 91 per cent reckoned they would lie.

It is in this context that we should judge Mr Major's instruction to his Cabinet colleagues to 'take a long, cool look' at our continued acceptance of the European Convention of Human Rights. The first thing to decide is whether or not we are really human.

Saturday, December 9, 1995

Just what we need

MANY will have been haunted, as I was, by the photograph of Gilbert Terrero, 19, the former altar boy who has been accused of stealing the Duchess of York's necklace at Kennedy Airport.

Gilbert, of Puerto Rican and Dominican background, is a luggage handler at JFK, famous for being the most burgled airport in the world. In his baggy Miami sweatshirt, jeans and trainers, he seems to have a strange affinity with the Duchess, in her baggy Mickey Mouse sweatshirt, jeans and trainers.

Is it just because they are both young? In fact, the Duchess is much older. Yet somehow they complement each other. Looking from one photograph to the other, I cannot make up my mind which is more deserving of the diamond necklace. Could they not share it out between them?

The point about Gilbert Terrero is that he is young, foreign and poor. He is exactly the sort of person the British Tourist Authority is trying to attract to Britain.

The idea is that we should wipe out Britain's 'fuddy-duddy' reputation among young foreigners by promoting a hyper-trendy image abroad. Particular attention will be given to the

65

nightclubs of Leeds, surfing in South Wales and hanging out in the Camden Market. Youngsters are told there is more to Britain than castles, quaint villages and lukewarm beer.

These are the people we hope to attract to our shores. They are also the sort of people the Conservative Party is trying to recruit as candidates in the next general election. As a former altar boy, Gilbert Terrero is obviously the right stuff: young, lower-class, not too elitist in the educational field, almost certainly a Eurosceptic. Fergie must bring him back to England and persuade the Queen to ask him to form a government.

Monday, December 11, 1995

Planning for old age

AS PEOPLE become more and more boring about their health, there is a certain comfort to be derived from the latest edition of *Population Trends*. It reveals that while life expectancy continues to increase at an alarming rate, more and more Britons are heading for a life of miserable ill-health in their extra final years.

Modern medicine can keep people alive almost indefinitely, but it cannot help them enjoy life. For that, we have only the inanities of television, nearly all of it specially devised for American teenagers with a mental age of seven.

I have a vision of these 'bonus years' being spent speechless, in a semi-coma, fed by a drip, recumbent on a bed, recognising nobody. Preparation for old age should be taken more seriously. I observe that Sir Andrew Lloyd Webber plans to farm ostriches in Hampshire. I have often thought of doing the same thing in Somerset. They are not very friendly animals, but they provide good meat, and everybody is growing tired of beef, lamb, pork and chicken.

I could talk to them in my dotage, but I could scarcely play with them, nor is any of my five beautiful grand-daughters likely to enjoy playing with my ostriches, but if ever, as they grow older, one of them wants an ostrich feather for her hat, the supply should be almost endless. I think I will wait and see what happens to the Lloyd Webber ostriches before taking the plunge.

The inheritors

MANY Britons will experience violent and contradictory emotions on learning that some of the great art collection at Castle Howard has been sold partly in order to buy off a younger son. There can be no doubt that these magnificent country houses and the society they supported were Britain's greatest contribution to human civilisation after Shakespeare.

In the new democratic age it is sometimes pretended that we are a nation of footballers, but it is no good pretending we are much good at football. Even today, far more people visit a stately home every year than ever attend a football match. They are the quiet majority, recognising that the country house was our greatest collective achievement.

But it is no good denying that the system was founded and sustained by an elementary injustice – the cruel and unnatural system of primogeniture, whereby the eldest son grabs all the family loot and turns his brothers and sisters out to make their own ways in the world.

This may have resulted in beautiful houses, well-managed estates and contented peasants, but it also created half the social problems that afflict us: an angry exiled urban intelligentsia prone to foolish Left-wing opinions, hatred of the rich, class snobbery and all the rest of it. No other country in the world sees a person's death as sufficient reason to confiscate most of his estate; no other country has ever proposed 98 per cent as the top rate of income tax where the income is derived from savings.

If the English country house culture must be destroyed, what, I wonder, will take its place? The football culture will never appeal to more than a noisy minority, but there must be something to emerge from an intelligent and ingenious race reduced, by foolish education policies, to making Plasticene worms. I think I see the beginnings of it in the Wallace & Gromit animated models. Their brilliant creator, Nick Park, is a Prince of our new Plasticene age. Wallace and Gromit are the inheritors of everything our former pride had planned.

Tipping's Law

Happy the man whose wish and care
A few paternal acres bound
Content to breathe his native air
On his own ground

ALEXANDER POPE wrote his famous *Ode on Solitude* before the Ramblers Association arrived on the scene. Under draft legislation to be presented in the new year by a Labour MP called Paddy Tipping, Ramblers can march in gangs of 20 or 30 on anyone's private land, subject to a few prohibitions, making as much noise and looking as ugly as they please in their terrible multi-coloured apparel. Under the Paddy Tipping rule, the only place where a poet will have any prospect of solitude will be in the lavatory. This may explain some of the disgusting rubbish already being written in the name of poetry.

No doubt these Ramblers think Paddy Tipping is a fine fellow. They will drink his health in condensed milk from tin mugs, banged solemnly together before they pull up their shorts and start rambling anew. But for every Rambler who is made happy by being empowered to stride over someone else's land or along someone's stretch of river there will be at least one small landowner who, with his family, will be dispossessed, at least one country dweller whose favourite spot is invaded by these unpleasant gangs of strangers.

The more that townspeople force their unwelcome presence on the countryside, the more hostility they will encounter. Already the police are finding it hard to recruit spies to inform on their neighbours in the countryside. Informing on neighbours used to be a major country sport, but increasingly the law is seen to be on the side of the enemy: animal activists, urban environmentalists, Ramblers and busybodies of every sort.

'The real requirement by the police is good intelligence, good information on who exactly is committing the crime,' says Supt Keith Akerman, a divisional commander in Hampshire. 'If people themselves are not interested in helping, we might as well pack up and go home.' Quite so.

68

Delighted us enough

MANY will have been disappointed that Europe's leaders, meeting in Madrid, neglected to adopt this column's suggestion that the European currency should be based on the old silver denarius, now worth 10p or a florin. This would enable the French to call it a franc, the Britons a penny, the Dutch a florin, the Germans a pfennig, and everyone would have been happy.

Nothing but sorrow can come from calling it a Euro. The plural form 'Euri' sounds dangerously like 'urine'. This will provide a major debating point to the Euro-sceptics. In fact, it would have been better to call it a Sceptic, in tribute to the intensity and the high intellectual level of the debate which has attended its introduction. We have heard Mr Redwood worried about the confusion it will cause to shopkeepers who may have to adjust their tills – although I can't think why, since the new currency will presumably be decimal. Others rejoice that they will not have to pay a 10 per cent charge on changing their holiday money. But that is not what the new currency is really all about.

At long last the penny seems to have dropped, at least with nice Mr Major and his clever Foreign Secretary, Mr Rifkind. Acceptance of a common European currency will involve a virtual surrender of economic and financial control by the British Government. This is exactly what the country needs. For 50 years our politicians have presided over our industrial and economic decline by devaluing the pound against our more successful competitors – effectively by printing more money.

The burden of this has been borne in large part by the country's savers, who have seen the value of their savings reduced to 10 per cent of their former value, and also in part by the gradual erosion of living standards – including health and education – in relation to our more efficient trading partners. The common currency, call it Sceptic or what you will, offers us our first opportunity to stop the slide. We will have as much money as we can earn.

Of course Mr Major and Mr Rifkind are terrified of losing any pretence of control. So far as economic management is concerned, the new currency will make them completely redundant. They have delighted us enough.

Something to celebrate

IT IS sad that a schism has arisen in the Airport Vineyard network of 600 charismatic churches in Britain and America. The Toronto branch, headed by John Arnott, has been excommunicated from its parent body, headed by John Wimber of California, over the correct interpretation of the Toronto phenomenon, in which worshippers writhe on the floor, laughing, barking, shaking and roaring.

According to Wimber, these activities merely indicate the presence of the Holy Spirit, whereas Arnott's supporters believe that the noises they make as they crawl about the floor represent the roar of the lions of Judah, or possibly Ezekiel, who also roared in his closet. Crowing sounds might herald a new dawn of Christian belief, or something of the sort, they feel.

But the really bitter theological struggles of our time still tend to involve lavatories in churches. One such dispute, at the 11th-century Norman church of St Peter and St Paul in Oxton, Notts,

has gone to the Lord Chancellor, Lord Mackay, for a decision on whether the parish council should be allowed to install a lavatory in the vestry.

The vicar, the Rev Michael Brock, explains: 'There is need for a toilet in the church for little ones, the elderly and people coming from afar to weddings and christenings.' In the previous 850 years of the church's existence, little ones, the elderly etc.

presumably made homely accommodations which are no longer considered acceptable.

But Mr Brock also pointed out that the facility would be out of view, and in this he seems to miss the point. The lavatory should not be a hole-in-the-corner affair, as if the church were ashamed of it. It should be given a place of honour, possibly beside the high altar. A new liturgy must be devised to show the world that Christians, after 850 years of shame, are proud to celebrate their natural bodily functions. Members of the congregation should dance around it, clapping and making bullfrog noises.

Starvation in London

IN THE glut of information available about every aspect of our national life in every newspaper and magazine, it is sometimes hard to believe we are all living in the same country. Mary Killen, writing in one of the Murdoch newspapers, solemnly proclaims the death of the dinner party. Instead, people nowadays give supper parties, sitting down at 9.45pm to little more than a leg of lamb, a Thai chicken, some jelly and cream.

She explains that they are taking advantage of the great national mood of exhaustion to hide the fact that they can't afford anything better, having lost all their money on Lloyd's. But the exhaustion is genuine, too. In the Nineties, she says, people are too exhausted to meet new people. They are physically and mentally reduced by their days at the office. They can only meet old friends. 'New people just drain your energy and we have lost the skill of coping with bores. The dinner party is dead. Enter, *faute de mieux*, the age of the supper party.'

Does Mary Killen live on the same planet as the rest of us? Everybody I know in London or the country sits down to a five- or six-course meal every evening. They start at half past seven and end at 11.30 sharp. Increasingly, these meals are attended by foreigners whom nobody could possibly have met before. I think this may be something to do with the European Union. Where Killen might have a point is that many people nowadays no longer eat a proper luncheon. This may explain their exhaustion in the evening. Is it not time the Government did something about it?

Occupational hazard

MRS BOTTOMLEY is a most attractive and persuasive woman, and it would be easy to agree with her decision not to spend £50 million of National Lottery money on building a new opera house in Cardiff. The Cardiff Bay Opera House scheme, which would have cost £90 million, was to have been the 'jewel in the crown' of Cardiff Bay's £3 billion plan to regenerate the economy of South Wales, but the scheme did not recommend itself to the people of Cardiff.

Opinion polls conducted by local newspapers and by the South Glamorgan County Council showed that by three to one, local people preferred a £55 million Lottery plan for Cardiff Arms Park, the Welsh Rugby headquarters.

So in the end they will get neither, and the economy of South Wales will remain unregenerated. This seems a sensible and fair solution, although the Welsh opera stars Dame Gwyneth Jones and Dennis O'Neill have said it represents a 'slap in the face for Wales and Welsh culture'. In fact it represents an acceptance of Welsh culture. If the Welsh prefer their own loutish, proletarian amusements to the opera, then it would be wrong to force opera on them, let alone the hideous modern building which comes with it.

The only depressing aspect of Mrs Bottomley's wise decision is that the *Sun* claims it as a victory for its revolting campaign against any form of higher culture.

'The *Sun* stops £50m lotto handout to opera' it gloated in its headline: 'Delight as toff scheme is ko'd: a barmy proposal to give £50 million of Lottery cash to an opera house for toffs was ditched yesterday after a *Sun* campaign . . . More than 16,000 jammed our "You The Jury" hotline to protest.'

If the *Sun*'s editor seriously imagines that an intelligent woman like Mrs Bottomley was influenced for one moment by what his readers thought about Welsh opera, then I fear he may be in danger of losing his marbles. This will probably turn out to be an occupational hazard for *Sun* editors. The best advice might be to stick to ball games.

They will never know

ON MONDAY, British viewers will be able to see a most interesting programme made by the BBC's Arena team on the subject of Elvis Presley's diet. It throws important light on the American mass culture which we must imagine will soon take over the world.

The Burger and the King, describes how young Elvis, growing up in a family of poor whites in the black district of Tupelo, Mississippi, originally survived on a diet of greens, sweet potatoes, deep fried squirrel and boiled or baked opossum (a small, rat-like marsupial). When he became rich, and moved to Memphis, Tennessee, his mother kept him fed on hamburgers and jelly sandwiches.

According to the programme-maker, Presley never learnt to use a knife and fork easily, preferring food he could eat with his hands. When he ate steak, he had it cut up for him like a child in bite-sized pieces. As a result, he never went out to restaurants, never met anyone socially and never grew up.

By the early Seventies, he was living an entirely nocturnal existence and sleeping by day. Throughout the night, he had three enormous meals, often adding up to 94,000 calories, enough to keep an office worker going for five or six weeks.

They included a 'supper' of five double hamburgers and five peanut butter and mashed banana sandwiches fried in butter. Staff at Gracelands, his Memphis stately home, watched in anguish as he slowly turned into a hamburger and died. This was in 1977 when he was 42 years old and weighing 25 stone.

I say that we will be able to see this programme on Monday, but the Americans will never see it. The Presley estate has threatened to sue any television company intending to show the film in America for 'infringement of copyright' in the Presley name. The BBC has withdrawn the American showing, despite believing that the estate has no case in law.

This may be because they have observed that un-American litigants rarely win cases against Americans in the American civil courts – least of all when, as in this case, Britain is threatening the integrity of an American icon. So perhaps the Americans will never learn what happened to their hero, will never learn of the effect which hamburgers and jelly sandwiches can have. It is a sobering thought.

Saturday, December 30, 1995

No one to vote for

LADY Mallalieu's assurance that Labour peers will defeat any Bill against hunting may persuade people to decide that if a new Labour government genuinely offers no threat to hunting, we have nothing to fear from it. But of course the House of Lords is so reduced in its powers that it can only delay things for a few years, and a new Labour government might easily abolish the Upper House in any case.

Nobody who has watched the Conservatives' performance over Europe can suppose they are fit to govern any longer, and if Mr Major seriously intends to honour the surviving Beatles with knighthoods and other gew-gaws, there can be no question of voting for him.

Only 'Paddy' Pantsdown, of all the party leaders, talks sense on Europe, but nobody who has lived in Somerset under the Pantsdown Terror at County Hall can possibly vote Liberal Democrat. Sadly enough, the Liberal Democrats seem to combine bossiness and silliness with an unscrupulousness seldom previously seen in British politics.

Norris McWhirter, chairman of the Freedom Association, complained in Thursday's newspaper that a single currency will hand control of our national economy to unsackable, unelected foreign bankers. That has always seemed to me the strongest point in its favour. McWhirter continues: 'In Britain, we, the once-sovereign electorate, have sacked our government eight times since the introduction of universal franchise in 1929.'

So we have, to be sure. But in those days there was some point in sacking the government, because there was an alternative choice. Events have moved on. The parties are now indistinguishable, as are the candidates, many of them 'classless', talking a language no one understands, scarcely to be recognised as fellow human beings, let alone fellow Britons. There can be no question of voting for any of them. Foreign bankers would make a much better job of running the economy, because they would not always be trying to buy other people's votes with our money.

Monday, January 1, 1996

A start to the New Year

IN BRITAIN, the best way to keep numbers down is to go on smoking. Even this public-spirited activity comes under attack today. The anti-smoking fanatics have chosen New Year's Day to spread their dismal message, spending millions of pounds of taxpayers' money in the process.

One plan is to embarrass us out of the habit by showing us pictures of John Cleese. Another is to hire child decoys who will test whether shopkeepers are willing to sell them cigarettes. The shopkeeper will then be prosecuted and can be fined up to £2,500.

Is children's evidence reliable? A better plan might be to make John Cleese dress up as a revolting schoolboy and try to buy cigarettes. There is something slightly repugnant in the idea of training up children in the role of *agents provocateurs*. In America, a young woman of 25 called Birdy Jo Hoaks dressed up as a 12-year-old boy and achieved great success claiming to have been abandoned by her parents at a bus stop. People offered money, gifts and a home. A newspaper set up a trust fund.

Then it was discovered she had tried the same trick two years earlier in Vermont, where she was imprisoned for 23 days for posing as an abandoned boy. Now she is held in Lake City Utah, facing charges which could land her with a 15-year sentence.

The Americans take this sort of thing very seriously. Kids are sacred. Soon, I expect, President Clinton will make child impersonation a capital offence. If we follow their lead, as we do in so many things, and if Cleese is charged with impersonating a child smoker, it might end up with his judicial execution by hanging.

Despite my anti-capital punishment sympathies, I do not feel that on that occasion I could object very strongly. Protection of children from child impersonators and suchlike must come first.

Saturday, January 6, 1996

Take the strain

WE MUST take off our hats to the Consumers' Association researchers who discovered that in nine cases out of 10 they were given the wrong advice by railway staff on cheap tickets. Another problem is to identify any advice at all through the various barriers of language and temperament which separate members of the public from ticket sellers.

Railway staff who suggest the more expensive tickets might show a touching loyalty to their employers, since I am reluctant to believe they receive a percentage, but I fear the real motive is misanthropy. They are irritated by the need for a five-minute conversation with every traveller to establish exactly the right degree of concessionary fare.

The muddle goes back to when the last Labour government, when, under the chairmanship of Sir Peter Parker, the fares structure was seen as a tool for social engineering, an instrument for furthering social justice. Everybody should pay what he or she could afford. Hence the immense complexity of the present system, with a different fare for every age group, every time of day, every marital status, sexual proclivity and trade or occupation.

Telephone calls are met by a recorded voice. Where there are information desks, they are marked by 45-minute queues while a succession of monoglot foreigners tries to explain its travel requirements to a monoglot Hindustani information officer.

Everything would be solved by a simple system of set fares, with a first, second and much cheaper and less comfortable third-class rate for every journey not covered by a season ticket. It is too much to expect a commercial firm to operate Sir Peter's private welfare service.

Monday, January 8, 1996

Thought for food

NONE of us had ever heard of the violet click beetle until last week, when English Nature announced that it was threatened in this country. Now we are to spend £15,000 planting trees for it on Bredon Hill. 'The violet click beetle is so rare that we know little about its life-style, and the adult has only been seen five or six times,' said Dr Peter Holmes, the English Nature Conservancy officer.

None of which really adds up to a good reason for spending £15,000 on a home for it. It is rather like the Department of Trade and Industry handing £750,000 to Rowntree for additional research on their fruit pastilles. As it happens, I have always been rather partial to fruit pastilles, although I have not seen the best ones – Callard and Bowser's Citrus Fruits – in any of the shops I use for the last six months or so.

Perhaps they have gone the way of the violet click beetle. Although I am not sure I believe in the existence of this beetle – it is not mentioned in any of my reference books – endless brooding on the subject has given me a strong desire to eat one. If anybody can provide me with a genuine violet click beetle in fresh condition, I will pay £10 for it.

The joke's the thing

CAN IT really be true that the National Lottery undermines capitalism, as well as causing untold misery to the unfortunate people who win it, destroying charities, making politicians and bishops unhappy, strengthening the corporate state, causing endless squabbles between arts and sports lobbyists?

77

Why, then, does one persist in thinking it is the best thing the Conservatives have done? The answer is to be found in the distress it causes to the puritans and self-proclaimed 'meritocrats' who hope to carry all before them.

Many of these 'meritocrats', as we can easily see, are ignorant, wrongheaded and conspicuously untalented, as well as being priggish and conceited, but let us suppose that a few of them do, indeed, possess some superior merit which has enabled them to climb to positions of wealth, power and importance.

Why is it less unjust that they should enjoy such privileges as a result of having been born with unequal merit than that Lord Clarence FitzSnotty should enjoy them as a result of inherited wealth?

It causes more resentment, not less, if we must believe that everybody richer than ourselves is richer in virtue, too. In fact, society becomes unsustainable under any such assumption.

The Lottery, which dispenses vast sums with no pretence of merit attached, is the perfect answer to this problem. Mrs Bottomley described the prospect of a £40 million prize as great fun, but it is more than that. It is the supremely excellent joke of our times. I find myself laughing whenever I think of the possibility of winning it. The misery it causes its winners is a small price to pay for retaining our national sense of humour.

Wednesday, January 10, 1996

Congestion

WE SHOULD not be too alarmed by the new claim that one in two motorists – perhaps up to 17 million in all – have defective eyesight and should be prevented from driving. It emerges from a survey conducted by Eyecare Information Service, rather than by anyone else, and one can understand that any organisation devoted to Eyecare would take a rather strict view.

Certainly no reflection is intended on the scientific accuracy or seriousness of this survey when I observe that there is a strong spirit abroad in the land trying to stop other people from driving. Other people's cars have become an abominable nuisance.

Opposition to them is necessarily disorganised, not to say at odds with itself. The heroic campaigners against a Newbury bypass, who have taken to the trees and built tunnels to further their struggle, are bitterly opposed by many, if not most, inhabitants of Newbury, who see the by-pass as a means of reducing congestion.

Perhaps the strongest pitch comes from those who claim to be worried by the dangers of drink on the roads, despite the fact that we have the lowest incidence of drink driving and the lowest road fatality rate of all developed countries. If the campaigners had their way, nobody would be permitted to drive who had drunk one glass of wine in the previous four hours.

That is all very well if you are a teetotaller with faultless eyesight living in London, but you don't need to be a half-blind drunk living in the country to feel threatened. Safety standards are high enough for there to be no justification for mass exclusions. The only way to reduce the number of cars is through making it more expensive to drive. If petrol cost £10 a gallon and the annual road tax is £1,000 – lorries over 10 tonnes £10,000 – life would return to normal. It is just a question of which we resent more, the congestion or the cost of avoiding it.

Holiday planning

AT A TIME of year when everybody is thinking where to go for their summer holidays, several obvious choices seem determined to rule themselves out. New Zealand, one of the pleasantest spots imaginable, with good food, friendly, comprehensible natives and some of the best wine on earth, seems to be going through a silly phase politically.

There is talk of abolishing knights and dames from the New Zealand social scene. One meets many more of them in Australia and New Zealand than one ever does in Britain, and although we tend to laugh at knights in this country and pinch their bottoms if we get a chance, there can be no question that people in the former colonies enjoy a title.

To withdraw from this benign system suggests a more general retreat from conviviality and humour, into pomposity and self-importance. This may not be the best moment to go there.

Similarly, the south Malaysian state of Johore, which many of us may have been thinking about, has suddenly announced that any Muslim caught committing adultery or cohabiting, will be caned. That is all very well, but if, on holiday, one suddenly fancies the idea of committing adultery, one does not necessarily wish to be caned for it – nor to have to convince some imam or other that one is not a Muslim.

Perhaps the best thing is to stay in Britain and go to the seaside. A new competition among English resorts for the most polluted beach has been won this time by a cove at Silverdale, Lancashire, with 166 items of litter per metre. By comparison a long stretch near Bideford, Devon, has fewer than one item per metre.

One of the problems about filling a beach with refuse is that seabirds and mammals – including dolphins, whales and sea turtles – will come and eat some of the best litter or take it away. One defence might be to poison the sea first. This would dispose of all the seabirds, dolphins, whales and sea turtles. Then we can lie down and sunbathe in our own little area of rubbish, surrounded by drink cans, sweet bags, crisp packets and plastic cups.

Saturday, January 13, 1996

Declining powers

BELIEF in hell as a form of eternal torment has declined in direct proportion to the greater comfort of people's lives. The old message to recalcitrant members of the underclass was that their existence might be uncomfortable now, but it will be much worse in the hereafter if they did not toe the line, respect other people's property and smile deferentially at the well-to-do.

By the same token, those of gentler, more privileged background were prepared to entertain the idea of eternal torment as a reflection of their social insecurity and residual guilt. Privilege involved obligations, and those who abused their position on earth would have to suffer elsewhere.

At a time when everyone outside a small minority of self-elected social outcasts enjoys an extraordinary degree of home comfort, with food, warmth, hot water and colour television to hand, the fear of discomfort has all but vanished, let alone the fear of eternal torment vindictively applied. That may be why, in part, so many young people seem happy to stab each other and kick each other to death for no particular reason. I do not know.

But I am not sure the Bishop of Newcastle has quite got it right when he tries to substitute the idea of annihilation – non-existence after death – as the ultimate punishment for a badly spent life. Intellectually active people may find the idea of their own extinction repugnant, but less active minds accept the idea quite happily as an extension of the sleep experience.

Perhaps the best way to communicate the idea of punishment attendant on a selfish and futile existence would be in the threat of an infinitely extended old age: eating nothing but salad, drinking nothing but goats' milk, reading nothing but idiotic suggestions in *The Times* for prolonging a miserable, pointless existence still further.

National pastime

PRESSURE on Mr and Mrs Clinton seems to be mounting from various quarters, but the most obvious area of concern connected with this young couple is still ignored throughout the length and breadth of their great country.

The President has been told that he cannot claim executive privilege and will have to face charges that, as governor of Arkansas four years ago, he exposed himself to a woman called Paula Jones in the Excelsior Hotel, Little Rock. It now looks as if he will have to answer these charges at the time of the November election, when they may prove a sad distraction.

At the same time Mrs Clinton is under ferocious attack for alleged lies and evasions to the Whitewater inquiry. An immensely distinguished political commentator in the *New York Times* called William Safire – America's equivalent of Sir Peregrine Worsthorne, Lord Rees-Mogg and the late Peter

Jenkins all rolled into one – has claimed that she has 'a habit of lying' and is at the heart of a 'web of deceit'. Strong words to use against a First Lady.

But the questions which absolutely nobody is prepared to ask are about who murdered Vincent Foster, the young White House attorney found with a bullet in his head in a park outside Washington; who arranged for a forged suicide note to be found among his effects many weeks later; who forged it and why.

For some reason Americans who are happy to consider whether their President may be a sexual exhibitionist or their First Lady a habitual liar are not prepared to ask themselves these questions. I think I understand the reason, and it is rather touching. They think it would be bad for their country's image.

But they need not worry. We all know perfectly well what America is like, and follow their national pastimes on television. Most people spend most of their time punching each other in the face, shooting each other and chasing each other in cars, one of which usually drives over a bridge or a cliff. Then they chase each other to the top of buildings until one of them falls off. Nothing can shock us, and we still love Americans, for all the jokes we make about them from time to time. Many of us are simply jealous.

Uses for women

ALTHOUGH we must all be pleased by the industrial tribunal ruling that Labour's notorious all-women shortlists are illegal, it does nothing to explain why they were thought necessary in the first place.

Was it that Labour MPs missed the female company in a House where fewer than one in 10 Members is a woman? In fact there are plenty of attractive and obliging young research assistants in the Palace of Westminster, for those who like that sort of thing.

No, I do not think that the pressure for more lady members came from the existing MPs. Few, in my observation, even notice the gender of the person they are talking to, so absorbed are they in themselves. The pressure came from Labour women, who felt they were being excluded from positions of power and importance.

Even so, it does not explain why it was necessary to rig the system in their favour. The sexes are more or less equally divided in this country, and apart from the disturbing episode of Mrs Thatcher, we have no reason to shun female leaders. Yet fewer than one in 10 MPs is a woman.

The explanation must be that although political ambitions are nauseating enough in a man, they are even more unattractive in a woman.

Politics is about bossing other people around and exerting power. Where a man puts himself forward for this task, we feel that at least we can punch him on the nose if he becomes too objectionable. With a woman we can't do that, but have to listen politely to all her fatuous pronouncements. Women make surprisingly good steeplejacks and pub bouncers, however.

Monday, January 15, 1996

The biggest threat

BERNARD QUINN, the amiable-looking former aircraft engineer from Weston-super-Mare who has chosen the eccentric hobby of 'stalking' the Princess Royal, told a policeman that he had once crashed his car while having sexual fantasies about her.

One cannot help wondering how many crashes take place where fantasies about the Princess are a factor. Is it beyond the ingenuity of science to devise a machine to measure these things. Might not the police be empowered to stop any driver whom they had reason to believe was fantasising about the Princess Royal and apply certain tests?

This could result in further injustice. There is no reason to suppose that just because Quinn crashed his car while fantasising about the Princess, he crashed *because* he was fantasising about her. He might have eaten something that affected his judgment.

Paul Firth, Liverpool city's stipendiary magistrate, was quite right to declare that Quinn had no case to answer on the charge of threatening a breach of the peace. It is reassuring to find a magistrate of such sturdy independence, unprepared to be browbeaten by all the rubbish put in the newspapers by police public relations.

On the train after his ordeal, Quinn was photographed eating a pasty. One may not like the smell or taste of these things much, but nobody has yet suggested they do you serious harm.

One hopes and prays he can stay away from more harmful substances. A long report on killer viruses in *New Scientist* contains this stark warning: 'In the 21st century, the biggest threat may come from contaminated hamburgers.'

Of course one cannot expect the Government or police to do anything about this threat. There is too much money in hamburgers, and the police seem more interested in monitoring our sexual fantasies. If only they would use some of the vast sums they spend on advertisements to urge people to eat pasties instead.

Saturday, January 20, 1996

Dishy Days

TRAVELLING east out of London on Wednesday I could not help noticing how many of the poorest, ugliest and dirtiest homes had been further disfigured by the presence of a satellite dish aerial, often stuck immediately above the front door like some sort of armorial achievement.

It was explained to me that people needed these ugly objects in order to watch sport on television. They were not proudly announcing that their household was uneducated and uncultured, although they plainly invited others to reach this humiliating conclusion.

Under the circumstances, Robert Atkins's call for a £5 levy on the BBC licence fee to pay for sport might seem humane and sensible. He was speaking at a London conference on the future of television sport. The only contribution from other Labour and Conservative MPs present was to accuse sports administrators of financial greed in selling television rights to the Murdoch-dominated satellite channel BSkyB. They suggested it was somehow unpatriotic not to sell them for less money to the BBC.

But why should sports lovers be forced to watch Murdoch's other rubbish, and disfigure their homes with his horrible emblems? The £5 sports levy on a BBC licence only makes good sense if those like me and my dear wife who detest sport can opt out of paying it, otherwise it becomes a simple case of extortion.

People should be able to devise a television set which does not receive BBC sport. By the same token, on a system of levies, people would be able to exclude all BBC programmes about pop music, politics, the Royal Family, modern art, the north of England, all American thrillers and love stories, and so on according to taste.

At one time we used to watch the Grand National, the Oxford and Cambridge Boat Race and the Wimbledon finals, but one grows out of these things. Television without sport would be a distinct improvement, but if they plan a compulsory levy on the television licence, they would have to build an enormous number of prisons to accommodate all the women who will refuse to pay.

Too much controversy

THE LEAST we expect Christians to do in this irreligious age is to agree with each other, if only within their own denominations. Wherever one looks, they are squabbling like jackdaws.

This week Cardinal Hume launched a book written by the Canon Law Society, seeking to undermine the Pope's instruction 'the Church has no authority whatsoever to confer priestly ordination on women, and that this judgment is to be definitively held by all the Church's faithful'.

One may doubt whether it would be legal to create this new job opportunity – the woman priest – if men were forbidden to apply for it. Like the Labour Party, with its women-only candidate shortlists, the Church would be left with egg all over its face.

A vicar in Mossley Hill, Liverpool, is at war with local members of the British Legion over his plans to use his church as an aerial for a mobile telephone company. They point out that drug dealers and other criminals use mobile telephones. The Legion's Maureen Brindle, 52, puts it this way: 'This is so hypocritical. Folk will be praying to God in the church and above their heads the aerial on the tower will be doing the work of the Devil.'

The vicar, Rev David Wills, said that normal telephones were used for drug deals. English Catholics, meanwhile, have been debating a claim made in court by the former headmaster of a Catholic school in Southsea that it is a 'normal thing' to bite boys' bottoms when chasing them to bed. Does the suggestion that it is normal make it more or less acceptable?

The worst clashes this week took place in Coventry Cathedral, where a young woman described as Angel Quercus, 28, in the *Telegraph*, and as Lucy Pearce, 35, in the *Times*, exposed her naked body, covered with slogans, in protest against a service to celebrate the car. The Rt Rev Simon Barrington-Ward, Bishop of Coventry, said it was a pity she could not have carried out her protest with more dignity and restraint.

Bishop Simon misses the point. What we all want to know is whether it would have been theologically and canonically correct – whether it would have been *normal* – for the bishop to have bitten her bottom.

Saturday, January 27, 1996

Progress

ON Wednesday's BBC2, I listened to a conversation between Andrew Marr, the journalist, and a strange philosopher called Peter Singer, possibly an Australian. Singer was of the opinion that animals, as sentient beings, should be regarded as having equal rights to humans, with regards to discomfort and death.

Marr pushed him a bit, but not hard enough. If there is only one life support machine, needed by a sick baby and a sick chimpanzee, and if the chimpanzee has the better chance of surviving, which should have it?

But the idea that animals are our equals, if not our superiors, is one that has gained ground under the New Education, and when next day I saw a delightful picture of Joanna Lumley taking a baby pig to the Palace of Westminster, I assumed she must be planning to ask Speaker Boothroyd to accept it as a Member of Parliament.

In fact, she was merely demonstrating her opinion that such

animals ought not to be exported. I must admit that I found myself agreeing. Perhaps it is because I am confined to a health farm, my mouth watered as I looked at the little thing. Why should the foreigners have it? Lumley was working on behalf of Compassion In World Farming. Perhaps these people have some good points among all the rubbish they talk.

There is much to be said for having a House of Commons composed of pigs and other animals. The public much prefers animals to human beings. This explains why nearly half of all television time seems to be devoted to them.

Almost any animal would romp home in an election, but perhaps we should settle for a parliament of pigs to preserve some vestige of the 'One Nation' idea. They would be less irritating than the present incumbents even if they turned out to have the wrong ideas about Europe like so many Conservatives.

Monday, January 29, 1996

American way of death

READING that the American Centre in Paris – a 65-year old showcase for the country's culture – is to close for lack of money, I was reminded of my note last Monday about the closure of the US consulate in Bordeaux after 200 years. This was explained partly by lack of money, partly by the fact that Americans have learned to make good wine for themselves. 'Everything they do, they do well,' I commented.

Brooding about this, I feel that a reservation should be entered on the subject of food. Most American food appears to be either tasteless or revoltingly over-spiced and over-ketchupped. Perhaps one should not feel too much sympathy for killers about to be executed, but I tremble with pity when I read about their last meals.

John Taylor, the child killer executed by firing squad in Utah, chose a pizza 'with everything on it' to accompany his last Coca-Cola. That should have been a fairly safe choice, and the execution seems to have been arranged with commendable efficiency.

But before he had smoked his last cigarette on the walk through snow to his execution chamber (Utah does not allow people to smoke in public buildings), he announced that he had an upset stomach. They gave him medication for it in the short time left before they shot his heart out. But nothing, really, takes the place of a decent meal.

Taylor, whose crime was committed in 1989, was the first American to be executed by shooting since 1977, and may be the last in Utah. Another record of sorts was set in Smyrna, Delaware, last week with the execution by hanging of Billy Baily, who killed an elderly couple in 1979. This was the first hanging in Delaware for 50 years.

For his last meal, Baily chose steak, baked potatoes, rolls, butter, pear and vanilla ice cream, presumably in that order. It may sound all right, but I trembled.

Reports of a third execution in the United States last week – of Richard Townes, in Jarrat, Virginia, for the murder of a shop assistant 11 years ago – for some reason do not carry details of his last meal. They merely mention that the execution was delayed for 22 minutes while medical orderlies tried to find a vein for the lethal injection.

We hear rather less of the electric chair nowadays – possibly because Americans have finally decided that, like socialism, it doesn't work. Perhaps judicial execution is another of those things the Americans do not do very well.

Wednesday, January 31, 1996

Noisy toys annoyance

WE SHOULD not become too morose and sentimental at the suggestion made by Mr David Howitt, director general of the

British International Toy and Hobby Association, that the poor buy all the most expensive toys.

'They know that times are hard for their families and in the very nicest of ways they try to protect their children from the hardship by spoiling them.'

To what hardship does he refer? Hunger? The money would be better spent on food. Cold? Buy them warm clothes. Homelessness? Tell the local housing committee. Children are not, by law, allowed to be homeless.

It is true that poorer homes often lack the amenity of a 'crying room', where crying children can be put until they stop crying, but the simple truth is that the main reason that poorer parents tend to spoil their children is that they lack the intelligence to do anything else. This may in part explain what sociologists ironically describe as the cycle of deprivation. Few spoilt children will rise to occupy such important jobs as director general of the British International Toy and Hobby Association.

The best news to emerge from the 47th International Toy Fair at Harrogate has been that an EC resolution plans to set a limit on the noise made by children's toys. Thank heaven for the bureaucrats of Brussels. British politicians would not have dared to make such a suggestion in a hundred years.

Smoke up, smoke up

BRITAIN's first American-style retirement village, to be built in Essex at Thorpe-le-Soken, near Frinton-on-Sea, will have a fitness centre, swimming pool, nine-hole golf course, restaurants, hospital, library and business centre, but it will lack any appearance of a fortress. There will be no high fences patrolled by private security guards.

'We want to integrate it into the wider community,' explains Mr Jeremy Tasker, of Chesterton, the estate agents.

I wonder if that is wise. In the great antipathy between the generations which is developing all over the world, I should have thought that elderly people in Britain needed more protection than they do in America. In America, oldies are at least allowed guns to protect themselves against the envy and avarice of the young. Even without security guards, they could give a good account of themselves against gangs of marauding louts on motor bikes. In Britain they are forbidden any weapon at all.

The greatest problem in Britain is that people are living too long. There are two aspects to this. In the first place, the state can no longer afford to look after them. If it tried it would have to tax the younger working population out of existence. In the second place, as they live longer they spend all the money they have saved on looking after themselves. The longer they live, the less the younger generation will inherit. Many will inherit nothing.

Unless people are prepared to make a determined effort not to live too long, there is bound to be growing friction between old and young, as the young see their expectations shrink and disappear.

Our rulers do nothing about it apart from evicting 98-year-old ladies whose money has run out. They would do better to mount a campaign urging us to smoke more cigarettes. If we lived less long, this would remove young people's anxieties and help restore the feel-good factor. With the extra revenue from tobacco tax they could then splash out on buying some votes.

Saturday, February 3, 1996

Birmingham the beautiful

LONDON's atrocious new logo, which will spearhead an £8 million worldwide campaign to attract more tourists, shows three sketchy figures, one blue, one yellow, one red, engaged in what might be some sort of dance to make a shape vaguely suggestive of fancy dress headgear.

This absurdity is said to have cost £100,000. How can anyone justify such a sum for a commercial doodle? I suppose the different colours of the figures are intended to give some idea of the exciting ethnic mix which London offers.

The whole world would be falling over itself to come here as soon as it saw the logo if only it had included the elegant smog masks which Londoners wear as fashion accessories. It has recently been discovered they afford scant protection against the exciting petrol and diesel fumes. But I am not sure that London really needs any more tourists. They crowd the pavements, take up all the places in restaurants, grab all the taxis and add nothing to my own enjoyment of London, or that of many millions of others. Perhaps they make a few people richer, those who sell them ice creams, soft drinks and T-shirts, but they certainly don't make me any richer.

The greatest anxiety of everyone in London who is not an ice cream seller is to prevent the wretched millennium celebrations from being held in the nation's capital. It will bring nothing but sorrow and irritation. Birmingham, on the other hand, is ideal. It also has similarly exciting diesel and petrol fumes, and a similar ethnic mix.

I have asked Mr Rushton to design an irresistible logo for Birmingham which will persuade the whole world to visit the jewel of the West Midlands instead of London. Here it is:

Things fall apart

ANYBODY could have pointed out that as soon as the police were given weapons they would start shooting each other by accident. It used to be accepted wisdom in the Army that when you give troops ammunition you will suffer a monthly loss of some two per cent killed or wounded by accidental discharges.

I am in no position to mock the police, having shot myself quite severely as a young soldier in Cyprus. But it occurs to me that the latest incident, when three marksmen of the élite Tactical Firearms Group were wounded trying to clean a Heckler and Koch sub-machine gun in Bishopsgate police station, raises some worrying questions.

Members of the TFG regularly guard the Queen, other senior members of the Royal Family and the Prime Minister. How long will it be before one of them is accidentally shot by a Heckler and Koch sub-machine gun? The Prime Minister may be replaceable easily enough, although we would miss him, but we can ill afford to lose the Queen before it has been definitely decided who shall succeed her.

Perhaps the most worrying story of our growing incompetence as a nation was told in the Old Bailey this week, where it was alleged that six prison officers, unable to stop a prisoner from having sex with a female visitor, whose throat he threatened to cut, watched him through an observation window while he had his way with her. Then the deputy governor arrived and ordered the officers to break into the room, whereupon the prisoner allegedly cut the poor woman's throat. I hope this story does not discourage prison visiting.

Monday, February 19, 1996

Leadership qualities

MY experience of watching television is too small for me to pontificate often on the subject, but I was interested to read a review of a new quiz show called *Carnal Knowledge*, described as 'possibly the single worst programme in the history of British television'.

'It is hard to come up with a comparison to make sense of quite how cretinous, vulgar, amateurish, adolescent and mind-bendingly boring this new quiz show is,' wrote Matthew Norman in the *Evening Standard*, explaining that it consists of four unattractive exhibitionists talking dirty, while everybody shrieks with laughter.

I am afraid I believe him. The great question is *why* anybody makes or shows this dismal rubbish. Have Britons degenerated so far that they now prefer it? My own guess is that they would be equally happy to be shown something much better. These programmes are made and shown because the educated middle-class has lost control, the yobs have taken over.

Some of the blame must attach to the country's leadership. Although nice Mr Major is fast becoming a love-object on this column – his beautiful manners, his kindness, his patience and common sense – he fails the Way of the World leadership test, and fails it dismally. This is determined by whether the candidate would look impressive as a Roman or Greek marble statue in the nude.

Major would look absurd. He has no leadership qualities.

Only one figure in public life seems to have the necessary grandeur. When we were both younger and he was Prime Minister, I used to see Edward Heath as a petulant, chippy little fellow. I used to mock him and throw packets of peanuts at him to emphasise his humble origins.

Now, as he approaches his 80th birthday in July, his stature has grown with him, until he has become a giant on the political scene. Everything he says is true, everything he writes is well written and wise. He would make a splendid nude statue in Trafalgar Square or anywhere else. I hope it is not too late to ask him to lead us into a United Europe with a new spirit of pride in our achievements and confidence in the future, greater fecundity among our women and a higher sperm count among our demoralised males.

The scaremongers

WHENEVER I am offered the editorship of a national newspaper, I tend to turn it down, having no interest in huge areas of the contemporary scene, from popular music and modern art to science, sport and business. Who apart from God is to determine what is news and what is idle gossip or scaremongering?

In the *Independent* last week I read a headline 'Mother's diet affects child for rest of life', over the suggestion that mothers who eat too many potatoes in pregnancy will produce babies who develop heart disease in later life. The same newspaper carried an even more lurid report, produced by a gaggle of child agencies, to the effect that there were 4,000 known or suspected paedophiles in Britain.

If there are really only 4,000 of them in a population of 58.2 million, would it be reasonable to ask the newspapers to stop boring us about them? They are an insignificant minority engaged in a statistically insignificant activity. It is the nation's apparent obsession with child sex which is worrying.

I think we should also be worried about our failing sperm count. British men now have only half the sperm count of the Finns. The most likely explanation is not pollution of the environment, but a general lassitude which has fallen on us all as we contemplate the American future. To some extent, the leadership must be held responsible. If Mr Major is not prepared to do anything about it, he might consider that what we need is a mature bachelor who has been saving himself all these years. Ted Heath will show us the way out of this lassitude. He is the only politician left in Britain who talks and writes sense.

Monday, February 26, 1996

Resist the hairless future

THE SCIENTIST who has discovered a laser beam which offers men the prospect of never having to shave again may suppose he has made a significant contribution to human comfort.

Professor Marc Clement, of the Swansea Institute of Higher Education, accidentally exposed his arm to laser light, and later noticed that the area remained completely bald, the hair never growing back. A laser light, tuned to the correct frequency, will fry the hair follicle in a way that is thought to be permanent.

Shaving is not a particularly enjoyable occupation, although it has become less tiresome since the invention of the electric shaver. Its essential function is to remind the shaver of his gender, of his function in the scheme of things – to cherish and protect his womenfolk. A man who does not shave or grow facial hair will soon degenerate into a whimpering, childish thing, expecting to be coddled and protected by his women. This will add to nobody's happiness in the long run.

The treatment is also said to offer women the promise of silky smooth legs without discomfort. Is this really what they want? Perhaps they do not agree that a lower leg without any touch of prickle is like champagne without its spritz. It all seems to be leading to a general attack on hair. Before long they will announce that hair is insanitary, germ-ridden and dangerous.

The thinning head can be most attractive, I agree. My colleague and friend, Christopher Booker, would not look nearly so distinguished without a certain lofty elevation to his brow, and Gerald Kaufman would be unrecognisable if he suddenly grew hair again.

But as Trollope remarks in *Ralph the Heir* (*not* Ralph the Hair): 'There is a baldness that is handsome and noble, and a baldness that is peculiarly mean and despicable.' Can we not leave it at that?

Saturday, March 9, 1996

Keep them away

THERE is no reason to rejoice and every reason to feel despondent at the news that 23.6 million tourists flooded into Britain last year – an increase of 12 per cent on the all-time record of the year before – unless you happen to earn your money selling them soft drinks, T-shirts or whatever. London in particular is made almost uninhabitable for large parts of the year by this invasion of tourists.

Of all the many arguments for retaining and cherishing our monarchy, the claim that it encourages tourism is quite easily the worst. If it stood alone, it might even prove sufficient reason for abolition. The main functions of the monarchy are to give us pride in our identity, to preserve a small corner of London from developers, to keep us amused and give us something to talk about.

The present Royal Family fulfils these functions brilliantly. I do not think we can really blame them for this appalling plague of tourists, who are mostly attracted by what they see as favourable rates of exchange. Favourable to whom, one wonders. The abject state of our currency is far more a matter of national disgrace than the Princess of Wales's sporting admission about the cad Hewitt.

Our currency is valueless as a result of Kenneth Clarke's obstinate policy of low interest rates. For the price of appeasing a handful of incompetent businessmen and a slightly larger number of domestic over-borrowers he antagonises the majority of conservatism's traditional supporters – the savers and the elderly.

Clarke suggests that the feel-good factor is about to reappear. I wonder if he lives in the same country as the rest of us. Journeys by train, car or underground are now a nightmare. Practically nothing seems to work. Britons in the street, if you can spot any, are not only miserable and quick to anger, they are also looking for revenge.

When they go abroad, they face humiliation from every side: not just for the worthlessness of their currency or because of the oafish manners of their compatriots, but for other reasons, too. Even the fishes have noticed. Why should a British tourist harmlessly swimming at Heron Island off the Barrier Reef suddenly be attacked and seriously mauled by a ferocious Tiger shark? I suspect it was infuriated by a certain air of lassitude it may have detected in the British swimmer. This may also explain why so many Britons are murdered in Florida.

Our best hope may be that foreigners will realise what a hell-hole Britain has become and keep away. The rest of us had better learn to stay where we are.

Sheep opportunities

MANY wise old heads were shaken over the news that scientists have managed to produce two identical sheep by cloning. When applied to humans, we are assured, this will surely lead to a fascist dictatorship, rather than produce a new breed of attractive, amiable, intelligent, healthy people.

Before we decide, I feel there are many experiments, not to say practical jokes, which should be tried on these two sheep. At present they look pretty well alike, but will they look the same after they had been in a field for a couple of years? More particularly, will they be the same after they had been put in different fields?

All arguments about the rival influences of heredity and environment will be settled if one of these sheep is sent to live as the pet of a duchess, frisking on the lawns of some stately home during its holidays from Eton; the other is sent to live in a rundown council estate in Liverpool.

Will the Scouse sheep develop unexpected musical talents, or have motivational problems in school? Will the Etonian develop a charming, self-confident manner and a certain vagueness about whose turn it is to pay for the next round of drinks? I feel we are on the verge of great discoveries. This no time to turn back.

Monday, March 11, 1996

The living arts

BEING in Somerset over the weekend, I missed the opportunity to inspect the naked actors and actresses on show in glass cases at London's Hayward Gallery. It was the brilliant idea of Peter Greenaway, the controversial film director, to introduce Londoners to high art in this way. Actors were available for inspection on Saturday, actresses on Sunday.

The glass cases were closed on only three sides, so art fanciers were able to talk to the works of art, although not to touch them. Works of art are not things to be touched by the public. But many people unmoved by high art are still quite interested to talk to people with no clothes on.

This seems a humane arrangement, so far as it goes. A society in which a huge and growing proportion of adults live alone must somehow come to terms with its own sexuality. I do not see that massage parlours do any harm, so long as their presence is not intrusive; the same is true of pornography.

It may be intolerable to display lewd material in public where it can cause offence to elderly, refined or religious sensibilities, but to have it discreetly available on demand seems a matter of social common sense.

Westminster Council officers who spend their time visiting massage parlours and prosecuting those that offer extra services would be better employed – if they must be employed at all – ensuring that the establishments are disease-free.

But it seems sad if Londoners cannot achieve even the limited degree of intimacy afforded by Mr Greenaway without pretending to be interested in modern art.

Monday, March 25, 1996

Try almost anything once

MANY people will have been shocked by the story of Philip Hall the ornithologist who made a long trek to the banks of the river

Niger in search of the incredibly rare Rufous Fishing Owl, only to be shown the remains of one which had been eaten by villagers the night before.

I hope he took the opportunity to ask if he could nibble at the remaining leg. Ornithology is a respectable science, and gives many people pleasure, but gastronomy is the more important of the two, affecting, in its way, the whole human race.

If the Rufous Fishing Owl proved exceptionally delicious, it might be worthwhile to mount an expedition to secure a pair and breed them up for the table. Somebody always has to try these things first or we would never know, for instance, that rabbits are good to eat, rats are not.

Being a bird-lover should be no impediment. It may not be completely true that every man eats the thing he loves, but I, who am Founder, President and only known member of the Dog Lovers Party of Great Britain (and a patron of the Canine Defence League) once ate dog in Manila. My attempts to eat giant panda in China were frustrated, and I caused grave offence once in Adelaide by asking where it was possible to eat koala, but I think one has a duty to try everything.

The answer to our present beef crisis is obviously ostriches.

I ate ostrich several times in South Africa, and liked it, while mentally taking off my hat to the person who tried it first. Another suggestion is that we should eat alligators from Florida. I ate crocodile once in Cuba – it tasted halfway between lobster and pork – but am not sure I would welcome its cousin from Florida. There are times when we have to allow health considerations to come first.

Sorely missed

WAY *of the World's* annual Business Award this year goes to Madame Tussaud's, always one of London's greatest attractions, which, in reopening its famous Chamber of Horrors after a £1m facelift, has decided to dispense with American horrors.

Previously, visitors were able to study a waxwork of Gary Gilmore, who chose to be executed by firing squad rather than continue the interminable process of appeal, and Bruno Hauptman, sitting in the electric chair waiting for American technology to take its erratic course. Instead, the exhibition now concentrates on British and European murderers.

This seems eminently sensible. No native Briton wishes to see American horrors, when we have only to turn on our television sets at any hour of the day or night to see Americans punching and shooting each other. Similarly, there are unlikely to be any further American tourists to please in this way.

London is really no place for the American tourist nowadays, what with our mad cow disease, or bovine spongiform encephalopathy, our Creutzfeldt-Jakob disease (very catching), our incurable new super-TB, our bulimia and our IRA bombs going off the whole time. They will be sorely missed, but we will quite understand if they prefer to stay at home and watch their own domestic horrors unfold. Already, in the United States, people can watch their fellow citizens being executed, whether in real life or on television. They have no need of waxworks to give them the idea of it. Everything is done better over there.

Wednesday, March 27, 1996

Road to ruin

ONE of the tasks which this column has set itself on behalf of its readers is to keep an eye on the European sperm count. Recently, it may be remembered, experts in Britain, France and Denmark announced that if the present rapid fall continued, European males would be completely sterile by the middle of the next century.

This provoked a response from the sisterhood that women could perfectly well have babies by themselves through a system of cloning, and we all kept rather quiet.

Now a group of American scientists has announced that as far as the greatest country on earth is concerned, sperm counts are actually rising. So it looks as if the main European breeding stock will be in America, while Europe is inhabited by asexual clones.

Any discussion of population trends is bound to be fraught with pitfalls. The latest figure for abortions in Britain is 160,000 a year. One pregnancy in five is ended in this way, about the same proportion as births to single mothers. For a long time it was fashionable in conservative circles to revile these single mothers for upsetting the social fabric, but it seems to me they should be recognised as the heroines of our age.

Whatever attitude one takes to the matter, it cannot be altogether healthy that one in five pregnancies is now ended by abortion. Perhaps our falling sperm rate is nature's – or God's – revenge. One of the least attractive aspects of a society which disposes in this way of so many of its babies before they are born is the nauseating sentimentality which attaches to sick children.

It would be a poetic irony if this sentimentality about sick children were to cause our government's bankruptcy, the disappearance of our agriculture, the destruction of our economy, the downfall of the nation.

Is this America?

AFTER my comments on the decision of Madame Tussaud's to remove the electric chair and other American execution scenes from the new Chamber of Horrors – Americans can see live executions if they want, and have no time for waxworks – I was not surprised to learn that Bob Dole, the Republican contender, had toured Death Row in San Quentin prison to learn how it was done.

After staring at the 424 prisoners on Death Row awaiting execution, he made a speech promising to curtail Death Row appeals, speed up executions and execute juveniles where necessary.

At a press conference held outside San Quentin as part of his campaign to beat Pat Buchanan in yesterday's Republican primary, he complained that more San Quentin inmates died of old age than died of lethal injection, which is the method of execution preferred there.

'Is this America?' he demanded. 'Do we believe in justice?'

Saturday, April 6, 1996

The sun, the sun!

SINGLE mothers who do not inform the Child Support Agency of the name of their child's father will lose nearly £20 of their £46.50 a week personal allowance under a new clampdown proposed by the Social Security Department.

I wonder if these are the right people to penalise. When one in five pregnancies in this country ends in abortion, as I pointed out the other day, these women might be seen as heroines. There are 50,000 single mothers on income support who have not produced the father's name. It occurs to me that many may not be absolutely sure who the father is, or may have forgotten his name. A few may be the victims of rape, although rape by a stranger is very rare, so far as anyone has been able to establish.

A much bigger problem, affecting millions, is the inability of many single people to achieve any form of physical intimacy with a member of the opposite sex. I am not saying this is a worse problem than rape, but it is a much, much bigger one. We hear many public speeches about rape, but none about this terrible inability to get together, which causes so much misery, bitterness and anger.

Perhaps it is the recent cold weather that has produced what looks like a giant national revulsion against sex. I was alarmed this week to see pictures of Mr Howard, flanked by police officers, touring what were described as 'streets with the most notorious criminal reputations in Britain'. On examination, these turned out to be in Soho, where I have had an office for 26 years. Soho's occasional strip shows and hostess bars can't be as bad as all that. Where is he going to clamp down next?

Perhaps all this will change with the weather. I can see London going mad with joy when spring finally establishes itself.

Insult to dead cows

THE most hopeful suggestion for disposing of the four million cattle that will have to be slaughtered as a result of Mr Hogg's ghastly mistake is that they should be turned into electricity. An ingenious firm called Fibrowatt, which runs power stations in Suffolk and Lincolnshire based on chicken manure, has revealed that far more energy is available from dead cattle.

Electricity is almost entirely benign in its application to human affairs, even if it cannot actually create milk, butter, or cheese. It is only in its more recent applications, such as the powering of the Internet, that all these dead cows may come back to haunt us.

The Internet enables people to communicate without the faintest physical awareness of each other, even that provided by the sound of a voice. They can send each other dirty messages and on-line porn, even accuse each other of sexual harassment, but the absence of sight, sound and touch strikes me as the ultimate denial of any real human relationship. The participants exist only in each other's imaginations.

American research has shown that the Internet is dangerously addictive. In a survey, 17 per cent of its users said they spent more than 40 hours a week on the Internet. The average was 20 hours. Nearly half acknowledged that their work might have suffered, and nearly all agreed that it interfered with their normal life of work, family and friends.

It was with some sadness that I read a column by my friend Alexander Chancellor on Saturday, writing in another newspaper, which revealed that he had decided to join the Internet. The reason given was his loyalty to an American friend, who has started a new cyberspace magazine that will be available only on the Net.

I fear this means that Alexander will be lost to his other terrestrial friends. He, in particular, will be haunted by the ghosts of all the dead cows providing the energy for his new pleasures. When I come to power, I think I will ban e-mail, if only out of respect for all the cows that have gone into it.

Wednesday, April 10, 1996

Reform of Parliament

IT IS depressing to learn that Labour's first priority, on coming to power, will be to strip hereditary peers of their voting rights in the House of Lords. One might have hoped they would have thought of something more interesting than this stale and unpleasant gesture during their 17 years in the wilderness.

Votes in the Upper House will then belong only to people appointed by the Lower House, exercising what they laughingly call 'the will of the people'. There are already signs that newer, younger members of the House of Commons, many of whom are unable to read or write, are getting above themselves, fretting against any restrictions on their behaviour.

At present, their only slight restraint is represented by the Serjeant-at-Arms, whose duty it is to accompany unruly members out of the Chamber. His office is under attack from young members on both sides of the House. David Shaw, the 45-year-old Conservative MP for Dover, up from the City of London Polytechnic, says he wants a 'co-ordinating chief executive to be brought in, someone who is forward-thinking, to promote Parliament and make it more efficient'.

I think he means he wants another of these 'meritocrats' who are gradually bringing the whole country to a standstill. A Labour MP said of the office of Serjeant-at-Arms: 'I've had cause for complaint. They're very high-handed. They have the attitude:

"What's this nerd approaching me for?"' Obviously he would prefer to see a fellow nerd in the job.

Tony Blair should take a long, hard look at the House of Commons. Is it perhaps more a source of temptation, an occasion of sin, than an instrument of righteousness? If Christians must vote at all, they should surely vote for the immediate abolition of the House of Commons, its replacement by a House of Lords reduced to hereditary members. This reformed Upper House would have no powers whatever, but would be responsible for keeping the Palace of Westminster nice and tidy.

Count our blessings

BY COINCIDENCE, my wife and I were guests of a hereditary peer and his family over the Easter weekend. After the shock of Labour's announcement about hereditary peerages, consternation was also caused by an advertisement showing the photograph of a white rhinoceros called Notch, similar to one called Juillet which, it was said, had been killed by poachers in the Garamba National Park on March 28.

'Juillet's death brings the number of northern white rhinos alive in the wild to just 29,' the advertisers announce, launching a Garamba Rhino Emergency Appeal to tackle the poaching and to save the rhinos from extinction: 'We're asking every reader to support this appeal. £30 could keep a specialist surveillance team in the air for one more day. Please help if you can. The future of the northern white rhino may depend on it.' We are asked to send our £30 donation to an address in Godalming, Surrey.

Various questions are raised by this appeal. How can these animals be said to be living in the wild if they all have pet names like Juillet and Notch, and are forever being counted and surveyed by animal enthusiasts from the air? And what sort of specialist surveillance team can be kept in the air all day for £30?

Having brooded about the matter, I have decided not to give any money to these Garamban rhinoceri. Easter, as Dr Carey reminds us, is a time of hope and optimism. Let us hope for the best for these animals in their distant country, wherever it may be, and for all the airborne surveyors. I am sure they will survive somehow. Closer to home, we have our own endangered species in the hereditary peerage.

For convenience, we should perhaps try to persuade all the

world's threatened species to live together, possibly in somewhere like Godalming, where we can count them to our heart's content and survey them from the air whenever necessary. Hereditary peers can probably be counted from ground level.

Far better to find out where the nearest hereditary peer lives and send him £10 through the post. I am sure that is just as useful as sending £30 to an address in Godalming to enable a poor white rhinoceros to be given a silly nickname and counted twice a day from the air.

Sign of hope

MUCH attention has been devoted to the fact that future officers in the Royal Air Force are to be given lessons in ballroom dancing, but the more important development must be that they will also have oral communication classes, to teach them the basic skills of conversation.

This is by order of Air Chief Marshal Sir Michael Graydon, Chief of the Air Staff, who discovered that new cadets at Cranwell lack these basic skills, answering polite inquiries from senior officers monosyllabically with 'OK' or 'yeah'. One does not have to be a senior officer in the RAF to have noticed this unfortunate failing in our young, who are rapidly making Britain the laughing stock of Europe. Most of us may have noticed it already, but Sir Michael is the first Briton to have done anything about it.

I hope that if at some time after the next election it becomes necessary for the military to take over, the Air Chief Marshal will still be around to guide the nation out of its difficulties.

Saturday, April 13, 1996

Preparing for it

WHEN Tony Blair comes back today from his visit to the United States, he can congratulate himself on having created an 'unprecedented wave of fascination', according to the *Daily Mirror*. A mass-circulation magazine called *People* read by 25 million Americans, gave him a four-page profile. *New Yorker* magazine gave him 11 pages. He appeared on the TV show *Good*

Morning America, seen by half the nation's households. Even the *Washington Post* mentioned him as 'premier in-waiting'.

One can't help wondering what exactly he was doing there. The *Mirror* suggests that his purpose was not to secure any electoral advantage so much as to strengthen ties between our two countries. If so, this was very civil of him, although the only clue he gave before leaving suggested that his purpose was to inspect Hillary Clinton, the President's energetic wife, with a few to ensuring that his own wife, called Cherie, does not become like her.

I do not know how well this went down with the Clintons, who received him at the White House yesterday morning. My own fear is that he went to America to look for a job. Tens of thousands of better-off people are moving abroad at the moment in terror of the tax reforms liable to be introduced by Gordon Brown after a Labour victory in the next election. They have to have been abroad for a full tax year in order to qualify for relief.

Others might suppose that Tony Blair would regard the prospect of a Labour victory with some equanimity, as he is the leader of the Labour Party and would automatically become Prime Minister, a job with many useful perks. But he is no fool, and realises that the voters will not simply be voting for him. As soon as Labour is in power, every twisted, embittered schoolteacher or polytechnic lecturer, every social worker and Left-wing ice-cream seller will also reckon to have come to power.

Blair may not last more than a few weeks, even if the military, under the admirable Air Chief Marshal Sir Michael Graydon, do not decide to intervene. This may be their best opportunity to teach us the social and conversational skills we are in danger of losing.

It would be quite understandable if Blair took a leaf from the book of his fellow meritocrat, Andrew Neil, and started inquiring about jobs available in New York for disc jockeys or television presenters. My own feeling is that it may be a waste of time to go abroad to avoid the horrors of a Labour government. It would be more dignified to hold a gigantic mass suicide, as they once did in Jonestown, Guyana, in protest. Poisons might be supplied by the NHS, as its last benign function. Private medicine is now prohibitively expensive.

Ostrich futures

WHEN I recommended ostrich to replace beef on the national diet some weeks ago I did not intend to cause a panic in the financial markets. Live breeding birds started changing hands at £14,000 each, which is an absurdity. Ostrich should be cheaper than beef, since the birds are more efficient protein-converters – they need less grass – and produce more offspring.

Personally I prefer beef, but ostrich meat can be tasty and surprisingly tender if young and not overcooked. What really appealed was the thought of English fields full of ostriches' pattering feet.

Even those with little or no experience of the countryside must admit that cows look very boring as one counts them through a train window. Ostriches could run beside the train and keep up with it, even engage children in what passes for conversation.

I hope the businessmen come to their senses. The proper price for a breeding female ostrich is £620. Meat should retail at about £6.50 a pound for the breast of a young bird.

Monday, April 15, 1996

Unsound neighbours

THE latest idea for treating violent young offenders is to give them vitamin pills. I wonder if it would not be as good an idea to give them large doses of margarine, now once again thought by the 'experts' to be better for us than butter.

On Saturday we read about Mrs Kay Potts, a mother of ten, who was finally evicted from her home on a council estate in Wythenshawe, Manchester, after the family had amassed 500 complaints from the neighbours.

Community leaders who organised the protest were presented with bouquets by the council 'for standing up against a nuisance which has caused so much misery'.

Poor Mrs Potts is now homeless with her ten children, who were accused of burglary, vandalism and threats to kill. They were rudely described in the County Court as 'neighbours from hell'.

Nobody at any stage offered them extra vitamins or margarine. Mrs Potts may reflect bitterly that her face did not fit, she was considered unsound.

Many people have suffered from this, among them the great Sydney Smith (1771-1845), essayist and wit, appointed Rector of Combe Florey in 1829. He is the subject of an article in the current *Spectator* by Paul Johnson, the distinguished historian and polemicist.

Johnson reveals that he, too, has suffered from being thought unsound. This may explain why he has never been offered a job in the Cabinet, as his talents undoubtedly command. He now lives in Somerset, only a few fields away from the village of Combe Florey, where my family lives. He has never burgled or threatened to kill any of us, nor have any of his children, although it is worrying that he continues to boast of his unsoundness.

'I am all for unsound men, not least because they are nearly always right,' he wrote of Sydney Smith. 'All my own life I have been dismissed as "Oh yes, he's a clever fellow, but not sound, you know."'

Perhaps we should send him some vitamins. That would be a neighbourly gesture, and safer than margarine.

Disconnect

TOMORROW *The Daily Telegraph* launches a free weekly tabloid called Connected. I was excited by this, imagining it would be a rival to *Hello!*, the brilliant weekly whose galloping success has revolutionised magazine journalism in this country.

Unfortunately, it will be addressing technological matters and what it describes as the 'on-line world of the Internet', with reviews of computer software and hardware.

I do not suppose I shall understand a word of it. When I decided 15 years ago to take no cognisance of advances in computer or digital technology, I was aware that I was also taking a risk. The general opinion was that it held the secret to the future. Now it seems to me we should acknowledge that computers, despite their many qualities, do not actually work.

They spend a large part of the time frozen, crashed out or in remission, unusable in any way and liable to wipe out all the information they have been given. This misbehaviour is not the result of user-error, but simply a question of mood.

Now they are proposing a computer in Darwin, Northern Australia, which will automatically kill the user when he or she presses the appropriate button. This is thought to complement the Northern Territories Euthanasia Act by sparing doctors from responsibility.

Which is all very well, but what happens if the user mistakenly presses the wrong buttons when trying to discover the birthday of the Duchess of Kent or when the computer is simply feeling in a bad mood? One can live a happy and fulfilled life without having anything to do with these machines, which grow more unpleasant and threatening every day.

Wednesday, April 24, 1996

Give us the guns

I CANNOT believe I am alone in feeling a deep sense of shame at the news that Walt Disney is planning to build its first non-Hollywood cartoon and film studios in Britain. This is a means of circumventing a European quota on American-made television programmes.

Britain has resisted enforcing the quota in any case, as part of its babyish anti-Europeanism. Now we learn that other Hollywood companies are eyeing up Britain as a means of infiltrating Europe. While Disney considers a £200 million 'entertainment complex' in Battersea Power Station, Warner Bros is seeking planning permission for studios in West London and Twentieth Century Fox has designs on Elstree.

Any suggestion that the nauseating rubbish churned out from Hollywood will be somehow improved by production in Britain is scotched by senior spokesmen who talk of 'tampering with a winning formula':

'We have built our worldwide success on quality control. We aren't going to throw that away to humour a bunch of Eurocrats who have never told a good children's story since Hans Christian Andersen. We are not going to produce Euro-puddings.'

Another attraction is that we have some of the most 'flexible' labour laws in Europe, which, being translated, means that we have lower wages, longer working hours and less job protection than anyone else. These may be things of which we can be proud. Nothing the Government has done is as wicked as its deliberate, planned urbanisation of the English countryside, but I think this sell-out to Hollywood may come a close second.

The most alarming aspect of both plans – to destroy the

110

countryside and surrender our culture to Hollywood – is that there is no opposition to them. All opposition is centred on defence of our national sovereignty against the European Union, but it is our own national leadership which is betraying us.

Sadly enough, the United States exports only the nastiest elements of its culture – the lubricity, sentimentality and violence of a Hollywood with Murdoch at its helm. There is no suggestion that we copy the things that really make America great – the efficiency and desire to please, the freedom of the citizen to bear arms and shoot any burglar, sanitary inspector, or government planner who threatens to invade his home.

Whisper who dares

NO CHILD has ever been so cruelly exploited as Christopher Robin Milne, who died on Saturday at the age of 75. I never met his father, A A Milne, creator of the fictional Christopher Robin who has sickened generations of English boys since his first

appearance in the Twenties, but I believe him to have been an exceptionally unpleasant man.

A A Milne led the pack against P G Wodehouse during the war, denouncing that gentle, kindly soul as a traitor after he had been tricked into making some innocent broadcasts on German radio. When Milne died in 1956, he left the copyright on his ghastly oeuvre – *When We Were Very Young*; *Winnie the Pooh*; *Now We Are Six* and *The House at Pooh Corner* – to be shared between the Royal Literary Fund, Westminster School and the Garrick Club, with only a quarter going on the death of his widow to the only son, whose life he had ruined.

As a result Christopher Robin Milne, who might have been very rich, lived a life of comparative penury as a bookseller in Dartmouth. I do not know whether it occurred to him to sue the estate. Whatever A A Milne may have owed to Westminster School or the Garrick, he would have been nothing but a minor hack on *Punch* if he had not discovered the poor young boy to dress up in frocks and exploit.

A modern six-year-old would probably have dialled 999 and had him arrested for mental abuse as soon as *Now We Are Six* appeared in 1927. For once, I feel that modern youth would have been right. If Christopher Robin Milne had beheaded Winnie the Pooh, garotted Eeyore and pulled Tigger's tail off, he might have been better prepared for life's vicissitudes.

Wednesday, May 1, 1996

Help is at hand

IN SMART London circles it is normal to deride Susie Orbach, the American psychotherapist, as representing and encouraging a whole race of women who spend their time being taught to talk about themselves with a silly tone of voice and in an irritating jargon. However, in my single dealing with Orbach, she seemed polite and cheerful, and I feel she should be given the benefit of the doubt. She is also an attractive woman, which helps.

Now we learn that she and other psychotherapists are setting up an organisation called Antidote, designed to increase the 'emotional literacy' of politicians by teaching them to open up and explain their feelings to one another. They feel that the British stiff upper lip hampers communication and leads to foolish legislation and blinkered views.

'We will question what makes some MPs hold on to the idea of Little England and become very anti-Europe,' she explains. Antidote's director, James Park, enlarges on her point: 'Until they reveal the emotional part, we will never have a healthily run country,' he says. 'But put people in a hotel for three days and give them space to open up – and they do.' We may not approve of psychotherapists for ordinary people, but for politicians they just may be what is needed.

Monday, May 13, 1996

What they all want

THERE is something rather sad in the news that spinach sales have doubled for the second successive year, following re-runs of Popeye cartoons on television.

One reason it is sad is the evidence it affords of how telecentric (a better coinage than wretched Polly Toynbee's 'stupidvision') our society has become.

What makes it even sadder is that a cartoon should exert this influence – further evidence of what has been called the Disneyfication of our culture. Saddest of all is that young boys seem to believe they really will become stronger and more like superman if they follow Popeye's example.

The main point about British boys to emerge from all the studies and reports on them is that they are physically weedier than ever before. They take no exercise; many of them watch television all day while others have been brought up on a diet of lettuce and other vegetables.

Poor things! One does not wish to fall into the trap of saying that Hitler was a vegetarian. We all know that some of the kindest, sweetest and loveliest people in the country are vegetarians. Equally, one does not wish to let these youths suppose that their problems will be solved by eating a certain amount of tinned spinach.

What they want is a cold bath, a cold run, organised games in the cold and a thoroughly good hiding.

Wednesday, May 15, 1996

A jolly good cry

THERE may be lessons for us all in the case brought by 13-year-old Julia McLaughlin against America's oldest school, Boston Latin, for refusing to admit her despite her doing better in the entrance exams than 149 pupils who were admitted. She was refused a place because the school is bound to a quota of 35 per cent blacks and Hispanics. As the racial mix varies, so will the quota, and a report by the Census Bureau in Washington prophesies that by the middle of the next century there will effectively be no white majority.

In Britain, of course, we have no such problems, so there is probably no lesson for us in any of this. It becomes harder and harder to participate in any of the issues which preoccupy our cousins across the herring pond. Recently the country which boasts the biggest legal brothel in the world sent a young student to prison after she photographed her four-year-old son in the nude.

At present, the country is rent by a dying teenager who expressed a last wish to shoot a rare Kodiak bear in the forests of Alaska. Americans always enjoy a little sentiment, and it so happens that there is a charity, called Make-a-Wish, devoted to granting any child who is about to die his or her last wish.

But there are also thousands of animal-rights agitators and millions of ordinary animal sentimentalists who are appalled at the thought of the teenager, called Erik, polishing off a bear with his last breath. One does not really know what to advise, except that those who wish to cry about the teenager should get together with those who wish to cry about the bear, and they should all have a jolly good cry.

Healthy regime

AT LAST, I see, scientific opinion is waking up to the dangers of inflicting 'healthy' diets on small children. A survey of more than 1,000 mothers throughout Britain revealed that 80 per cent of them were feeding their babies on fresh fruit and vegetables, fruit purée, low-fat yoghurt and all the rest of the rubbish they have been reading about all these years in the *Sunday Times* and other publications. No doubt a few have even inflicted undressed lettuce and other salads on the poor little mites.

As a result of this high-fibre, low-fat diet, the children are pale, listless and stunted, as if they were the product of London's pre-war slums, and grow up with learning difficulties. Many find it difficult to absorb perfectly ordinary minerals and vitamins.

What the growing child needs is plenty of sugar, starch and fat for energy. The best diet would consist of meat and potatoes, followed by apple crumble and custard or cream, then a little Camembert, brie or Somerset chèvre and a teaspoonful of port. When they are ill, they should be given some aspirin.

Saturday, May 18, 1996

Banquo's ghost

IT WAS not a good idea for Buckingham Palace to publish the guest-list and seating arrangements for the state banquet on Tuesday night to welcome President and Mrs Chirac.

Although there were one or two stars present, the guests were for the most part a dreadfully dull lot. It must be a depressing thought for the younger generation that at the top of the ladder in this country, nothing awaits but boredom.

My own complaint is more specific. Seeing that I was not on the list of those attending, many of my friends assumed I must be ill. All this week, my telephone has been ringing with their tender inquiries and condolences. Others observed that the Princess of Wales was absent, too, and supposed I was dining tête-à-tête with her. Would that it had been so.

No, the simple truth is that on Tuesday evening I dined quietly in my club, perhaps brooding about an empty chair only a few hundred yards away in the Palace ballroom. It is a sad day when we can't even organise a state banquet without the invitations going astray.

At least they did not make the president eat beef, as a loutish gesture. What people in this country do not realise is that the French are genuinely worried by Stephen Dorrell's hedging on the question of BSE's transferability to humans.

The European ban is entirely the result of Dorrell and his 'expert' adviser, Professor John Pattison. It has nothing to do with French hostility to Britain. My own abiding memory of President Chirac's visit (not having been at the dinner) is how well the French tricolour and Union flag looked fluttering side by side in Whitehall.

Monday, May 20, 1996

Love story

MANY will have wept to read of the charming couple, Bill and May Hill, threatened with separation after 60 years of marriage because their savings have run out and they can no longer pay £2,000 a month to their nursing home. Social workers ruled that only Mr Hill was in need of full-time care, so Mrs Hill would have to move out.

The new insistence that we must be prepared to give up our life's savings and life's achievement before being eligible for NHS care in old age has prompted a correspondent to suggest that NHS care should be available to the young only if they are prepared to pay for it by working as child prostitutes.

In truth it is all part of a historic betrayal. In an age of longer life expectancy and soaring medical costs, the welfare state will never be able to provide care for everybody at any stage, let alone from cradle to grave. We can vote until we are blue in the face and tax ourselves out of existence, but it can't be done. Nor, for that matter, will we ever find a government prepared to cut taxes and cut public expenditure. They will never do it.

So the whole idea of democracy nowadays is a bit of a fraud, to the extent that it pretends to offer a choice. It doesn't matter how you vote. The only way to beat the process, in an individual case, is to cause a fuss in the media. This is called a public outcry, and in the case of Bill and May Hill, it has won a reprieve. The couple may stay together.

The trouble is that after all the weeping and the indignation, one begins to have terrible doubts. The Hills are much too polite to make the point, but I wonder whether at the age of 85, after 60 years of marriage, they might welcome a change. My wife and I have been married for only 35 years, so the problem does not yet arise, but it occurs to me that in 25 years' time she might welcome a different face, a change of scene, the promise of a new adventure.

I hope the Hills were properly consulted.

Wednesday, May 22, 1996

Better in private

PERHAPS not everybody is aware that this week is being celebrated as Breastfeeding Awareness Week. As a male without a baby of the appropriate age – even my five grand-daughters have been weaned long ago – I may not be able to do much about this, but I felt I should draw attention to it.

As the result of a 12-month campaign by the Natural Childbirth Trust, a list has been drawn up of 4,700 shops and supermarkets that allow breastfeeding in public – anywhere and any time – as well as a list of those that do not encourage the habit. This second list includes Marks & Spencer, Waterstone's, the book chain, and Harrods.

There can be few more affecting sights than that of a mother feeding her child, even if it is no part of our cultural tradition to make a public exhibition of it. One might see it as an improvement in our national life to have mothers feeding their babies all over the place, but only in the right setting. Tranquillity is essential to the scene.

Perhaps it is convenient for mothers to feed their infants while they are in the process of shopping. I am surprised that this should be so, and will be very surprised if many mothers take up the invitation to bring their babies to Asda, Boots and Burton Menswear at feeding time. Mothers generally look harassed and furtive under these circumstances.

But it is not the mothers we should think about so much as the babies. Should they really be introduced at such an early age into the disgusting British habit of endlessly eating snacks in public? The smell of steak and kidney pies and hamburgers is bad enough – at least one has the consolation that those who indulge in them are probably doing themselves some incurable harm – but nobody who has sat in a train opposite someone eating an egg sandwich will ever forget the horror of it. Are the nation's mothers determined to bring up another race of monsters?

Not a bad man

NOBODY should be surprised or shocked to learn of claims that Lord Jenkins of Hillhead, as Roy Jenkins has almost imperceptibly become over the years, had one or two romantic adventures in the course of his happy and successful 50-year marriage to Dame Jennifer. It would be nice to think she had had some, too, although I have no particular reason to suppose that this is so, except that she is an attractive and spirited woman.

But I do not see that anything useful is achieved by digging up 30-year-old affairs and parading them before an oafish, sexually bemused modern television audience. This is what BBC2 plan to do in a documentary about him, called *A Very Social Democrat* to be screened at 9.05pm tomorrow – guaranteed to produce nothing but jealousy and resentment.

It is in the spirit of the times to try to diminish our great men. Roy, at 75, should be looking forward to an old age surrounded by pretty nurses. As a young man I used to think a nurse's uniform the most attractive garment in the world, and I am sure one returns to that view in old age. Unfortunately, a recommendation put forward by the Health Services Management Unit, backed by the National Association of Health Authorities and Trusts, would abolish nurses altogether, as well as unqualified health staff, replacing both by semi-qualified 'generic health workers', who would prevent patients 'being constrained by out-of-date role demarcations'.

We all know what these generic health workers would be like.

The only bad thing Roy Jenkins ever did was to fail to become Prime Minister and put a stop to all this nonsense. Now he must suffer for it.

Exciting work

STUNG by criticism of his plans to urbanise the English countryside, John Gummer, the Environment Secretary, has announced that in the summer he will launch a programme to encourage people to live in the cities.

In order to help the construction industry, he will call for the building of 4.4 million new homes by the year 2016, of which half will be built in towns. 'The central tenet is to bring back the excitement of cities,' he said.

By putting up 2.2 million hideous, jerry built new homes? The construction industry has already ruined nearly all our towns, before Gummer decided to let it loose on the countryside. That is why so many hundreds of thousands of young people are being driven to seek a lonely life in the countryside.

The main advantage of town life (now that the shops have moved out) is in the chance to meet people – a polite way of describing sexual opportunity. But Ann Widdecombe, the born-again Home Office minister, has announced a crackdown on that sort of thing. She plans to cut off the telephone lines of anyone who advertises in a call-box for the purpose of meeting people. Councils already employ people to go round taking down the cards, complaining of an inexhaustible supply of out-of-work actors employed to put them back again.

I do not think Mr Gummer, straight from his campaign to gummerize Somerset, is the right man to bring excitement to the towns. Instead of acting as Minister for the Construction Industry, he should see the industry as an anti-social force, and prevent it from putting up anything new. Unemployed construction workers could breed spaniels, or earn a little money putting up cards in telephone boxes, helping people to meet each other.

Monday, May 27, 1996

Watch that Siegfried

MANY people must have been alarmed to read the report in Friday's newspaper quoting an unnamed Whitehall source as saying that Mrs Bottomley had fallen out with Lord Gowrie, chairman of the Arts Council over the distribution of National Lottery money.

The suggestion was that Mrs Bottomley thought the grants had been too elitist, and was bringing pressure on Gowrie to make them more popular. This would have been in line with the *Sun*'s objection to any spending on the arts or old buildings. My own feeling is that money which is not spent on restoring old buildings (and possibly demolishing new ones) should be given back to the punters in the form of higher jackpots and other prizes.

The problem with giving money to the arts is that it has to be channelled through the various artistic establishments, all of which are full of power-mad second-raters, dedicated to blowing on the dead embers of the modern movement and producing rubbish. When the design for an extension to the Victoria & Albert museum is awarded to a Polish-American for a neo-cubist construction called Boilerhouse, the time has surely come to call a halt on the public funding of such absurdities.

But at least we learn in a letter from Lord Gowrie that there are no tensions between him and the fair Mrs Bottomley. They are both prisoners of the same system, he writes, and the frustrations are shared. They frequently put their heads together, he reveals. I understand. Mrs Bottomley is an attractive woman and Gowrie can be most persuasive: 'Like a battered Siegfried, I am trying to hack my way through . . . in order to reach the Secretary of State and gratify her desires, which we share.'

I hope it is all right. These artistic people sometimes have a funny way of talking.

Unfair advantage

OXFORD University has been alarmed to discover that women undergraduates' examination results, across all degree classes and in almost all subjects are poorer than men's. It has launched an official inquiry.

The same phenomenon has been observed at Cambridge. Dr Margaret Spear, who is to conduct the study, said: 'Among the theories that have been put forward are that women are less intelligent than men, they cope less well with the stress of final exams, and have lower expectations of themselves and their careers.'

My own theory is that the women are distracted by a hopeless yearning for male company, and cannot concentrate. Men have been so terrified by all the feminist and politically correct propaganda from America that they now shut themselves up with their work, and do even better at exams as a result.

Some women have become so desperate that they have taken to playing golf as a way of meeting members of the opposite sex. Even there they are mocked by men who have had sex-change operations to be like women, and who thrash them at the game. Now they have changed the female handicap to favour only those women who were female at birth.

122

Dr Spear says she is looking for factors which can be changed 'so that women have an equal chance of securing a first class degree'. I suppose this will mean some form of positive discrimination. Even there they may be frustrated by male undergraduates who wilfully undergo sex-change operations in order to compete on more favourable terms.

Monday, June 10, 1996

New world problem

THE NEW fashion among American churchgoers for taking their communion in hermetically sealed individual plastic containers – one for bread, the other for wine – is apparently prompted by health anxieties. They are nervous of catching diseases from a shared chalice, with the wine, or from the priest's hands, with the bread.

This neurotic terror of disease, which has developed as a major feature of the American culture, does not suggest any great degree of confidence in the promise of an after-life. Instead of awaiting their Saviour's call with joy, they spend most of their time and vast amounts of money fighting against it.

Twenty-five million of these special containers are being distributed to churches each month. The spectacle is bound to raise the question once again (among those still interested in such things) of whether Americans can be said to have immortal souls. If not, they might be seen as disposable, like their own plastic communion cartons, or paper handkerchiefs.

The question is then bound to arise: when an American sneezes, which should be thrown away, the paper handkerchief or the American? To the extent that a sneezing American represents a serious health hazard to his neighbours and to the community at large, the only responsible answer must be: both.

Wednesday, June 12, 1996

Three dangers

NOBODY who reads this column will be surprised to learn that a gang of middle-class white teenagers in Fort Myers, Florida, who planned to shoot black tourists visiting DisneyWorld, also proposed to dress up as Mickey Mouse and other cartoon characters for the purpose.

Many have remarked on the sinister effect that cartoons can have on a national character. There are many wonderful things about the New World culture, but most of the things that are less wonderful can be ascribed to a mixture of Mickey Mouse and hamburgers – to which some might add mobile phones.

There has been an unexpected development in the case of an English girl said to have contracted CJD from eating hamburgers. Her friends say she has never eaten hamburgers, or any red meat, and would go to a hamburger restaurant to eat chicken burgers.

She may prove to be the first authenticated case of the baleful effects of passive hamburger eating. It seems unlikely that she has CJD, which has nothing to do with cows or meat, but she has shown many of the classic symptoms of ordinary hamburger poisoning – irrational, inarticulate violence, kicking desks in the middle of class, short temper and depression.

Mobile telephones are now known to cause cancer as well as uncontrolled garrulousness. Personally, I find them a harmless diversion when people use them in trains, but scientists in Los Angeles are now embarking on a research programme to establish the consequences of passive mobile telephoning.

This is caused by sitting next to someone who is using his machine. The symptoms include irrational rage. It is thought that people can become infected even if they only shake hands with someone who has been using a mobile telephone.

Saturday, June 15, 1996

A question of decency

FOR various reasons I have refrained from joining the great national debate about whether the new slimline Lord Lawson is to be preferred to the old roly-poly Nigel. It was Lawson who appointed me Political Correspondent on *The Spectator* nearly 30 years ago.

We worked together happily for three years. Then, it is true, he went mad and sacked me. The National Union of Journalists had to drag him to court and force large payments out of his wretched magazine, which had already rehired me by the time of the hearing.

Even so, it does not behove a former employee to discuss his patron's waistline in public. My second reason for ignoring the great debate is that it seems to me that once politicians have retired from the political scene, they should be allowed to live in decent obscurity, like people who have been sent to prison, however vile their crimes. We do not need to keep a baleful eye on people who have been removed from doing further harm.

This elementary decency is no longer observed in our murdochised press. The *Sun* recently told us about Rosemary West: 'Evil Rose becomes slimline sex siren for her lesbian jail love: Dumpy House of Horror killer Rose West has lost more than a stone in a bid to wow her lesbian lover in jail. The 42-year-old bisexual monster has become a keep-fit fanatic who wears trendy skin-tight cycling shorts.'

Even *The Times* – once such a good newspaper – reports: 'Owen Oyston, 62, the multi-millionaire jailed for six years for rape . . . has been set to work with his hands and is paid £7 a week.'

Perhaps this keeps the punishment freaks happy, but it has nothing whatsoever to do with Lord Lawson's weight. I shall preserve a decent silence on this subject, whatever I may think in private.

A good idea

TAUNTON, county town of Somerset, has been made virtually unvisitable by the ruling Liberal Democrats, who are turning the centre of the town into a gigantic shopping precinct with traffic reduced to a single file, permanently blocked.

Bypassing it on Friday afternoon, I found myself stuck in a traffic jam for 20 minutes beside the car of Mr Paddy Pantsdown, the world statesman.

My dear wife and I were going to stay with some friends in Gloucestershire; Pantsdown, with a grim-faced female chauffeur, was no doubt headed for his home in the sink of depravity called Yeovil. He spent all 20 minutes rapping orders into a mobile telephone.

It occurred to me that these people who have taken over the old Liberal Party have nothing whatever in common with old-fashioned liberalism. They are bossier, as well as stupider, than any other political party has ever been. Perhaps they are part of our general decline.

This is not a subject we should dwell upon. What we need is some natural catastrophe, such as has happened to the Spanish in Madrid, which has been invaded by millions of large moths from North Africa, soon to be followed by billions of giant caterpillars. Crowds of moths enter homes every night, covering

television screens, blacking out street lights and pursuing cars. A challenge of this sort might at least take our minds off Euro '96.

No, but seriously

I COULD spot only one journalist among the 1,041 names on the Queen's Birthday Honours list. An MBE went to Dr Thomas Stuttaford, the medical correspondent of *Oldie* magazine, and it couldn't have gone to a nicer man. A former MP, he believes that smoking even one cigarette cuts off much of the blood supply to the male genital area. If true, this would suggest a solution to the notorious Westminster sleaze factor that is preferable in every way to the alternative suggestions being considered. These involve compulsory castration of all MPs.

Otherwise, it has been a wonderful week for journalists, with the editor of the failing *Independent* writing a letter to the editor of *The Times* complaining about *The Times* having lifted an article from the *Daily Mail* criticising an article in the *Independent* which attacked the *Daily Mail* for considering running an article about the private social arrangements of Miss Polly Toynbee, social affairs correspondent of the failing *Independent*.

Frank Johnson, in his wise and witty account of it all in Saturday's newspaper, suggested it was time for Toynbee to shut up and stop telling us about her close three-year relationship with a man who looks like a squirrel. Speaking for myself, I can't hear enough on the subject. It should be set to music. This is what Andrew Marr, editor of the *Independent*, wrote to *The Times*:

'I was disgusted but unsurprised that the editor of the *Daily Mail* chose to punish her [Toynbee] in this way; but I was genuinely saddened and very surprised that *The Times* has seen fit to follow. Was this really fair play?'

On a more serious note, it occurs to me that if journalists are regularly to feature in sex exposés – no doubt the public is as happy to read about the sex lives of unknown hacks as the sex lives of unknown MPs – proprietors may decide to take action. They do not want their newspapers reduced to the level of the House of Commons by these allegations of sleaze. They should insist that all journalists in their employment smoke cigarettes, as they always used to do in the good old days, when everybody knew his place.

Monarchy in peril

NOBODY who read Adam Nicolson's interview with the amazing 'Paddy' Pantsdown in this week's *Sunday Telegraph* magazine will be surprised to learn that the Liberal Democrats propose to strip the monarchy of all its remaining constitutional powers. Although last year Pantsdown rebuked his colleagues when they proposed to abolish the monarchy altogether and establish a republic, one can well see that he will tolerate no impediment to his foul plans for turning the whole country into a shopping precinct and making us all wear jerseys.

People may have been more alarmed when a gang of hooligans describing themselves as 'Right-wing Tories' launched a vicious attack on the Princess of Wales. An unsigned article in a Conservative magazine edited by Sir George Gardiner, the 'Eurosceptic' MP for Reigate, describes her as 'not much of a princess' and calls for her withdrawal from public functions. 'The future of the monarchy is the Prince of Wales,' it explains.

We should not be surprised that there are some people in the Tory party nowadays whose feelings of personal inferiority, social or sexual insecurity, class envy or general rancour make them unable to give thanks for the Princess of Wales. Where they might do harm is in planting the suspicion that this loutish attack was inspired by friends of the Prince of Wales.

It seems inconceivable that the Prince could involve himself with such people, even at several removes, but I must admit that staying this weekend with friends in Gloucestershire, I began to have doubts. The neighbouring village of Daglingworth, in a protected area of outstanding natural beauty a long way from Highgrove, has been virtually gummerised by this man. The Duchy bought some allotments in the centre of the village and then sold them to a developer. Three hideous executive-style houses, completely out of scale with the rest of the village, and four smaller houses, all with repulsive brown window frames, followed. Now the Duchy has obtained outline planning permission for two more new houses next to them in the conservation area.

I hope the vulgar newspapers never get to learn about this appalling business. By all means let us keep patriotically silent. But there is really nothing to be gained by insulting his wife.

No misogyny here

ANYBODY who follows the Washington scene will be deeply interested in the way American press and television have turned against Hillary Clinton, the First Lady who banned smoking in the White House. Her critics concentrate, as usual, on alleged financial irregularities.

I would like to think that the real motive behind these attacks may be found in the Delayed Smoker's Revenge syndrome, which is more or less self-explanatory: we smokers, who are unable, in the present climate, to defend ourselves against our enemies on that issue, bide our time and attack them from the side about something quite different.

I hope there is no element of misogyny in this. The simple truth, which I have often observed, is that American women are nearly always superior in every way to American males. They all know this. It is a horrible thought that the worm may be beginning to turn, and the American male is poised for his revenge.

I also hope there is no element of misogyny in the opposition to the plan for Exeter College, Oxford, to include women in their all-male chapel choir for the first time in 450 years. They will replace boys from the Christ Church Cathedral school.

Undergraduates voted unanimously against it, but the go-

ahead chaplain won the dons over. He hopes that women will attract more undergraduates to his services, but he is probably too holy to have looked at many Oxford women recently. I would be surprised if his innovation had that effect.

Time for action

AS LONDON'S Tube drivers propose to join with postmen in a strike on Thursday, which will close both the Underground and the Post, we all find ourselves in the position of judge and jury to decide who is in the right.

Postmen, alas, can no longer be said to provide a very useful service. Practically nobody writes letters nowadays. The post is unreliable, and brings little but bills and unwanted announcements. It will be sad to lose them, but if they are asking for too much money I feel we should let them go. Faxes and other machines are cheaper and better.

Tube drivers, on the other hand, who have rejected a 3.2 per cent increase which would bring their salaries to £25,436, perform a very useful service to Londoners, which becomes all the more useful as London's streets become more and more congested. Nor can it be very pleasant to spend all day underground. I feel they should get 7.5 per cent, or at any rate 5 per cent.

MPs are slightly different. Although they are demanding a 30 per cent increase in their basic wage of £34,085, taking it to £44,310 (this is before adjustments to their allowances of £42,754 for 'office costs' and £11,267 for living in London), they have not threatened to strike. I wonder why not?

The last thing we want from MPs is greater productivity. Since 1979 alone, they have passed enough footling and oppressive new laws to last a hundred years. They should be offered half the money for half the hours, with an open invitation to go on strike for the rest of their natural lives.

Monday, June 24, 1996

How many must die?

IF John Major asked himself why there were no cheering crowds to welcome him back to England after his resounding victory in

Italy, where he forced the rest of Europe to accept its original conditions for allowing us to resume beef exports after the BSE epidemic, the answer is obvious. Under normal circumstances he might have expected to be pulled from Heathrow to Downing Street in an open carriage by stout cheering men from Essex in Union flag shorts, singing *Here we go* and other patriotic songs. On this occasion, all their enthusiasm was bound up in these wretched football matches.

There are many tribulations in a politician's life, but the worst of all is to be ignored. Nice Mr Major is doing his best. However much our leaders must pretend to enjoy football, just as they pretend to enjoy kissing babies, they cannot be expected to put up with this sort of insult for long. In fact there are good reasons for banning attendance at football matches, for safety reasons.

At a Walsall inquest on a football fan who was crushed to death under a coach during a drunken fight between Crystal Palace and Manchester United supporters, the coroner demanded a new law which would forbid coaches destined for football matches to stop at a pub on the way. There is already a law preventing them from drinking inside the coaches, he said. It made no sense that they should be permitted to drink outside them.

This scratches at the surface of the problem. It does not matter where people get drunk. The point is, they want to get drunk before attending a football match, and where there is a will, there is a way. After Hillsborough (where nobody was drunk) we must ask ourselves how many young men and children must perish before the Government takes effective action, and insists that football matches should be seen only by television audiences. It simply will not do to say that most of the casualties at Hillsborough were from Liverpool. Liverpudlians need protecting, too.

The police have not been shy to demand a total ban on the private ownership of handguns after the Dunblane tragedy. Perhaps Michael Howard is nervous that a ban on attendance at football matches would be electorally unpopular, but only a tiny proportion of the population ever attends a football match. Many more visit historic houses owned by the National Trust. If we could all forget about football, we might pay more attention to the important things Mr Major, Tony Blair and John Redwood have to tell us.

An economist writing in the current *Spectator* demonstrates

131

that success at football always presages a national economic collapse. Failure can do immense harm to the feel-good factor. Perhaps it would be better to ban football altogether.

Let us be grateful

PEOPLE should not be too alarmed to learn that Hillary Clinton, wife of the American President, now spends much of her time on the top floor of the White House, holding imaginary conversations with the late Eleanor Roosevelt, wife of President Franklin Roosevelt, and Mahatma Gandhi. She talks to Mrs Roosevelt about her concern for children's welfare, and asks her why some people insist on doing down the needy.

Mrs Clinton is undergoing something called virtual therapy with a female counsellor, Jean Houston. Houston believes that she is some sort of spiritual descendant of the ancient Greek goddess Athene, with whom she holds dialogues on her computer in a procedure known as 'docking with one's angel'. Houston and another counsellor encourage Mrs Clinton to join with her female staff to turn the White House into a 'creative teaching-learning community' where women can do physical and mental exercises together to nurture one another and reverse 5,000 years of male-dominated history.

All this is apparently on tape belonging to Bob Woodward, the celebrated Watergate reporter, and will be brought out in a forthcoming book, called *The Choice*. As I say, European readers should not be worried. It is not necessarily a case of virtual insanity. Many Americans are like this nowadays. If it does them any good, we should be grateful.

Wednesday, June 26, 1996

Unfair advantage

THE British Medical Association is to debate whether doctors should be permitted to have sexual intercourse with their patients. My own feeling is that it would give an unfair advantage to doctors. Not only are they held in an absurd degree of reverence, not to say awe, by their patients, who see them as God-like figures possessing the powers of life and death. But there is another reason.

A doctor can always suggest to a patient that she removes her clothes, and she will nearly always comply readily. That is what I mean by an unfair advantage. Of course, nothing I say applies to attractive young women doctors. They should be free to do what they like. That is what the sexual revolution was all about. That is what we mean when we talk about consenting adults.

But where male non-doctors are concerned, the business of persuading women to undress, or be undressed, is often half the battle. We can always pretend to be doctors, I suppose, and suggest they take their clothes off for medical reasons, but I believe it is a criminal offence to impersonate a doctor in this way.

If the BMA decides to change the rule at its annual meeting in Brighton tomorrow, it must also see to it that the rules are changed that forbid private citizens to pretend they are doctors. Otherwise, health fascism will have gone too far, and Britain will scarcely be distinguishable from Nazi Germany.

Saturday, June 29, 1996

Let us all give thanks

I NEVER knew Anthony Chenevix-Trench, the schoolmaster who left an indelible impression on many of my contemporaries, but I feel I have known him for nearly 40 years. Their memories are of an active, violent sadist – whether at Shrewsbury, where he was a housemaster, or Bradfield, Eton and Fettes, of which he became headmaster in turn.

His career was a monument to the secretive English tradition which marked the 75 years of public-school ascendancy in this country. It is thought that his mind may have been unbalanced by his experiences as a prisoner of war of the Japanese, building the Burma Railway, but he was well known as a sadist when he left Shrewsbury.

Many of my friends, now quite eminent in their fields, had to confront the Trench choice of whether they would prefer to be caned with their trousers down, and receive fewer strokes, or with their trousers up, and receive rather more. Like good public schoolboys, they wanted only to please the man, but it was hard for them to decide which would give him more pleasure.

There are various versions of the events which led to his being

133

sacked from Eton. The one I heard at the time was that he had brutalised the son of a Wiltshire neighbour into within an inch of his sanity. The neighbour happened to be a Cabinet minister at the time . . .

But the important thing is that nobody at Eton breathed a word of this when he later took up the headmastership of Fettes, where he remained until his death. Private citizens are impeded by the laws of libel – any number of goody-goodies can be found, even now, to testify that he was faultless – but employers' references, in those days at any rate, were privileged.

Much has happened in this country since the collapse of the public-school ascendancy which is truly horrible. At least there is less terror around. Sadism and brutality are no longer protected by an iron code of *omerta*. Let us be thankful for that. We might even be thankful for the *Sun* newspaper.

Monday, July 1, 1996

All the circumstances

IS IT my imagination, or is it the case that as the national mood of infantile self-congratulation over England's defeat at Wembley recedes, the newspapers are fuller than ever with descriptions of atrocious violence? On Saturday, we learnt of a teenager who was happily burgling a house in Lewisham, when the 75-year-old, half-blind owner approached him. The teenager was forced to stab him repeatedly in self-defence, as he later explained in the Old Bailey. It was unfortunate for all concerned that the old man died. The youth was detained at Her Majesty's pleasure for the usual gruelling course of holidays in the Far East etc.

Many will agree with the Birmingham judge who criticised West Midlands police for having cautioned two youths who pleaded guilty to robbery at knifepoint, and another two who pleaded guilty to rape: but we must remember we do not know the full circumstances.

Perhaps all these youths were handicapped by having had parents who smoked. A society which refuses to take such children into care cannot really complain when they go to the bad. Certainly, we are in no position to punish them.

In any case, we must keep prison cells available for really serious infringements of the law. Remember the case of the 21-

year-old man in York who found a dead badger by the side of the road and took part of it home to put in the fridge. He received only three months in prison. That was in September, and the miscreant is presumably at large again. We owe it to all our dead badgers to keep at least one cell empty (at a cost of some £26,000 a year) in case he re-offends. With crimes of this sort, one does not really care whether the offender's parents were smokers. They are inexcusable.

What future for cats?

THE Cat Protection League has always struck me as one of the more admirable bodies in Britain. It specialises in helping people who have lost their cats and has some of the nicest members of any league in Britain. Everything I have heard about it has been entirely to its credit.

Now for the first time it is beginning to show RSPB tendencies. It has produced a report claiming that more than 10,000 cats were injured by air-guns in the past year – 10,390 to be exact – and demands a new law raising the legal age for ownership of an air-gun from 17 to 21.

I owned an air-rifle perfectly legally from the age of 11, and I think I can honestly say I never shot a cat. But if I had been told I had to wait 10 years because some cat lovers had passed a law forbidding me to own one until I was 21, I know exactly what I would have done as soon as I got one. There would not have been a live cat left for miles around.

People are not persuaded to behave well by bossy and oppressive laws, only by being introduced to good behaviour from an early age. It is nearly always a bad idea to keep people under tight control for years and suddenly give them freedom to do what they want. This explains the terrible drunkenness among our 18 to 19-year-olds, as well as the eccentric behaviour of some Catholic schoolgirls when released from their convents. It is also what worries me most about the prospect of a new Labour government.

Labour will have been out of power for nearly 18 years. It seems almost certain that when they are suddenly given it at last, they will run amok, enacting fatuous and unpleasant new laws at the rate of 20 a week. Pretty Mr Blair has always struck me as too good to be true. Have we any reason to suppose he is sound on cats?

135

A new diversion

TODAY Hong Kong enters its last year under British protection. It is hard to be sentimental about such an unsentimental place, although many of us, I dare say, have happy memories of times spent there. But nobody has yet explained Mrs Thatcher's acceptance of bad advice from her Communist-infiltrated FCO to give the whole Crown Colony to China.

It is not true, as many people seem to believe, that Hong Kong was held on a 100-year lease from China. The entire island, and most of Kowloon on the mainland, were ours in perpetuity. Only the New Territories – an agreeable addition – were subject to a lease, and they are obvious candidates for leasehold enfranchisement. If China tried to cut off water, that would be an act of war, and China has no protection against nuclear submarines under the South China Seas, let alone in the depths of the Pacific ocean.

The only explanation the FCO could offer was that our presence in Hong Kong was an anomaly. The real anomaly is to be found in our continued possession of these hideously expensive nuclear submarines, especially if we are too frightened to draw attention to them, let alone use them. They should be converted for luxury underwater cruises, allowing rich South American widows, water profiteers, Borstal boys, deprived children from the inner cities and other privileged individuals to gape in amazement at the giant squid, sea snakes, porcupines and other wild life on the ocean bed.

Wednesday, July 3, 1996

Other pleasures

SCOTTISH heritage enthusiasts have expressed disquiet over today's sale at Christie's of £6 million worth of Bute treasures from Mount Stuart, but I do not really see that it is any business of theirs. If the private ownership of property means anything, it must confer the right to dispose of it.

Lord Bute's ancestors acquired these things for their own pleasure and that of their children. If the present marquess, who prefers to live in Ladbroke Grove and be known as Johnny Dumfries, the racing driver, finds greater pleasures elsewhere, he would be foolish not to sell. The treasures will continue to exist, and give greater pleasure to other owners.

The sad truth may be that the joy has gone out of owning a large house and a priceless collection of art. If you possess works of art, it seems to grant a licence to heritage enthusiasts and art experts to sniff around them, telling you boring facts you don't want to know and behaving as if they were the owners. Anything of any value is liable to be burgled on any day or night of the week. Private property is an almost meaningless concept nowadays.

If you live in a large house, it is as likely as not to be plagued by bats. Since the bat lobby has made it a criminal offence to disturb or frighten them, you have to live with their presence, which is most unpleasant. If you have a single bat in the house, you can't switch on the burglar alarm, because the brute will set if off every five minutes. One always hopes the bat will be rabid and bite a burglar to the bone. Then, in his death agony, he can be charged with the serious crime of annoying a bat.

But revenge is an unattractive solace and I can't really blame Johnny Dumfries for preferring to race motor cars.

Saturday, July 6, 1996

Those potty exams

THOSE of us who have held driving licences for the best part of 40 years could not help smiling to read that future applicants will be expected to sit a written exam on the theory of driving. Those who came out of the first tests this week were smiling, saying they were a doddle.

Perhaps these people do not quite realise what is being done to them. The exams are arranged on the 'multiple choice' system, now almost universal in the United States, whereby candidates are asked to choose between one of four answers as the correct solution.

There can be no argument that the solution designated as correct is the correct solution. A book of 600 questions liable to be asked is available at £9.99, with the correct answers supplied.

What the system ensures is that the candidates are brainwashed into accepting the 'correct' answers, whether they agree with them or not. If they give an incorrect answer they risk failing the test.

This imposes a degree of conformity that would be unacceptable to any liberally educated person. It also explains the extraordinary gullibility of our American cousins and the whole sad phenomenon of political correctness. The liberal European would find it repugnant that there should be a 'correct' answer to every question. The liberal American mind can see no alternative.

At least the system is now worked by self-conscious liberals. If the question were: the American Negro fails to excel in academic examinations because (a) he is kept back by the weight of inherited racial prejudice, (b) he is intellectually and morally inferior, (c) he has too much sugar in his diet and takes too much dope, or (d) he has no ambition – there can be no doubt that the correct answer would be 'a'. But it needs only a small shift in the power structure for the correct answer to be 'b'. What is slightly frightening is that people who now tick 'a' would be equally happy to tick 'b' if they thought that was the answer expected of them.

Monday, July 8, 1996

Hazards of country life

SENTENCING three men to prison for organising a cockfight in Kelloe, County Durham, the stipendiary magistrate, Mr Ian Gillespie, condemned a 'barbaric and illegal practice which is apparently widespread throughout the United Kingdom'.

He is right. These cockfights have been an established feature of country life in Britain for as long as I can remember. Word is passed around and aficionados gather, with great secrecy, in some barn or other. The only sign that anything untoward is happening is usually a huge number of cars parked for no apparent reason in an unlikely spot.

I have never been to a cockfight in England, but I once went to one in Manila, where they are a regular Sunday morning diversion, and found it very boring. A cock, when all is said and done, is no more than a male chicken. As a fighter, it lacks dignity, poise, intelligence or any of the attributes of nobility.

But that is no good reason to stop other people diverting themselves in this way. I was interested to learn that although the practice has been illegal since 1835, this was only the fourth prosecution of its kind to go before a British court in the past 50 years.

This may be seen as a tribute to the taciturnity of country folk. In fact, the law is a monument to the way town dwellers think they can control the life of the countryside. Their influence is increasingly resented, as villagers on Dartmoor showed last week when they prevented a tourist centre from being built there. Plans included a visitors' centre and café and a 70-space car park but, despite these wonderful promises, the local inhabitants announced that they simply do not want to be visited.

The worst threat to townspeople wishing to visit the West Country does not come from hostile natives, however, or even from the danger that they might be mistaken for male chickens and put to death with great cruelty. It comes from the bracken. This is one of the most poisonous plants in the country. According to the Bracken Advisory Committee (a useful body set up by the Government), it causes cancer and harbours a type of flea that induces Lyme disease. Bracken has now taken over most, if not all, of the West Country, and many areas outside. British holidaymakers should stay at home or go to the Costa Brava, where there is no bracken at all.

Saturday, July 13, 1996

Cautionary example

TWO reports on British schoolgirls – one from the Office for Standards in Education combined with the Equal Opportunities Commission, the other from Gardner Merchant, the catering firm – confirm what we always suspected: that schoolgirls are much pleasanter than schoolboys.

They work harder, try to please their teachers more, and have overtaken boys in English and maths in nearly every age group. Some people may be saddened to learn that so many of them are becoming vegetarians, but it is my observation that some of the kindest, funniest, most beautiful women in England are vegetarians.

What is more worrying is that they unnecessarily replace regular meals with continual snacking. Inevitably, the nutritional standard of their diet is declining. Chocolate and

139

fizzy drinks are their mainstay. This is bound to have an appalling effect on their appearance.

Perhaps they have adopted this course of action from the highest moral standpoint, in order to discourage the paedophiles who, if we are to believe our newspapers and the speeches of men and women in public life, threaten them from every quarter. What was once a minority taste among a few schoolmasters would appear to have become the greatest threat to our children since smallpox, scarlet fever, tuberculosis and polio.

My own feeling is that the dangers of paedophilia have been exaggerated, both by the tabloid press, seeking sensation, and by the childcare agencies, seeking money and power. As a result, schoolgirls come more and more to resemble baby vultures. If only, instead of all the rubbish they are taught at school, they could be persuaded to learn Belloc's *Cautionary Verses*:

The Vulture eats between his meals
And that's the reason why
He very, very, rarely feels
As well as you and I.

His eye is dull, his head is bald
His neck is growing thinner,
Oh! What a lesson for us all
To only eat at dinner.

After the break

THE Clinton administration is making a mistake to ban Rupert
Pennant-Rea, the former deputy governor of the Bank of
England, and Sir Patrick Sheehy, former chairman of British
American Tobacco, and their families from entering the United
States. This is in revenge for being directors of a company that
has allegedly used confiscated American property in Cuba, but
both men are genial fellows – especially Sir Pat – and life in
America will be poorer without them.

It means I will have no chance of seeing them during my brief
visit to Los Angeles next week. I hope the Home Office responds
by banning at least a hundred American businessmen and their
families. Then the Americans can ban a couple of hundred more
and we can ban a thousand or so. Eventually every American
without residence in Britain will be banned from coming here,
and all Britons will be banned from America.

This seems an admirable idea. I am going only to see a
daughter in Los Angeles, but under the new arrangement she
would have to come back to England anyway. Way of the World
should resume on Monday July 22.

Monday, July 22, 1996

A loyal toast

HOW MANY of us, if we are honest, were a little disappointed to
learn that gunshots heard around the villa in the South of
France where the Princess of Wales is staying emanated from
Prince William shooting at clay pigeons, rather than from
French police shooting paparazzi?

This would have been an unworthy emotion, of course: the
paparazzi are only doing their job; it is not a capital offence to
persecute beautiful women; we cannot be sure that any
paparazzo who dies in this way is ready and prepared to meet his
Maker.

On the other hand, it seems an odd time and place to be shooting at clay pigeons. The French police tend to be stricter with miscreants than our own delightful 'bobbies'. If there are some unmarked graves in the garden of the villa Clos de Meaulx at Seillans, they might bring some comfort to the many millions of Britons who feel abused by endless sneering attacks on the Princess of Wales in this country. She has become more than a national icon and national skittle. In a nation which is rapidly becoming as bad at games as it is at work, she has become our only point of reference for the rest of the world's population.

I was in Los Angeles when the news broke of her public humiliation at the hands of the Palace establishment, and of her prompt response in resigning from 100 public duties. Finding American newspapers unreadable and American television incomprehensible, I could follow the news only in headlines. They were enough to demonstrate not only that British public life will be immeasurably poorer for her absence, but the rest of the world will lose all interest in it too.

The country is bitterly divided and there can be no agreement between those who hate the Princess of Wales and those who love her. So far as the latter are concerned, this humiliation of a much loved public figure humiliates us all. I see no reason to accept this new directive from the Palace. If they succeed in driving her out of the country, there will be many glasses raised in the years ahead as secret toasts are drunk to The Queen over the Water.

Wednesday, July 24, 1996

Hatred of tourists

SPANISH experts have been quick to point out that ETA, the Basque terror group, has nothing to gain by blowing up British and other tourists, since nearly all its professed aims have been secured long ago. It does not seem to occur to anyone that these outrages may be explained by a simple dislike of tourists.

Yet this is one of the strongest emotions in the modern world, from where I live in Somerset to the East End of London – one of the least obvious tourist destinations in Europe – where residents of Whitechapel and Spitalfields have won curbs on tourist trips to visit the sites associated with Jack the Ripper.

The truth is beginning to emerge that 100 years of social progress – towards greater prosperity more equally shared – have been a catastrophic mistake. Too many people with too much money to spend on trying to have a good time create nothing but a hell of noise, ugliness, foul smells and pollution for themselves and for everybody else.

This hell may be worse in a small island, but it is only a matter of time before it spreads to the whole world. For the past 50 years, idealistic, well-disposed people have imagined that the kindest thing they can do is to help the poorer countries of the world, such as India, to get richer.

Yet India, with nearly 600 inhabitants to the square mile, has almost exactly the same population density as the United Kingdom. It would be the unkindest thing in the world to destroy that country's innocence in favour of the congestion, noise, sights and smells we have inflicted on ourselves. Idealistic people should concern themselves with preventing the Indians getting any richer. An obvious first step must be to ban tourists. If the Indian government won't do it, local patriots will almost certainly take the law into their own hands.

A future with Fish

ON THURSDAY, the mighty Vivian Ellis prize for the best original musical submitted by young composers was chosen out of over 100 entries. To immense acclaim from the distinguished audience which included Herbert Kretzmer, Tim Rice, Trevor Nunn, Ned Sherrin and the whole of the musical establishment, the prize went to two brothers, Alexander Waugh, 32, and Nat Waugh, 27, for their musical *Bon Voyage*, combining a beautiful love story with complicated black comedy, set in 1735 aboard the world's first luxury cruise.

This is very good news for the authors' proud father. When *Bon Voyage* eventually opens in the West End, I think I may retire from journalism and sponge off the two young geniuses as some sort of consultant. These are not good days for journalists.

My first scheme is for a musical on the Polly Toynbee saga, which seems to have disappeared from the newspapers while I was in America. It will tell how Toynbee's passionate affair with an unknown man who looks rather like a squirrel led to heartbreak for the nice young editor of the *Independent*, Andrew Marr, when he discovered that everybody was laughing at him.

Next in line will be the *News of the World's* great scoop which dominated all world news on the front page this Sunday: 'TV Weather Man Cheats on Wife with a Redhead: Michael Fish in sexy romps with mistress.'

Fish, denounced as a 'stinker' by the odious hypocrites who produce Murdoch's rubbish for him, will be the hero of the new musical, with Mrs Fish and the redhead as joint heroines. It will be set in wild weather, with grotesque errors of forecasting as a sub-text. Generations yet unborn will be tapping their feet to the strains of the Waugh brothers as they re-tell the stories of Toynbee, her squirrel, Fish and the redhead. We will be riding on the shirt-tails of history.

Saturday, July 27, 1996

Badly advised

PERHAPS it was just tact which prevented anyone spotting a connection between the lightning which struck down guests at a Buckingham Palace garden party this week and the Queen's public instruction to her eldest son that he should divorce his wife and the mother of his children.

I am surprised that the *Catholic Herald*, at least, did not spot the coincidence. The Church of England, of which the Queen is head, is, in fact, even stricter than the Roman Catholic Church on marriage, allowing fewer grounds for annulment. Many regard broken marriages as the greatest force for destruction in modern society. When the Queen openly champions divorce, many will see the lightning strike as a terrible warning.

Personally, I see it as a reaction to the proposal to drop the Princess of Wales from the Anglican prayerbook, where she features in prayers for the Royal Family. This will appear to most people who revere the monarchy as a gratuitous act of spite, causing many who take this sort of thing seriously to boycott church services.

I don't think the Queen is being well advised by anyone, least of all by Lord St John of Fawsley, whose adulation is counter-productive. Her decision to snub the BBC by giving the Christmas Message to ITN in apparent revenge for the *Panorama* interview with the Princess of Wales will upset no one. Above all, it seems to invite counter-reprisals from the BBC. I would love to see the

Panorama interview screened again and again, and so would many other older people whose children have left home and who can't work the video-recording machine without their help.

Perhaps it would be irresponsible to suggest that the BBC screen it on Christmas Day at the same time as ITV is screening the Queen's Message. But it would be irresponsible only in the sense that the BBC would never do it – they are all far too wet.

It is tragic to see how badly advised the Queen is today, whereas the Princess of Wales, who has no advice at all, goes from strength to strength, with occasional setbacks.

An end to all job chances

ONE CAN easily understand the Government's decision to withdraw the magazine *Jobsearch* from Jobcentres and 10 Jobclubs around the country after a prying Labour MP pointed out that it carried advertisements for men and women to work as gigolos or as female prostitutes.

On the other hand, it is hard to see what sort of job is open to young people after so many years of state education, especially if they are unprepared to consider the option of cleaning shoes. As I never tire of pointing out, there is endless opportunity for shoe-cleaners in an age when nobody wishes to clean his own footwear, and the nation's shoes are getting dirtier and dirtier.

Shoe-cleaning is generally thought infra dig, however. Many of the unemployed prefer to sell *The Big Issue*, which is a useful thing to do, as it has been quite a good magazine up to now. I certainly would not suggest they become journalists. These are bad times for journalists. All money and power in the newspaper industry has moved to the accountants.

When *The Big Issue* was looking for a new editor this week, it settled for a former editor of the *Observer*. This may seem something of a step down in the world for *The Big Issue*, but I suppose nobody else was prepared to look at the job. Being an editor nowadays is too much like cleaning other people's shoes.

But the sex industry, for those with no religious objections, might still provide a useful service without requiring too much effort or training. In the New Britain, where more and more people live alone because they find the rest of the human population too selfish, too bad mannered or otherwise unpleasant to share with them, demand for sex services of this sort is bound to increase.

Labour's employment spokesman, Ian McCartney, who demanded the withdrawal of *Jobsearch* because he disapproved of two advertisements, has effectively hindered its readers in finding out about any other jobs. I don't suppose it matters: soon they may have no choice.

Monday, July 29, 1996

History is made

NOBODY has yet blamed smoking for the explosion at the Olympic Centennial Park, Atlanta, where a thousand people were listening to rock music. I do not know whether visitors were allowed to smoke, but I observe that alcohol was banned at that dismal function, and that may have been a factor.

Since the opening of the Olympic Games there has been a deluge of hostile reporting from the foreign press, particularly the British. One bitter complaint concerned the inadequacy of transport supplied by the Olympic authorities for visiting journalists.

This shocked me, rather. The British Journalist does not wait to be carried around in a charabanc. He takes a taxi at his newspaper's expense.

But as I never tire of pointing out, these are bad times for journalists. Many of the reporters were probably not given airline tickets to get out there, while others had to suffer the unspeakable indignity of Virgin Atlantic Economy Class smoke-free accommodation.

When I was a young reporter on this newspaper more than 35 years ago, all journalists, however humble, travelled everywhere first class at their employer's expense. This was insisted on by the National Union of Journalists. Does the NUJ still exist? When I tried waving my NUJ press card towards a surly Virgin Atlantic receptionist at Heathrow recently, on my way to Los Angeles, I could not help noticing that it had expired four years earlier. But something of that name continues to make depredations on my bank account.

As I say, these are bad times for journalists and I cannot help wondering whether their disgruntlement might not influence the general perception of world events. By the standards of our own American-sponsored IRA, the Atlanta bomb was very small beer. Americans are killing each other by the score – both accidentally and deliberately – with every hour that passes. That two Americans should die in a rock concert in Atlanta may be sad, but it is not big news. In fact, one of the victims turns out to have been Turkish.

I dare say the explosion was caused by hamburger gases escaping from a reveller's satchel. Such accidents are not uncommon in the United States. Then the disgruntled, alcohol-starved foreign press decided to present the explosion as a second Nagasaki. Is this how the history of our times will be written?

Crime wave

IT WAS also sad to learn that a 10-year-old boy from Narborough, Leicestershire, is most unwell after being bitten by an adder which he tried to pick up from a rock in a park. His hand and arm are badly swollen and he is in hospital, suffering from shock.

Even sadder is the thought that on recovery he may face criminal prosecution. Adders (or vipers, as they are known) are now protected animals, and it is an offence to disturb or annoy them in any way.

At least the lad is too young to be sent to prison, unlike the 23-year-old who was jailed for a month by Stockport magistrates last week for chopping up his son's pet lizard, or the poor man who took home a bit of a dead badger he found on the road and was sent to prison for three months.

Michael Howard has just initiated a £90 million emergency building programme to help to accommodate our enormously expanded prison population. Soon, if the economy is really picking up, as Mr Major claims, we may be able to imprison anyone who pulls a rude face at a horse.

Saturday, August 3, 1996

Why so inadequate?

WE HEAR much about the inadequacy of British children at the

end of their schooling. I was pleased to observe that the Professional Association of Teachers has finally got round to describing how bad they are when they first arrive.

The Association's conference in Cheltenham heard (as if they did not already know) about children who arrive at primary schools with limited language and communication skills, who have never been taught to play, share, or take turns, who throw tantrums and hit out when they are told not to do something, or want to do something else.

It is to escape such scenes that so many millions of people wish to leave the towns and build new homes in the countryside, according to the Rowntree Trust, whose study, *Where Will the People Go?* concludes that 'large scale use' of greenfield land is inevitable as people try to escape from poor environments, high crime and low school standards.

What these people do not understand is that they will bring their problems with them. It has already happened in at least one Somerset school which has been encouraged to receive children from Birmingham. Inner cities may well be dirty and horrible places – Trevor Nunn has sensibly proposed that homeless young beggars should be paid to clean them up, although nobody pays any attention to him – but what creates these generations of unemployable criminals in the first place is parental inadequacy.

I wonder why we have become a nation of such inadequate parents.

Monday, August 5, 1996

The British way

A HELICOPTER carrying members of the West Mercia Police was used in a dramatic raid on Summer Farm near the village of Wyre Piddle in Hereford and Worcester last week. As a result, officers were able to question Mrs Siwarn Kaur, a 65-year-old widow suspected of trimming, wrapping and packing spring onions without the appropriate work permit.

The raid was the result of months of undercover work across the Midlands. Police found many other Asian workers engaged in trimming, wrapping and packing vegetables, their ages ranging from 12 to 85. They arrested 31.

I wonder how many of the policemen involved thought they were doing anything useful. These illegal immigrants did not come here to sponge off our welfare services, as so many people like to believe. They could do much better on the welfare services of the European countries which they use as stepping stones.

They came here to work, something which many Britons are nowadays disinclined to do, particularly when it comes to trimming, wrapping and packing spring onions. By working hard for reasonable wages, they help to keep the rest of us agreeably overpaid, if we work, or enjoying reasonably generous welfare benefit, if we don't. Is it really worth harassing them with police helicopter raids and expensive undercover investigations?

That police action was called Operation Vesuvius. In Operation Sport, officers of the Derbyshire force visited some suspected brothels, and made a number of 'test purchases' to collect evidence. Five officers agreed they had paid money for sexual services which fell short of penetrative intercourse, but when the case came to trial at Derby Crown Court in January 1995, it collapsed because of witness problems.

Then a Sunday newspaper came to hear of these 'test purchases' and the Police Complaints Authority announced that the five police officers and one other would face charges of discreditable conduct.

It was only on Friday, after four days of hearing, that we learned how these charges, too, were dismissed. Once again, I wonder how many of the policemen involved thought they were doing anything useful. Police opinion seems, by and large, in favour of regulated brothels. Do they really care about illegal onion wrappers?

Next year, when the new Immigration Act comes into force, the authorities will be able to prosecute anyone who employs an illegal immigrant. That will ensure they are forced to live on welfare or, if that is denied, on crime.

It would be easy, in the face of all these half-baked and unpleasant new laws, to urge police to ignore the lot and use their common sense, leaving industrious immigrants and brothels alone. The trouble is, if you allow them to use their discretion they will ignore burglary, mugging, rape and almost any other form of crime except drink-driving.

150

Honouring Benjamin

SOME have been tempted to mock the councillors of Aldeburgh who expressed a preference for a birdbath over a statue to commemorate their greatest citizen, the composer Benjamin Britten, who died in 1976.

No doubt they are mindful of Kenneth Rose's dictum that modern dress (especially the modern trouser) is not suitable for commemorative statuary. A frequent solution is to show the person to be commemorated undraped, but this may not be suitable here. The councillors of Aldeburgh could feel they have no curiosity to see Benjamin Britten in the nude, and I understand their point of view.

A commemorative birdbath has possibilities, but so fickle are the masses, and so short is their memory, that it would probably soon be known as the Benjamin Birdbath monument, inviting confusion with Peter Simple's equally famous genius, Julian Birdbath. So far as I know, they are not related.

Various compromises have been suggested. Britten could be shown clad in those wondrous new underpants we have been

reading so much about, called Waist Sculpt. I fear that in 20 years' time we may have forgotten about Waist Sculpt, and wonder what on earth he is wearing.

I think a compromise is the answer – a nude statue with its modesty protected by a discreetly positioned birdbath.

That should please everybody.

End of St Helena

AN INTERESTING study of the recent arrival of television on the remote island of St Helena is said to confound those who claim that exposure to violence, sex and bad language on television corrupts children.

I normally keep quiet when this sort of thing is being debated because, although I have had many children, I practically never watch television and might be accused of not knowing what I was talking about. These last five days, however, being at a health farm in Suffolk, I have watched bits and pieces of some 20 television programmes, and can reasonably claim to be an expert on the subject.

It does not seem to me very probable that children are corrupted by the violence, sex and bad language on television because, on this visit, I have seen and heard none, unless you describe the USA versus China women's football match at Atlanta as an act of violence.

What corrupts them, I feel sure, is the affectation of television presenters. Nearly everybody on television appears to combine extreme vulgarity with a patronising air of superiority. I am not a violent man, but I feel a wish to kill them all.

For the less intelligent child, these grimacing morons represent a role model. This explains why one section of young Britain speaks, thinks and acts like an air hostess telling passengers to refrain from smoking, while another settles on a course of social alienation and criminal activity. St Helena must wait a few years for these results.

Wednesday, August 7, 1996

Properties of salad

AN OBVIOUS reaction to Britain's disgrace at the Olympics is to demand the Prime Minister's resignation, and his replacement by Mr Heseltine, unless Lord Howe is prepared to lead the Government from the Upper House. He would probably be the best choice, as the House of Lords is less implicated than the Commons in our national humiliation.

As for Iain Sproat, the Minister for Sport, he should plainly be sent to prison. His exact sentence should be decided by a national debate between ordinary men and women in the street, but there should be no question of leaving him at liberty while the shame is upon us, if only for his own safety.

Alternatively, we might set up a public inquiry into what exactly has gone wrong with our athletes. It will centre on their diet: have they been getting enough milk, or too much? Enough or too many fresh vegetables? Enough fibre? Since doing U-turns on almost every known foodstuff, the doctors have now announced that a high fibre diet may not prevent you getting cancer, as they originally said, and is bad for you in other ways.

No scientist – even in California – has yet discovered the dangerous poison contained in many forms of salad, particularly green lettuce and the bitter red leaf called radicchio. In my Suffolk health farm, I study little else but the effects of salad on human behaviour. Just because it does not kill you or give you cancer, like everything else, no one is interested, but lettuce and radicchio are notoriously bad for javelin-throwing, discus, long jump and sprinting at any length because they destroy all ambition, all competitiveness, all desire to win. In extreme cases, they have even been known to make women pregnant.

On the other hand, perhaps salad eating will also enable us to take our defeat in good heart, teach us a little humility and give us the grace to welcome and applaud these new, rather small countries which have done so much better than we have. Even so, there is much to be said for a diet of beef and Burgundy.

Let them eat coke

PRESIDENT Clinton's decision to allow Americans who are out of work for more than two years to starve to death, with their children, must be seen as a desperate bid for popularity before the November elections.

More people in America are employed than unemployed, and

the former show a growing spirit of 'zero tolerance' (as they explain to each other in their delightful language) towards those less fortunate than themselves.

In this country, some concern would be expressed about the children, since we must pretend to like other people's children and to feel sentimental about children generally. However, anyone who has seen American children (or 'kids') on television, will quite understand why it may not be a problem in the United States.

The reason why Mr Clinton is so desperate for favourable publicity at the moment may be found in a newly published biography of him by R. Emmett Tyrrell Jr, respected editor of *The American Spectator*. In it, Tyrrell accuses the President not only of complicity in a murder, but also of complicity in smuggling cocaine.

Nobody in America is much interested in political murders – witness the extraordinary lack of interest in Vincent Foster's fate – but cocaine smuggling is a serious offence. It will be curious if Mr Clinton is arrested and led away to serve 95 years in prison on the day he is re-elected President. The thing which worries me is: what will happen to Chelsea?

Monday, August 12, 1996

Repentance

'JOY shall be in heaven over one sinner that repenteth, more than over ninety and nine just persons, which need no repentance' (Luke XV 7).

Many of his friends might have despaired of Neil Hartley, 32, unemployed, of Huddersfield, when they heard he was in trouble with the law again. Neil already had 231 offences recorded against him for dishonesty, including 85 for burglary, when he pleaded guilty to stealing £27 from a purse in a farmer's car last December. He was sentenced to 40 hours community service and ordered to return the £27.

But it was not this savage punishment which persuaded him to turn over a new leaf. It happened because the farmer, Kenneth Hall, accidentally shot him as he was stealing the £27. Neil had to spend four days in hospital: 'Coming so close to death made me wake up to what I was doing. I will never steal again,' he said.

'Before this my life was going nowhere, but now I'm trying to get my life on the right track.'

After last week's trial of Mr Hall for defending his own property – if convicted, he could have been sent to prison for five years – Karen Earnshaw, a friend of Mr Hartley, said: 'This has had a profound effect on his life. He has kept out of trouble.'

The most encouraging thing to emerge from this episode is that there may indeed be nothing seriously wrong with our young people. All they need is a thoroughly good shootin'.

Wednesday, August 14, 1996

Give it a try

ALTHOUGH more than one in 20 Britons applied for tickets to attend the Oasis concert at Knebworth at the weekend – three million in all, we are told – I was not among their number. This was not because I prefer the music of Blur. Like the majority of people in this country I do not like rock music at all.

Nor did I relish the thought of the people I might meet there. Although I have never actually been to a rock concert, I imagine they are the sort of places where foreign tourists go to breast-feed their babies. It is not the breast-feeding one minds so much, as the people who turn up to watch it.

On the other hand, Knebworth is a beautiful and unusual house. We should not approach experiences with our minds made up. There is a distinct possibility that next year's crowd will be altogether higher class.

This is because the *Sun* has advised its readers to stay away next year. Readers complained of having to pay £6 for a burger. But the worst complaints of all were about the two-hour queue at the beer tent, and a 90-minute wait 'to use the loos', as *Sun* reporters delicately put it.

'A disaster . . . Knebworth '97 . . . don't bother,' was their conclusion. Perhaps one should feel sorry for *Sun* readers in their misery, but I don't really see why. What is life, after all, but a process of queuing for beer and waiting to use the loos? If there is the guarantee that no *Sun* readers will be present at Knebworth next year, any of us might give it a try.

Where guidance is needed

SHOULD we all cancel our subscriptions to the *Catholic Herald*? Accounts of the new Editor, Miss Deborah Jones, 48, are not encouraging. It has been said she intends to commission articles from Catholic bishops and church leaders, that she is an ardent advocate of modern church reforms (as the Donald Duck movement is called in ecclesiastical circles), and that she will 'have no truck' with traditionalists who want to turn back the clock.

This might all be a foul calumny, designed to discredit Britain's only intelligent Catholic newspaper. There are many good thinkers and intelligent writers who, for one reason or another, find themselves in the Roman Catholic priesthood, but none of them in recent history has been made a bishop. As an editor myself, I would no sooner ask a Catholic bishop to write an article than I would ask a cart horse to sing from *Un Ballo in Maschera*. Apart from anything else, it would be cruel.

But we must give Miss Jones a chance before cancelling our

subscriptions. A great challenge for all religious thinkers nowadays comes from the French campaign to prove that adultery is good for you. 'Infidelity, blamed for breaking up marriages, has become an ally for couples determined to stay together,' explains *Le Nouvel Observateur*.

This observation cuts across everything a celibate clergy has been taught on this subject. There may be a further problem in an age in which physical health is often confused with what is morally and philosophically correct.

There seem to be two questions here: is adultery good for you, and if so, should it be encouraged? If both answers are 'yes', they might seem to destroy the whole moral stance of the born-again Murdoch press. Last Thursday the *Sun* was happy to expose an unknown social worker, a married mother of three, who had been suspended from her job when a former lover shopped her to the authorities and then gave intimate photographs of her in underwear to the *Sun*.

I don't think it reasonable to ask Bishop O'Bubblegum to give readers advice on delicate matters of this sort. Miss Jones will have to think them through for herself.

Prophetic

THERE is something deeply prophetic in the decision of Michael Portillo's constituency Conservative Association to sell its headquarters to McDonald's, the American global chain, for a 'drive-thru' burger bar. McDonald's offer of £325,000 – thought to be £100,000 more than the asking price – is subject to planning permission. I cannot suppose that is a major problem in Enfield, although about 2,000 local people have signed a petition protesting about the sale.

'They are worried about traffic, parking problems, noise, litter and security,' said a spokesman for the residents. I can think of other things they might be worried about, but perhaps it would be unkind to list them.

If I were a Conservative activist, I would worry most of all that my beloved party will disappear entirely into the McDonald's empire. It used to be said that the Church of England was the Conservative Party at prayer, but that has not been true for some time. Nowadays we might with greater truth describe McDonald's as the Conservative Party at table.

My chief anxiety is that once these somewhat farouche young

Tories have discovered the joys of eating, they will never do anything else. The Palace of Westminster will be converted into a gigantic drive-thru McDonald's burger bar, where MPs will sit all day stuffing themselves with hamburgers and counting their money. I worry only for their health, of course. We would be much better off if they spent all their time eating burgers and never passed another law. Have the Conservatives of Enfield glimpsed this?

Saturday, August 17, 1996

Crime prevention

I DON'T know whether police computers have revealed a new pattern of assaults on Church of England clergymen. If so, I dare say they plan a special operation to rush police and resources to

the next clergyman in trouble. But since the Rev Christopher Gray was murdered in Liverpool and the Rev Nduna Mpunzi had a close shave in Palfrey, two bishops have suggested it might be necessary to remove all clergymen from the inner cities.

This seems unnecessarily defeatist. One alternative suggestion is to have panic buttons in vicarages, another that the new breed of female vicar or 'woman-priest' should carry a personal alarm.

The Bishop of Barking who supported the Bishop of Stafford in his fears that clergymen might have to be withdrawn from inner city areas unless security improved, said: 'We must have priests who can get out into the community and mix with people.'

How will personal alarms help them achieve that? Some might see these attempts to get out and mix with people as provocative. It is obviously unreasonable to expect the police to protect them if they indulge in this sort of behaviour. A much more sensible solution would be to allow clergymen to carry guns. Nobody should be ordained who cannot show his proficiency with a .38 Smith and Wesson.

This will allow police to study possible reasons for the new crime pattern. I cannot understand anyone wanting to attack a clergyman, although I suppose I might be tempted to have a crack at one of these new Australian 'bishopesses' if I bumped into one. Such temptation would be reduced if we filled our empty grouse moors with kangaroos. Is it against the law to shoot kangaroos in England? I can't see why it should be.

Monday, August 26, 1996

Gloomy future

IN RETROSPECT, there may be something terribly sad about those pictures which appeared day after day showing schoolchildren grinning all over their faces and hugging each other as they opened their exam results.

There are those who maintain that the extraordinarily high percentage of good grades was fully justified, that this year's children are brighter than those of previous years. Perhaps it is true that they are brighter. Their only problem, as the Institute of Management has pointed out, is that they cannot read or write or do the simplest sums.

'Over three-quarters of our members believe that current education standards are a threat to our economic competitiveness,' said Roger Young, the institute's director-general, pointing out that these young people do not have the skills to make them employable.

A robust alternative view is that we have no business to submit our children to school examinations as it encourages elitism, favours the more intelligent and creates an unhealthy feeling of failure in the less successful. This view is more or less accommodated in the present arrangement, where everybody, or nearly everybody, is given a 'pass' and most are told they have passed with flying colours.

But it does not solve the problem of what will happen to all these gleeful schoolgirls whom we saw hugging each other as they read their A-level and GCSE results. No doubt the declining birthrate has added to our sentimentality about children, but I detect a note of doom in the general hysteria.

Of course a few of the more adventurous among them may take to the streets, but many of these highly qualified school-leavers will probably fill their days as single parents in specially built accommodation, in the depths of the countryside, waiting patiently for their next welfare cheque.

All for the best

I AM not sure this was a good moment to open the splendid mausoleum at Frogmore where Queen Victoria lies beside her adored husband. It can prompt only melancholy thoughts at the present time.

Prince Albert, who was several months younger than the Queen when they married at 21, served for only 21 years as husband and Consort before he succumbed to the drains at Windsor Castle. It is a mischievous invention that she wore him out with her sexual demands, but it is true that he had to wait nearly 50 years of her widowhood before she rejoined him at Frogmore.

Albert is remembered by the great Gilbert Scott Memorial in Kensington Gardens, now being restored at a cost of millions, and the Royal Albert Hall. He was undoubtedly a good man, but he died absurdly young.

Our beloved Queen Mother, who was born in the reign of Queen Victoria, put in 29 years as a wife, later Consort, and has been working hard throughout the 44 years of her widowhood, will be remembered only by a peculiarly disgusting pair of gates in Hyde Park Corner.

No monument is planned for Prince Philip, so far as I know, although he is a grandson of Queen Victoria, who has put in nearly 50 years service as a husband, 45 as a royal consort. Perhaps it is all for the best.

Wednesday, August 28, 1996

Attention needed

LAST week, while I was in Tuscany like everybody else, my shotgun certificate expired in Somerset. To possess a shotgun and cartridges without a valid certificate is a criminal offence, punishable, under the 1994 Firearms Act, by four years in prison.

Even worse than that, in the hysterical mood of self-importance which has visited so many people since the Dunblane tragedy, the police are entitled to come in their helicopters with their submachine guns and tear gas, break down my front door, destroy every piece of furniture in the house, gas my pekingese if they put up any resistance, and shoot my dear wife of 35 years if she reaches for her spectacles in the general excitement.

This is unlikely to happen in Somerset, where we have a sensible and experienced chief constable in charge of a force which has few of the 'classless' power-maniacs who dominate other areas and threaten to take over the Association of Chief Police Officers.

Before Mr Howard starts waving his Union Jack and uttering strange Russian imprecations, he might like to know why my certificate has run out. Although I sent in the renewal form over a month ago, duly signed, accompanied by a cheque, with four photographs attested by a saintly local clergyman, the licensing authority never acknowledged its receipt.

Knowing that some government departments take at least 30 days to open a letter, I sent the papers by recorded delivery, but of course it requires only one over-zealous policeman to testify that the envelope was empty, or contained a swan's down powder puff . . .

As I say, I am lucky to live in Somerset, but even the long-suffering Somerset police may grow weary of my constant jokes about police overtime, as one of the greatest scandals in modern government. I am sure there was nothing sinister about their failure to acknowledge my gun licence renewal application, or do anything about it. They are on holiday like everybody else – probably in Tuscany. But perhaps I should stop making this sort of joke.

Saturday, August 31, 1996

Men as victims

IT LOOKS as if the worm is beginning to turn in the great sex war that has become such a distressing feature of our times. No man has yet successfully prosecuted his wife for marital rape, as women are entitled to prosecute their husbands, but men are beginning to complain of being stalked by women.

This week the World Congress, meeting in Stockholm to discuss child prostitution, heard about rich European widows who buy Sri Lankan male teenagers for their sexual gratification. It sounds less shocking, somehow, than the European businessmen who buy Thai and Filipina teenage girls, often in paedophile rings, but I feel sure we are right to keep an eye on this new development, too.

Where female stalkers are concerned, we have heard a long moan of complaints from television and radio presenters, disc jockeys and that sort of person, and many of us may feel they are fair game. But men who suffer unwelcome attentions from deluded and lovelorn women are not confined to these groups, even if they are the ones who are happiest to publicise their suffering. Many men are stalked by women. Often these women are their wives.

Since both stalking and marital rape have now been identified as crimes, we must insist that marital stalking is put on the list without delay. Then husbands will be able to have their wives arrested, just as wives and other female partners can lay information against men in their lives, or any man who may be a complete stranger.

More work for the police, more fees for the lawyers – the benefits are obvious and almost endless. The chief benefit, however, is to restore an element of fairness to the sex war. Every advantage so far seems to have gone to the women without a shot being fired.

Give him a chance

MANY years ago, in the mid-Fifties, when Lord Beaverbrook wished to persecute my poor father – in those days, novelists were thought worth persecuting – he sent one of his employees, the late Nancy Spain, to harass him in his Gloucestershire home. Spain telephoned to ask for an appointment, and when this was refused, turned up at the front door with a tall, gangling young man whom she introduced to the butler as her friend Rufus Noel-Buxton. One assumed she had bought him on *Daily Express* expenses.

When they were refused admission, an altercation ensued, which brought my father out of his library, red in the face and quivering with rage. Had they not seen the notice in the drive, he demanded, 'No admittance on business'?

It was at this point that Noel-Buxton produced a rejoinder that was to echo down the years. 'I am not on business,' he said. 'I am a member of the House of Lords.'

And so he was, the son of a Labour minister for agriculture raised to the peerage by Ramsay MacDonald in 1930. The notion that no member of the House of Lords could be refused admittance to anyone's home had a profound effect on social thinking in the 1950s and 1960s.

Now we learn of Rufus's son, the third Lord Noel-Buxton, that after becoming a solicitor, he lives in a Battersea charity flat with a regular income of £47 a week, signing on for income support once a fortnight. He has achieved fame at the age of 55 by almost managing to live on the welfare provisions available for single males – he is separated from his third wife – and the measly expenses allowed by the House of Lords on the few days of the year it is in session.

Of his father, Rufus, the friend of Nancy Spain, who described himself as a writer and painter and once worked on the editorial staff of *Farmers' Weekly*, we learn that he died of alcoholism, destitute, in sheltered housing, in 1980. That, perhaps, was only to be expected.

But the third Lord Noel-Buxton, who has been fighting the good fight through Alcoholics Anonymous, is plainly a most amiable person, part of the rich reserve of well-educated, intelligent, well-mannered Britons we all ignore.

I wonder if he would like to be *Literary Review*'s talent scout in the House of Lords. We don't pay much, but not everyone in this country is yet entirely eaten up with Thatcherite greed for money. I suspect there are many well-educated, intelligent, amiable people in that place, feeling rather left out of things.

Monday, September 2, 1996

Late summer diversions

AUGUST was a wicked month, full of bogus debates about the monarchy, calculated to turn that normally amiable institution into a focus for the nation's boredom and irritability. Even more inappropriately, many of us found ourselves overcome with scepticism, even derision, by the great paedophilia debate.

Polite concern would have been more appropriate, but it could scarcely survive Roger Moore's contribution. Moore, who is now 68 and chiefly remembered for having acted James Bond 20 years ago, told the World Congress of paedophilia experts in Stockholm about his narrow escape from an alleged pervert on Wimbledon Common when he was eight. The man wore a dirty mackintosh and made a lewd suggestion, so Moore and his friend walked away. When they returned, he had stolen their sandwiches.

One might have thought James Bond had had narrower squeaks than that. It is only in August that we have to listen to such people. Let us hope that next year we can think of a different subject, and a jollier place than Stockholm to discuss it.

After that we were all supposed to be living in terror of a 'dangerous' sex offender of 52 who has been in institutions since he was six, talks in a broad Lancashire accent, leans to the right when walking, has a pronounced nervous twitch and covers his ears with his hands when approached by anyone. He was once convicted of two charges of indecency against boys, so they took him from the secure psychiatric unit where he is held to the Chessington World of Adventures, in Surrey, after he had expressed an interest in animals. There, to everyone's indignation, he gave his accompanying nurse the slip and was found a few days later on the beach in Worthing, reading newspaper headlines about himself.

It seems to me that in our present obsession with paedophilia, we may have missed the point. Of course boys need protection, but so do animals. Is it proper treatment for someone suspected of an unhealthy interest in boys to be encouraged to take an interest in animals instead? Have the animal rights groups anything to say about this? Next August's subject for debate could be the growing scourge of bestiality. A World Congress in Tonga on the Sexual Exploitation of Animals might help to clear the air.

Wednesday, September 4, 1996

Sensitive matters

A MOST disturbing report from something called the Institute of Employment Studies – I wonder who pays for the institute, and how you get a job on it – reveals that the 'white' image of traditional universities is putting off talented black and Asian students and damaging their long-term prospects. Ethnic minority students feel under pressure to 'act white'. Some also feel alienated by a rugby club culture.

What, we may ask, can we do about this? The least we can do is to ban rugby at universities. This has always been part of my agenda since I, too, felt alienated by the rugby club culture at Oxford. I can see it would have been much worse if I had been black.

Students of racial sensitivity will also be interested to learn of yet another attempt to lance the perennial blister represented by Helen Bannerman's 1889 *The Story of Little Black Sambo*. Two black Americans, Julius Lester and Jerry Pinkney, have written Sam and the Tigers as a 'reconceptualisation', set in the American South of the 1920s, where a clever little boy called Sam outwits the tigers.

At the same time, HarperCollins is bringing out a new version of Helen Bannerman's book but with the names changed. It is called *The Story of Little Babaji*. Babaji's parents are called Mamaji and Papaji rather than Black Mumbo and Black Jumbo. Perhaps this will assuage the hurt feelings of us all.

Africans themselves tend to take a more robust line on these delicate matters. In a moving speech at the funeral of his son Earnest (sic) Thuthani, who died of Aids at the age of 41 earlier this year, Joshua Nkomo, the Vice-President of Zimbabwe, declared that Aids was brought into Zimbabwe by white people who intended to wipe out the black population and take its land and wealth.

According to Harare's *Sunday Mail*, he continued: 'Unfortunately, it back'fired because they, too, are dying of it, but still they have the knowledge of its origins and how it can be cured, but they just do not want to share the knowledge.'

Some whites in Zimbabwe might have been rather hurt by these suggestions, but Nkomo was obviously upset – fortunately, there is no Race Relations Board out there to persecute him – and at least he made no attempt to patronise the whites. If I were a member of some ethnic minority in this country, I think that what would make me angriest would be attempts by well-meaning people to patronise me.

People must decide for themselves whether the treatment of Helen Bannerman's book comes under this heading, but there can be little doubt, I fear, about the activities of the Institute of Employment Studies. Ethnic minority students resident in

166

Britain make up 12 per cent of university students, against six per cent of the general population. It is the white population we should all be studying.

Lest we forget

SOME derision was expressed at the English Heritage proposal for listing Sheffield's infamous Park Hill council estate, but it was proposed only to give the building Grade II status.

This means that this ghastly pile of rotting concrete will be protected from demolition or 'unsympathetic' development. It does not mean that people will be forced to refurbish its empty flats or occupy its disused shops, heavily shuttered against vandals.

This sensible recommendation would ensure that this building, already 40-years-old, is allowed to stand rotting away quietly for another 40, inhabited in parts by ever poorer, ever less house-trained generations yet unborn.

More useful even than that, it will serve as a monument to the foolishness and vanity of the English intelligentsia through much of this century. Perhaps pretty Mr Blair will change its name to Beveridge Towers.

Saturday, September 7, 1996

The right stuff

WAS it the world's worst party, guests asked themselves as they were ushered out of *Punch* magazine's relaunch celebration at Harrods on the dot of nine o'clock on Tuesday night?

The heat was intense, the drink in short supply, there were far too many people and too many of them were ugly, and unknown to anyone but themselves. But humorists are often ugly and nearly always unknown.

I was encouraged to learn that 90 per cent of the staff of the new magazine are smokers. Here we have a collection of proper journalists, I decided, unlike the goofy young substitutes who now make the newspapers so boring. I am sure they will produce a good magazine, and look forward to reading it when they get round to printing it in black ink instead of the present penumbral half-tone.

A little bit of old England survives under the benevolence of Mohamed Fayed, the proprietor. Everywhere else, people are working away to undermine it. This week the British Medical Association started a new campaign to persuade all British airlines to ban smoking.

So long as a few airlines stand out against this move, smokers can make a point of avoiding the bossy ones. But if ever these wretched doctors manage to persuade them all to adopt the nanny attitude, many Britons will decide not to travel at all by air, leaving large parts of the world the poorer for their absence.

Perhaps Mr Fayed would like to start a new British airline. By then, the demand will be so great that he will not even need to give a party to launch it.

Monday, September 9, 1996

Discussion time

AS I FEARED, Liam Gallagher, lead singer of Oasis and hero of our national yob culture, is failing to delight audiences in America on this visit, despite spitting on stage and grabbing the crotch of his trousers as he shouted insults at them in New York. By general agreement, the standard of our rebellious behaviour has declined since the days of The Sex Pistols and The Who. The Americans now do it better, but I fear we are stuck with this particular act for the foreseeable future.

Last week I was invited to join a panel on *Thursday Late Night Live* for Carlton/LWT to discuss a curious decision by BBC World Service to encourage British regional accents in foreign broadcasts. The decision interested me because it seemed a small milestone in the disintegration of our national culture. Some regional accents are proud and beautiful things, especially among Yorkshire women and West Country farmers, but they are essentially designed for communication within the region. Others, like the south London whine, reflect nothing but an awareness of social failure and rejection. The yob culture promotes these noises as an aggressive statement that there is nothing to be gained from education.

But a mixed audience requires a standard, correct pronunciation. I was hoping to argue that the essential difference between the snob culture we once had and the yob culture that threatens to overtake it is that in the snob culture, based on a class system, people tried to advance themselves and their families by improving themselves: the snob culture was preferable because, in encouraging us all to try to improve ourselves and our families, it also encouraged us to be honest, well-mannered and disciplined, and firm with our children and their teachers.

That, at any rate, is a summary of what I hoped to say. Unfortunately they decided to let in the public and the debate dissolved in uproar as we shouted glib, one-line insults at each other and at anyone trying to speak. It was good fun, for the most part, and well reflected the general standard of national debate.

Written in water

WHILE we are discussing the general standard of national debate, I feel we should challenge any assumption that the Church's disgusting advertisement, 'Bad Hair Day', was addressed exclusively to the country's half-witted, ineducable young. I feel it was addressed to the general standard of intelligence, education and intellectual curiosity to be expected of our tabloid-reading adults.

Whether or not it will work is another matter. The Church of England is understandably desperate to fill its churches. When I last discussed this matter, I helpfully suggested that the new female 'priestesses' should preach their sermons unclothed. It would be less useful to encourage male clergymen to perform in the nude, because women, for reasons which I cannot even begin to imagine, do not always delight in male nudity, whereas males are nearly always interested to see a female without any clothes on.

They must have misunderstood me in the north of England. The Bishop of Durham's decision to pay £200,000 (with help from the National Lottery) for a video in Durham Cathedral showing a naked male American emerging from water and then jumping back in again seems to grasp the wrong end of every stick, although I suppose it might encourage a few of the male homosexuals whom Archbishop Runcie wishes to avoid.

Perhaps the best way to fill the churches would be to turn them into swimming baths. An unclothed priestess could jump in and out at one end, as a metaphor of the human condition, while the rest of the pool could be occupied by members of the congregation, also unclothed, paddling around or swimming in circles. This seems as good a way as any to get the Message across.

All the rage

SINCE Roger Moore, the 68-year-old James Bond actor, revealed that he had been approached by a pederast on Wimbledon Common 60 years ago, other people's memories have come flooding back. Now a tribunal has been set up in North Wales under Sir Ronald Waterhouse, a 70-year-old former High Court judge, to examine allegations of child abuse going back 20 years.

In South Wales, police have set up a hotline, inviting anybody who thinks he may have been abused in a Cardiff children's home in the past 11 years to telephone and tell them all about it. 'They may well still be suffering from trauma,' says Chief Supt Phil Jones, head of South Wales CID, 'but we would like them to stand up and be counted.'

The *Sun*, on Saturday, called for all those men who had dirty thoughts about children to be castrated or jailed for life. More specifically, Paul Foot, the distinguished journalist, writing in the *Guardian*, recalled how he had been abused by the late Anthony Chenevix-Trench, the distinguished headmaster, at Shrewsbury some 45 years ago.

Chenevix-Trench escaped justice by dying in 1979. I wonder if it would please *Sun* readers for the body of this former headmaster of Eton to be exhumed and ritually humiliated in some pantomime of castration, possibly by the Home Secretary. Whether it pleased them or not, it might discourage them from following his example, and that is the important thing.

Wednesday, September 11, 1996

A position on gherkins

OPINIONS are bound to be divided on the subject of Sir Norman Foster's £550 million, 1,200ft tower, designed for the site of the Baltic Exchange blown up by the IRA in 1992. The building, which would be the tallest in Europe, was described by the *Guardian*, in terms of warm approval, as an 'erotic gherkin'.

Perhaps a 1,200ft erotic gherkin is just what Londoners need.

They certainly don't need the office space, since there is already a surplus of 8 million square feet of that in London. Against those who argue that it will provide a tempting target for the IRA, one can make the point that at least it will keep the bombers occupied, away from older, more handsome buildings in other parts of London.

It may be true that enormously tall buildings never look very well in our rainy climate. Some say that diseases lurk in them, that people develop melancholia and go mad, but that is a problem which affects only those who live and work there, and we have no reason to suppose that anyone ever will in this one.

It may seem mean to grudge London's gherkin fanciers their little treat. Few of us have any reason to visit the City of London and those who go there are interested only in money. I have never even visited Canary Wharf, which is only 800ft high and houses, with other newspapers, *The Daily Telegraph*. Canary Wharf does not resemble any sort of vegetable, although I have heard rumours that it has been taken over by swarms of power-crazed accountants.

There must be a case for having huge buildings, well off the beaten track, to keep these people together and out of harm's way.

Saturday, September 14, 1996

A new language

CAN it really be true that Ireland proposes to drop the shamrock as its national symbol? How will the Irish ever manage to explain the doctrine of the Trinity to each other without this ingenious device thought up by the wily St Patrick (a Welshman, born in Boulogne) in the 5th century?

According to the Irish tourist board, which is spending £30 million to promote a new image of Ireland, the shamrock 'has no place in the concept of a modern, prosperous country playing a pivotal role in Europe'. Noel Toolan, the board's international marketing director, describes some research undertaken among people who do not holiday in Ireland: 'Frankly, they did not really recognise the shamrock. But even if we get recognition, is it the right thing to build an image on?' He proposes instead to 'major on people interaction'.

What on earth does this mean, to major on people interaction, and why should it cost £30 million? Marketing experts are the new high priests of our demoralised, uneducated classless, unintelligent society, to whom we all listen respectfully as they talk their rubbish in a language nobody understands. In a properly established social system, these people would be trying to sell pieces of raw pig's liver to American tourists as being a miraculously preserved heart of St Kevin.

Occasionally I receive letters from *Telegraph* readers complaining that their beloved newspaper is becoming a bit pivotal in places. Now I know how I should reply to them, if ever the marketing directors can spare me some writing paper, envelopes, secretarial assistance and postage stamps. I shall say that we are majoring on people interaction.

Saturday, September 21, 1996

Our role in Europe

THE SIX Tory elder statesmen who told nice Mr Major he was leading the country to disaster if he failed to embrace the single European currency might have put their case more strongly. Generations of Britons yet unborn will curse the name of Major and that of the Conservative Party if they manage to exclude us from the European Union by their nervous dithering, and leave us out in the cold.

I now feel the new currency should be called the Euromark, in deference to the admirable country which will carry the main burden of supporting it and controlling the spendthrift habits of other members. If Germany supervises the economy, I feel that the French will teach us all how to enjoy life and the Italians might give us some useful tips on singing, perhaps.

Britain should supply the military protection. Fighting is the thing we are best at nowadays. On the other hand, my colleague Christopher Booker is right when he urges us to keep a close watch on our fellow Europeans. The French decision to produce champagne corks that make a whimpering plop when the bottle is opened is a case in point. They claim that the present cork is daunting to women, frightens the old and threatens the safety of children. Two-thirds of champagne buyers in France prefer an easy, safe method of removing the cork, they say.

172

I have always loved France and the French, but this can only confirm what many of us have long suspected, that they are tremendous cowards, now reduced to a state of terror by their own champagne corks. In the New Britain, by contrast, Essex man does not drink much champagne. He prefers to squirt it around when celebrating a sports victory or a wedding. To him, the loud explosion and projectile cork are essential parts of the ritual.

Perhaps the French will be less nervous when they and the rest of the European Union are protected by the might of the British Army. They will come to realise that these explosions do not signify another invasion, another occupation. We are all friends.

Monday, September 23, 1996

Saving the koala

NEWS that London is emerging as one of the richest places in Britain for wildlife – not just rabbits, hedgehogs and deer, but rare creatures such as water voles, dormice and marsh warblers – must have some social significance. In the old days, these animals were caught and eaten by the poor. Just show a water vole or a marsh warbler to your average, old-fashioned Cockney, and he would pop it straight into his mouth.

This may seem cruel, but at least it kept the numbers down. Nowadays we are constantly told that under nice Mr Major the poor are poorer than they have ever been, so I can attribute the present plague of water vole and marsh warblers only to the fad for vegetarianism.

Australia is facing a similar problem with koalas, whose numbers have increased up to ten times in some places, threatening the survival of the very eucalyptus trees whose leaves are the only thing they eat.

One proposal, to cull 2,000 of them in South Australia, created an outcry from animal lovers. Now the State of Victoria proposes to vasectomise as many as possible of the males, but I am doubtful about this. Roger Martin, a research fellow at Monash University in Victoria, points out that vasectomy won't work because 'koalas are highly promiscuous animals. You only have to miss one and he will fertilise all the females right through the summer'.

Strangely enough, it never seems to have occurred to anyone to eat them. On my first visit to Adelaide about 12 years ago, my hostess asked if there were any Australian delicacy I fancied. I said I would like to try koala. They all fainted in horror.

Now they know that koalas are an ecologically responsible thing to eat, the Australians should produce them at official receptions for visiting grandees like the Prince of Wales. This might produce an incentive for those of us who really want to know what they taste like to work a little harder and try to get invited.

Wednesday, September 25, 1996

Maggie Garnett

'YOU must never underestimate the stupidity of the British public,' said Simon Burgess, a former Lloyd's underwriter who now sells insurance policies to British women against the danger of having a 'Virgin Birth by Act of God' in expectation of a Second Coming in the year 2000. The policy, which costs £100 a year, has already banked £30,000 in its first two weeks. A further 723 women have insured against impregnation by an alien.

It does indeed sometimes seem that we have become a very stupid nation. I often cite the fact that our traffic lights are no longer synchronised. The fare system on trains belongs to a higher form of lunacy. An InterCity West Coast supersaver day return, spotted in this newspaper last week, allows passengers from Aberystwyth a 474-mile day trip to Euston station and back for only £34, but it allows them to stay only 10 minutes in London.

All these developments can be explained, I would suggest, by the historic shift of wealth and power in favour of the working man and his family. We are now governed by our non-commissioned officers. They define the culture, run the administration and make all the decisions. Despite their many sterling qualities, they are not really up to the job. Almost every policy decision made in the past 10 years has been the wrong one, at any rate since Margaret Thatcher lost her marbles.

Now we can read in the *Diaries of George Urban*, the former director general of Radio Free Europe and foreign policy adviser to Mrs Thatcher, how his admiration for Mrs Thatcher gave way to something like dismay: 'I was amazed to hear her uttering views about people and countries, especially Germany, which were not all that different from the Alf Garnett version of history.'

Garnett is a popular figure in British mythology. Admiration for him usually divides among those who see him as a brilliant satirical expression of mindless prejudice, and those who see him as a witty, fearless commentator with sensible views on most subjects.

It would seem that Mrs Thatcher, after her triumphs against the unions and in the Falklands, became impervious to criticism. Surrounded by sycophants, she concentrated on pleasing the second category of Garnett fans, who are now in the ascendant. It will be a shame if they manage to convince the rest of Europe we are all like that. If we must be left out in the cold, I can think of better company.

Not the greatest evil

THE new temperance offensive gathers pace. As I thought they would, the campaigners are losing no opportunity to drag children into it. When Sir Leslie Turnberg, the Salford physician, launched a savage attack on Manchester United football club for having its own brand of whisky, he particularly blamed it for associating itself with products which did the opposite of promoting healthy habits among children.

'Everything you do is used as a heroic model for the young in particular. I do hope you will reconsider your position in putting your name to an alcoholic drink.'

Now we have a survey from the Schools Health Education Unit at Exeter University in which a quarter of boys between 10 and 11 told researchers that they had drunk some alcohol in the week of the survey. John Balding, the unit's director, claims that a growing use of alcohol is among the most serious threats to young people's health.

It seems to me that if Mr Balding can believe alcoholism is among the most serious threats to the health of our 10-year-olds, he can believe anything. Most of us in this country worry about our young people. I was not particularly pleased to learn of the gang of six London teenagers, some of them thought to be as young as 14, who raped a 32-year-old Austrian mother of two and then threw her into Camden's Regent's Canal after she told them she could not swim.

My apologies to Mr Balding, but I am not so worried about 10-

year-olds who enjoy an occasional tipple at home. In fact, I wish them well.

Saturday, September 28, 1996

Behaviour problems

THE British Psychological Society may have scored a cheap point when it said that naughty children should not be diagnosed as suffering from attention deficit hyperactivity disorder. Very few children suffer from this disorder, whereas many have behaviour problems.

But we should not suppose that this entitles us to describe children suffering from behaviour problems as 'naughty'. In our sex-obsessed society, the only connotation attaching to the word 'naughty' is sexual. Even the expression 'naughty but nice', referring to chocolates, has strong sexual undertones, according to Dr Joan Smith, the acknowledged expert on these matters.

If you apply the word 'naughty' to children, you will set bells ringing which may bring a wild-eyed Esther Rantzen to your door. If you respond to a child's 'naughtiness' by smacking it, you will be lucky to avoid being shot out of hand by a special police helicopter squad.

Children's main purpose nowadays is to create jobs for education experts and the health and welfare officers supervising their homes, but as the word 'child' carries more and more a sexual connotation, the job may be handed over to the Vice Squad.

The more that children are seen as actual or potential sex

hazards, the more sense it makes to punish a six-year-old boy for sexual harassment if he kisses the cheek of a girl classmate, as happened in North Carolina last week. Let us hope Mr Howard keeps a jump ahead, and legislates against six-year-olds stalking each other on the way home from school.

There are many who feel these six-year-old boys should be castrated before they can get up to any worse harm, but perhaps Howard feels that a county court injunction should do the trick. I don't know. What do you think?

Beyond sex

LAST Sunday I bought a copy of the *News of the World* for the first time in ages, hoping to read the confessions of the bonking bishop – one is never too old to take Holy Orders – but all he said was that he had never done it.

Turning the pages, I was amazed by the repetitiveness of the 'news'. It was all about adultery. The erring husband is nearly always described in terms of deep loathing, as a 'rat'. Nobody is too humble nowadays to be denounced for sexual impropriety. Postmen and bus conductors must expect to be hunted down by Murdoch's hacks as much as MPs, clergymen and television stars.

Perhaps the tabloids think they are avenging the wronged wife, but not all wives can be made happier to see their marriages held up to public scrutiny in this way. When they run out of adultery stories, the tabloids now denounce similar postmen and bus conductors for cross-dressing out of hours or wearing women's underclothes under their uniforms. Where will it end, this obsession with sex, and what does it tell us about our society?

On Thursday the *Sun* had a major news story about a fireman and his wife in Pill, Gwent, who kept neighbours awake with the noise of their lovemaking. 'Fireman's Rumpy Pumpy makes All Feel Grumpy' was the inspired headline.

One can argue that nothing else is happening in Britain these days, but the reason so many people wish to read about sex, I fear, is that fewer and fewer people are getting on with it. While the *Sun* was describing rumpy pumpy in Pill, the quality newspapers were preoccupied with accounts of an alleged liaison between Harold Pinter and Joan Bakewell, 30 years ago. Soon any act of sexual intercourse, even between couples who have been married for 40 years, will be headline news.

177

Wednesday, October 9, 1996

Great vegetarian revival

SOME may be depressed to learn that there are now about four million people in this country claiming to be vegetarians, and that their numbers have increased by a million or so in the past year. Personally, I do not see that these vegetarians do the rest of us any harm.

Unlike the temperance movement and anti-smoking campaign, which include many of the bossiest people on earth, vegetarianism embraces some of the sweetest, kindest and best, who ask only to be left alone to eat their vegetables in peace.

The Vegetarian Society, which will celebrate its 150th birthday next year, believes the swing has been caused by the Government's muddle over mad cow disease. I doubt this being the reason. We now know that Creutzfeldt-Jakob disease, its human equivalent, is not caused by eating mad cows but more often than not by eating pituitary glands taken from corpses at post-mortems. This was thought to promote growth.

It is my experience that beef tastes rather better since the arrival of BSE. I wonder if it improves the meat. If so, I wonder if there might be a case for infecting cattle with it deliberately. This would make the French and Germans look very foolish.

The great vegetarian revival is more likely to be explained by the nauseating smell of hamburgers which make urban life so disagreeable nowadays. Every week we learn of new diseases caused by these terrible meat buns, but of course it is none of our business if people wish to take the risks and eat them. The terrible gases, which threaten the entire nation's mental and physical health are another matter. Even vegetarians must suffer this poisoning. There is no escape, but at least they try.

Saturday, October 12, 1996

Obfuscation

Readers will have observed how quickly John Major acted to scotch my rumour that Lady Thatcher will declare her support for James Goldsmith's Referendum Party before the next election. As the person who invented the rumour, I feel I should apologise for the scenes of kissing and cuddling which followed in Bournemouth.

In a world of rumours and hoaxes it is not easy for anyone to know what is really happening. What we are to make of the *Family Expenditure Survey 1995-1996*, from the Office for National Statistics, which claims the average family now receives £53 a week as cash in state welfare benefits? Who does the state get the money from, except from the average family? We must pay at least £150 a week, on average, to receive our average £53 a week; the difference being what it costs the state, in wages and expenses, to extort the money and supervise its redistribution. Does this make sense? Is it comprehensible?

On Wednesday I went to see *Phantom of the Opera* for the first time – 10 years after it opened. The production was magnificent, but I found I could scarcely understand a word of what was happening. The important thing is that the audience loved it, cheering their heads off and yelling for more. It was a joy to be among so many people enjoying themselves so much. Then we were all taken – about 1,000 of us, it seemed – and given oysters, foie gras and lobsters and champagne to celebrate the show's tenth birthday. It was a very happy gathering.

Brooding about it afterwards, I thought that anything which causes such happiness and generates such vast amounts of oysters, foie gras, lobster and champagne must be good. In the same way, the great welfare hoax, though impossible to understand, actually makes for a reasonably contented country, when compared with the poverty, crime, drug dependence, sexual depravity and disease that afflicts so much of the United States, for example.

Interpretation

Further assaults on our ability to understand anything are launched daily by the advertising industry. Thursday's newspaper featured a poster advertising the new Harvey Nichols store in Leeds. It showed the ugly double photograph of a bald model with a dog's collar attached to a lead round her neck, over the legend 'Harvey Nichols Leeds (Not Follows)'.

The women's committee of Leeds City Council is protesting on the grounds that the poster is an insult to women, tending to dehumanise them or showing them as passive, degraded victims. My objection, apart from the ugliness, is that I cannot understand the message. Why should that ugly picture and silly legend persuade anybody to shop at Harvey Nichols?

Why, in particular, did the model shave her head? I have often gallantly maintained that women do not really need hair, and we would love them just as much without it. On the other hand, like single motherhood, it might be seen as a condition requiring sympathy and support, rather than as one to encourage as an end in itself. Perhaps it is intended to reassure rather than mock such people as Princess Caroline of Monaco who have the misfortune to lose their hair. I do not know, but I feel it is in questionable taste.

Doreen Lewis, deputy 'chair' of the women's committee, said: 'Showing women in dog leads gives the message that women are not even human and that they need to be kept under control.'

I am not sure. It might also be an attempt to attract dog-lovers. The dog-lovers' vote is something which politicians neglect at their peril, as Jeremy Thorpe discovered in North Devon in 1979, and as Mr Major will discover when he is thrown out at the election for not having abolished our cruel quarantine laws.

Women and dogs can both be delightful, but in entirely different ways. It is foolish to confuse the two. Why can't they just say: 'Please shop at Harvey Nichols. It is a very good shop.' That, I think, is what they are trying to say.

Please stop buzzing

TOURISTS represent a threat to our national survival. According to the British Tourist Authority, nearly 24 million visited Britain last year, an increase of 13 per cent. They are increasing at a similar rate this year. One does not have to be good at arithmetic to see that the time is fast approaching when they will outnumber us.

Obviously we cannot expect to be allowed to shoot them, which would be wrong, but we must think of ways to discourage them. According to the chief executive of the BTA, they come here because they find us stylish, contemporary and vibrant; they like our modern architecture and our popular music and particularly enjoy the 'creative buzz' which we give off. Can this be true? What sort of people are attracted to these things? Personally, I always avoid any compatriot who gives off a buzz. Tourists must be putting themselves at unnecessary risk by seeking them out. Our overtaxed police force can scarcely be expected to protect an extra 24 million tourists from rape or murder, while still preventing us from frightening bats or collecting birds' eggs.

We English must simply learn to stop buzzing. The Scots may have something up their sleeves with this strange proposal to reintroduce wolves into the Highlands. Nobody else can think why they should wish to do anything so foolish, but I may have a pretty shrewd idea.

All-American potato man

GEORGE PATAKI, the Republican governor of New York, sets us a puzzle when he insists that the new doctrine on the Irish Potato Famine of 1845-1849 (as an example of British genocide) should be taught in all New York schools.

'The great Irish hunger was not the result of a massive failure of the Irish potato crop but, rather, was the result of a deliberate campaign by the British to deny the Irish people the food they needed to survive.'

Never mind that this is rubbish. The famine was a result of potato crop failure and Britain voted an unprecedented £10 million – almost the exact equivalent of £1 billion today – to help the Irish in their plight. Between one and two million used the money for assisted emigration to the United States.

Quite a few of the Irish Americans in New York and Boston are descended from these migrants. I can well understand that they should feel bitter against the British to find themselves in a country of lethal hamburger gases and filthy food when they could be breathing the pure sweet air of Ireland, eating her delicious pigs' trotters and potatoes.

As I say, we can understand the bitterness of Irish Americans, but what of George Pataki? His name suggests Greek descent, and the Greeks have no particular reason to hate us. Perhaps his sensitivity to the potato problem derives from his surname. The Greek word for potato – patata – becomes pataki as an affectionate diminutive: 'my little potato'.

It may be this which has driven him to the strange conclusion that potato failure has nothing to do with the presence of so many Irish in New York.

Free speech

AN EXCITING seminar on smoking and health was held at the Association of District Councils in Chapter Street, Westminster, on Tuesday, to which anti-smoking experts and agitators came from all over the country. At a given moment the chairman, Mr Tony Close, of the Health Education Authority, read a prepared statement:

'The seminar organisers were happy to agree to Mr Clive

Turner of the Tobacco Manufacturers' Association speaking at the seminar today on advertising and tax issues from an industry perspective . . . In the event, Mr Turner's participation was not acceptable to some of the other speakers so Mr Turner has agreed to withdraw from the seminar. We apologise to Mr Turner for the inconvenience and embarrassment he has been caused.' So the anti-smoking experts and agitators proceeded to hold their cosy little get-together at the taxpayers' expense.

I often wonder why it is that anti-smokers include not only the most unreasonable people in the country, but also the most odious.

Can it be that tobacco, in addition to its proven benefits in helping resistance to colds, Alzheimer's, obesity, nervous tension and other diseases, also makes its adherents nicer people? That the anti-smokers threaten us with a population which is not only demented in its senility, obese, becolded and twitching with nerves, but also extremely unpleasant? I feel it is time to hold a seminar on the question, being careful to ask the other side to put its point of view.

Wednesday, October 23, 1996

Three widows

IT WAS with a sinking heart that I saw John Major's name on all the headlines when I returned home from a visit to Spain over the weekend. Should his advisers not tell him that he has delighted us enough for the moment? If he is to give us the benefit of his opinions on every issue of the day there is a danger he will lose all the goodwill he earned at Bournemouth with his devastatingly witty jokes about young Mr Blair's education.

'Major Backs Widow's Crusade' shouted one of the tabloids. This might have referred to the campaign being waged by the widow Diane Blood who wishes to be impregnated with sperm taken from her unconscious husband before he died.

Equally it might have referred to Freda Adrian, the 74-year-old widow of a former prisoner of war in the Far East who has had her pension taken away after 50 years because he smoked. But I somehow don't see nice Mr Major taking sides on such a controversial point as this one, do you?

In fact it referred to Frances Lawrence, who is the widow of the murdered London headmaster, Philip Lawrence, and whose dignified appeal to the nation to pull itself together, look after its children better and generally behave itself touched the heart of every decent person in the country. By far the least interesting aspect of Mrs Lawrence's plea is that Mr Major supports it.

The danger in having an uneducated Prime Minister is that whenever he produces a fatuous or ignorant opinion, other people take him seriously. That is why we are going to lose the Stone of Scone. After 700 years in Westminster Abbey, as an awe-inspiring part of our national history, it is to be sent next month as a permanent museum exhibit to Edinburgh, where it has never been and where it has no business to be.

This may please a few Scots nationalists, but it can only be seen as a gross insult to the English, who have had the stone longer than the Scots. Mr Major is a nice man, and that is a rare phenomenon in politics. He might be preserved in some museum or cathedral for the general edification. But the time has come to leave him alone.

Saturday, October 26, 1996

What about self-abuse?

THE PLAN for a national register of suspected paedophiles strikes me as particularly barmy. Once again, these campaigners shelter under the moral umbrella of Dunblane.

The point about Thomas Hamilton is not that he was a suspected pederast but that he was something totally different and much rarer, a homicidal lunatic.

A suspected paedophile is someone who has been so designated on the basis of rumour, gossip or intuition. He has no defence because he is neither charged nor consulted.

When we have to listen to the NSPCC's solemn assurance that a million children are abused every year, that 'up to' 100,000 of these are sexually abused, and that child abuse costs the nation £1 billion a year, it is obvious that we have moved into a realm of what might politely be called fantasy. There are other unkinder words to describe the reliance on controversial statistics in advancing a special cause. None of them encourages confidence in the idea of a paedophiles' register.

If paedophile tendencies are thought to lead to infanticide in

the same way that marijuana is thought to lead to heroin, we may wonder what it is that leads to paedophilia and other sexual abnormalities in the first place. Has Mr Howard consulted the Catholic bishops on this issue, as they move into a position of authority in national politics?

When I was a boy, many vices were thought to stem from masturbation. A National Register of Suspected Masturbators might provide the vital clue which would prevent employers from taking on a potential paedophile, mass-murderer etc.

Information for this register would be provided by a hotline on which anyone could telephone their suspicions. Another useful source might be Catholic priests, who have to listen to this sort of filth all day in the confessional.

The teenage menace

THE ONLY sensible part of Michael Howard's £3 billion Crime (Sentencing) Bill, published on Saturday, is in the promise of three-year minimum sentences for domestic burglars on a third conviction. However, this 'tough' measure is subject to judicial discretion and applies only to offenders of 18 or over. Many, if not most burglars of the new wave, are in their middle teens. We read of streets in Manchester where gangs of marauding teenagers have reduced property values by 80 per cent, from £26,000 to £5,000, in 10 years.

Police can do little to protect the terrified inhabitants, because younger teenagers are sacrosanct. Despite Howard's many fatuous and ill-thought out initiatives in the fields of crime and punishment, his inability to do anything about the teenage menace will remain his most conspicuous failure.

These teenage offenders may not be named, they may not be charged with any but the most serious offences which might carry a 10-year sentence for an adult. Howard has increased the powers of the police to stop and search any of us at will, but why should they bother to stop and search a teenager? If the person they stop is bristling with combat knives, all they can do is hand the weapons back, because Howard says there is no legal way of distinguishing between a dagger and a table knife. But even if combat knives were made illegal, those under 18 would not be charged, because the offence would not be serious enough.

No doubt many if not most of these teenagers will end up eventually with life sentences under Howard's proposals, but not until they reach 18 and are set in their habits. This is the most expensive, as well as the cruellest way of dealing with the problem. A much better plan would be to sentence them on first conviction to four years in a public school. This would be cheaper than keeping them in prison or in an approved school, where they have to be waited on by psychologists and behavioural experts and are sent for extended holidays on the sun-kissed shores of the South Pacific.

A few years at public school would soon sort them out. Look at the late Matthew Harding, who managed to keep out of prison for over 20 years while he made £140 million as a reinsurance broker at Lloyd's at a time when half the underwriters were going broke. If he hadn't crashed in his helicopter on the way back from a football match, he would almost certainly be living free and out of prison today. That is what a public school education does for you.

More interesting

BRITISH Eurosceptics will probably feel encouraged by the recent polls in Germany which show that only 16 per cent of the Germans see any advantage in being a member of the EU, while 80 per cent believe that a single European currency would not be as stable as the mark.

They are absolutely right, of course, but by the same token the advantage to Britain is greater: the single European currency will be more stable than the pound, controlled as it is by the unscrupulous and incompetent spendthrifts who swarm over Westminster and Whitehall.

We should be grateful to the German government for paying no attention to German public opinion. The trouble here is that the wrong sort of people are attracted to politics in our popular democracy. At least we can say we have a nice leader in Mr Major, but it was a sad moment last week when Downing Street telephoned GMT to say the Prime Minister would be very happy to appear on television next morning and explain his Government's new policies, as outlined in the Queen's Speech. A spokesman had to explain that they were putting on a Tom and Jerry show at the time, and they were very sorry but viewers preferred the cartoon.

I have never said that Tom and Jerry would be any better at running the country, but I do think that everyone would be happier if nice Mr Major stopped trying to appear on television and explain how he is doing it. He should stay at home and watch the Tom and Jerry show like everyone else.

Time to telephone

THE House of Commons acted decisively against one of its members – Tessa Jowell, the Labour MP for Dulwich – who forgot to turn off her mobile phone during a debate on Friday. Hatred of mobile telephones seems a new rallying point for people in this country who resent the way things are going.

Perhaps I am the only person in the country who enjoys

listening to other people on their mobile phones, especially in the train, where their banal statements and self-important tones ring out over their cringing fellow passengers. It provides an insight into other people's lives and activities which would not be attainable in other ways without endless effort, and at much greater risk of boredom.

By contrast, speeches in the House of Commons, to which I had to listen for five years as a political correspondent, never afforded the slightest enjoyment. Although as banal and self-important as anything one is likely to hear in a train, they offer none of the pleasures of eavesdropping.

Voters might take a greater interest in Parliament if MPs made no speeches and asked no questions, but sat on their benches talking loudly into their mobile phones about what time they hoped to be home for dinner.

Wednesday, October 30, 1996

De-Gummerisation

JOHN GUMMER's assurance that he will contain the spread of suburbia and protect what is left of the English countryside from residential development would be more impressive if the development was not proceeding at a furious pace all around us. It would also be more impressive if he did not publicly accept the ludicrous figure produced by the Central Statistical Office for 4.4 million new homes 'needed' in the next 20 years.

Of course there would be a demand for any number of new homes if they were available at the right price. To say there is a need for them is rather like saying Moss Side needs caviar. Mr Gummer blames the demand for new homes on marriage break-up and adultery, but I don't think adultery has much to do with it.

The real reason why so many marriages break up – half of them do nowadays – is that Britons have become so disagreeable that they can no longer live together. They are not taught about good manners, and many have no idea what they are. Another reason may be that practically nobody smokes. This makes for bad temper and aggression, and almost certainly explains road rage as well. We all hate each other too much.

A final reason why even young and unmarried people have no wish to live together is that there is practically no sex. Any act of

188

sexual intercourse is automatically headline news. Where women no longer do the housework and both partners are earning, there is very little point in living together unless they wish to discuss whales and rain forests. How many people do?

When Mr Gummer blames adultery for the ruination of the countryside he forgets that divorce and adultery are two separate things. Before we start hearing about life sentences for persistent adulterers as a means of protecting the countryside, let them all reflect that the way to stop people building houses in what is left of rural England is to pass a law against it. Then Britons will have to make an effort to get on with each other again, instead of living alone in a selfish stew of resentment against everybody else. If this leads to more smoking and more sex, that is the price Gummer must be prepared to pay.

How to vote

ACCORDING to new evidence a recent opinion poll asking, among other things, how people voted in the last election came up with the result that Neil Kinnock won in 1992 by a margin of up to 10 per cent. People who take these things seriously are worried by the tendency of respondents to tell lies.

It does not seem to have occurred to anyone that they may have forgotten. The truth of the matter is that not many people attach much importance to voting, and few are interested in politics, or see much difference in the parties.

Only in this context can we understand the general excitement that one in 100 people is thinking of voting for Sir James Goldsmith's Referendum Party.

Someone who attended the party's conference in Brighton recently wrote of '5,000 serious minded people . . . listening to an impressive range of eloquent, fact-packed speeches.'

The trouble with this idea of a referendum on the European Union, as I sometimes point out, is that we have already had one. The only thing that those 5,000 delegates got out of it was an opportunity to look serious-minded.

One good reason for voting Goldsmith is that he seems the only party leader with any sexual prowess, unless you count 'Paddy' Ashdown's one moment of glory. A magazine called *Scallywag* made valiant attempts to fix nice Mr Major up with a girlfriend, but it did not really work.

Perhaps poor Bob Dole's chances will pick up in time for

Monday's presidential election now they have discovered he had an affair 28 years ago, but I am afraid they have left it too late. If I ever vote for anyone, it will be for Vladimir Zhirinovsky as leader of the British Liberal Democrats.

Saturday, November 2, 1996

Worth a riot?

DENIS HEALEY's solemn warning in the House of Lords that imposition of European Monetary Union will result in rioting in the streets should be seen in context. Healey, in fact, was the last Chancellor who actually had to preside over a genuine curb on public spending – imposed by the International Monetary Fund in 1975. There was no rioting in the streets then – in fact nobody seemed to notice apart from the public employees who are always baying for more money.

The last rioting we saw – apart from occasional outbreaks from animal lovers – was over Mrs Thatcher's poll tax. That was because people actually had to pay it, whereas the connection between EMU and some small increase in unemployment is remote and contentious.

The only item on the political agenda which is likely to produce prolonged and bitter rioting, in my view, is the suggestion for a minimum wage. This will instantly throw many millions of casual or part-time workers out of their jobs, just at a time when we are beginning to discover that casual or part-time work is best suited to our national temperament.

This policy is earnestly advanced by Bishop O'Bubblegum and his cronies as the best way ahead. It may work in Europe, but I cannot believe it will work here. Many will decide we have heard enough from the Euro-sceptics and should give a hearing to the Anglo-sceptics in our midst – those who simply don't believe it when politicians tell us that our currency is the healthiest in Europe, because we can see it buys nothing abroad; or that our economy is booming, when we receive virtually no interest on our savings; or that the withdrawal of services has anything to do with the government cuts, when there have been no government cuts.

Then we will see that the only real issue in domestic politics is to decide which set of politicians will preside over the dissipation

190

of our earnings and savings by these spendthrift public employees. It is not worth rioting about.

Such a very pleasant man

WEDNESDAY of this week marked the first meeting of a new secret society, composed for the most part of influential journalists and broadcasters. Called the Penal League for Howard Reform, it will continue to meet, as it met on Wednesday, in the private room of a Soho restaurant, for members to compare notes and make plans for the future.

It is committed to ensuring that no opportunity is lost for making jokes in public about the Home Secretary, Mr Michael Howard. Some will complain that this is not fair, that it will foster feelings of persecution in the Home Secretary which might be dangerous.

Others will argue that Howard is not a fit subject for jokes, as he spends another £3 billion of our money and proceeds towards his ultimate goal of a National Register of Suspected Masturbators, with life sentences for persistent adulterers.

Some seem to feel that Howard is the devil incarnate. Recently, when my godfather Lord Longford was addressing the

F. E. Smith Society in the House of Commons, Howard came up and introduced himself, in the pleasant manner he has, despite a long history of violent criticism from the aged Labour statesman. Longford, instead of offering his hand, made an elaborate sign of the Cross.

Despite an unbroken record of deferring to the police, giving them helicopters and submachine guns, more money and more powers every time they ask, his name was jeered and booed by Metropolitan police officers on Wednesday. But I am sure the best and kindest way to treat the Howard phenomenon is to see him as a joke. That is how we won the war, and built the bridge over the River Kwai. My terror is that he will find out about our secret meetings and somehow infiltrate one of them, possibly jumping out of a huge steak and kidney pie to shake us all by the hand.

Monday, November 4, 1996

Police priorities

IT WOULD be hard to imagine anything less conducive to affection for the police than the Appeal Court decision to allow four police officers to claim damages for post-traumatic stress after being present at the Hillsborough disaster in 1989. But I think that Mr Howard's new Police Bill, published on Saturday, may do even more damage, in the long run.

As well as making it legal for the police to break into private homes and plant bugs inside, it sets out to establish a national crime squad to deal with organised crime, both nationally and internationally. Presumably 'organised crime' embraces terrorism and drugs, to which gigantic resources are already committed – as well as 'paedophile rings' and international sex tourism. None of these things looms large in the life of the average citizen.

On the day before we were allowed to see the new Police Bill, we learned that the Chief Inspector of Constabulary had told police to work harder to solve domestic burglaries. Only 24 per cent of reported burglaries are now solved.

Every householder through the length and breadth of the country lives in fear of burglary. In my area of the West Country, where churches used to be left open and unattended all day, they now have to be locked for the first time in history. This, of course, is only a symbol of our national disintegration. The reality of it can be seen in housing estates – again all over the country – which are perpetually terrorised by teenage gangs dedicated to burglary, vandalism, violence and threatening behaviour.

The new national crime force will take up the time of 1,400 police officers and cost £90 million a year – this works out at £64,285.70p per officer – to tackle the organised crime about which the police talk so much. But few of us could give a toss for organised crime. It is the disorganised variety that is destroying our quality of life, not the drug smugglers, the terrorists, the sex tourists or the paedophile 'rings'.

Disorganised crime does not seem to interest them any more. At the end of the trial of two teenagers sentenced for murdering another teenager by kicking him to death in Stratford-upon-Avon, we learned how the mother of the victim had written time and again to the police asking for protection, only to be told they could do nothing without hard evidence. When the hard evidence arrived, it was in the form of her dead son.

Baldies unite and fight

MUCH has been made of the revelation of Jon Snow that when, at the age of eight, he discovered his mother was bald and wore a wig, he suffered from a sort of post-traumatic stress syndrome which turned him into the horrible person he has become.

The revelation is made in a fascinating new book, *Sons and Mothers*, edited by Victoria and Matthew Glendinning (Virago Press £16.99). Snow blames his mother for his inability to form close relationships, and reveals that when she had to be put into a home, he was 'ruthless in his refusal to make sacrifices for her'.

His brothers have complained that this is no way to write about a mother, but nobody has queried the suggestion that parental baldness can have this effect on a sensitive child. Is there no organisation of baldies prepared to put him to rights?

It is one thing to insult your mother in public – Mrs Snow, a bishop's widow, is still alive at 85, although in no position to answer back – but quite another to insult a group of fellow citizens who include many of the hardest-working and most respectable people in the country.

When pretty young Mr Blair comes to power, I hope he will make baldism a punishable offence, along with racism, ageism, heterosexism and all the other-isms which indicate persecution of

a harmless minority. Snow obviously has an obsession about hair. He says his only really happy memories of his mother were after he had had his hair washed, and claims that his great pleasure now is to have his daughters run their fingers through his hair.

The sentence of this court is that Jonathan George Snow be taken to a place where hair is cut and have all his hair shaved off, and that he shall not be permitted to let it grow again for so long as he may live.

Wednesday, November 6, 1996

The unanswered questions

STANDARDS are slipping in West Sussex where the market town of Horsham has decided to honour the poet Shelley, born nearby in 1792. He was the son of the local Tory MP but disgraced his family and the whole neighbourhood by becoming a libertine, a socialist – and worst of all, a poet! Many writers are disagreeable enough, but poets, as anyone who has had dealings with them will know, are an abomination.

For more than 200 years the people of Horsham have hidden their shame. This week they are distributing 2,500 gingerbread men in their primary schools and unveiling a huge monument which involves a fountain and fibre-glass sphere in constant motion. What has this to do with Shelley? What have the children of Horsham done to deserve so much gingerbread? Why has the grocer Sainsbury decided to pay for it all?

It would make more sense to explain that the gingerbread is designed to comfort the poor children for the horrible years ahead of them while the monument will serve as a salutary warning not to take their armbands off when swimming.

Shelley, of course, drowned in the sea. That is probably all he has to teach them. But this is not really the time to put up monuments, least of all to a poet who left some perfectly good verse for us to remember him by.

Saturday, November 9, 1996

The Howard agenda

AN American medicine, nicknamed the Fountain of Youth, is reported to have many beneficial effects: it reverses the ageing process and restores sexual vigour while preventing cancer and heart disease – or so its adherents claim. This would make it considerably better even than the traditional British aspirin, which has no effect on the ageing process or sexual vigour.

Until recently the new medicine, which is widely used in America, was freely available in Harrods at a price of about 50p a day for men, 33p a day for women. Now the Government has declared it is an unlicensed medicine, which means that it can be acquired only on prescription from a private doctor.

Many of us in this country may decide that this American medicine is just what we need. Why the restriction? Many political analysts will say it is another of the tough measures which the Home Secretary is not frightened of taking. If he can crack down on the sexual vigour of older citizens, the Home Office may be able to show a reduction in sex crimes in its next set of bogus statistics. No doubt Michael Howard put his colleague Mr Dorrell up to it.

One can't help wondering about Mr Howard's real agenda. An international survey by Professor David Warburton, head of

195

psychopharmacology at Reading University, reveals that Britons, while fairly high on the list of those who enjoy life, are also high on the list of those who suffer from guilt as a result of their enjoyment.

The Germans, by contrast, have fewer pleasures than anyone else in Europe, and feel guiltiest of all about them. If I understand Howard correctly, his purpose is to make us more and more like the Germans. The guiltier we feel, the easier it is to send us to prison for enormous lengths of time, the more malleable we are, the easier for politicians to boss us around. And just see how much money the Germans are making! If only we can learn a little of their guilt.

Significance of hair

AS political debate in this country centres on the problem of Tony Blair's baldness – which he admitted only after allegations in the *Financial Times* that he was changing his hairstyle to attract women voters – we might take a look at the other side of the Atlantic to see how the Clintons face this problem.

Neither the President nor Mrs Clinton shows any sign of losing hair – both presumably take advantage of this wonderful medicine (see above) so freely available in the United States. Their delightful daughter, Chelsea, seems, in some of her pictures, to have enough hair for three or four English teenagers.

But there is something odd about Chelsea's hair. One photograph which appeared on the front page of Thursday's newspaper, shows the Presidential Trio waving regally from the Presidential Plane at Little Rock, Arkansas, before flying to Washington to resume their Presidency. In it, Chelsea appears to have very little hair.

If she is indeed suffering from premature baldness, like Tony Blair, this may have a profound effect on world politics. No doubt she is considered too young to be given the American medicine which reverses the ageing process and promotes sexual vigour. Informed Arkansas opinion attributes her apparent hair loss to her father's habit of eating hamburgers at all hours of the day and night.

If Chelsea is going bald, it will soon be the smartest thing to be. Blair will be swept to power, as we always thought he would.

Tories will come to realise that rather than ban medicines which prevent people going bald, their best way to confront the

Blair threat would be to take away the vote from women.

I have seen no sign that it makes them any happier, and we must all agree it produces the most terrible political leaders. But it would be a proud day for those who are follicly challenged if Chelsea took off her wig and showed herself to Washington as she really is.

Wednesday, November 13, 1996

No meals

A NEW diversion of our no-meals generation is for its plainer young women to form gangs and attack any woman who is judged prettier than they are. Charlotte Reed suffered a 20-minute battering from a group of feisty young women who cut off her hair and stubbed a cigarette out in her face 'so that you won't pull boys'.

This happened in mid-Glamorgan. Violent female gangs are now a recognised feature of our exciting classless society, which is the envy of the world. When I was young and the middle classes were still in charge, plain young women tended to join feminist groups, read the *Guardian* and insult any unfortunate young man who came within range. It never occurred to them to assault anyone, least of all members of the sisterhood who happened to be prettier than they were.

197

A similar hatred prevails against anyone who might be more fortunate or more successful or (worst of all) more deserving in our prosperous proletarian culture. Recently a story appeared in this newspaper about a respectable working family in Stratford-upon-Avon whose presence so much annoyed other tenants in their council estate that they became prime targets for abuse and vandalism, bullying and taunts. These culminated, after many unsuccessful appeals to the police for action, in the battering to death of their 19-year-old son by a gang of teenagers.

A recurrent nightmare in these changing times is that perhaps there are elements in our brilliant, new classless police force which secretly rather agree with these sentiments – not, of course, with their unlawful expression, but with the general idea (promoted by the 'meritocrat' Andrew Neil), that such remnants of our liberal humane, educated bourgeois culture as survive need to have their noses rubbed in the new proletarian ascendancy.

A form of death wish?

ONE might have thought that urban sentimentality about foxes took a bit of a knock when a Croydon housewife went into the conservatory of her terrace house and found a fox starting to eat her five-month-old son in his pram. The lad was rushed to hospital with bites to his face, but the local pest officer made it plain that council policy was not to interfere with healthy foxes.

England has always been particularly plagued by foxes. They are cruel and vicious animals. The foxhunt, an English invention, may well have been inspired originally as a mark of hatred and defiance, as well as a sporting way of keeping the brutes down.

Those who live in towns, eat no meals and watch television all day may think they can afford to be sentimental about them, but foxes have already invaded the suburbs, where sentimental housewives feed them, and will soon be taking over inner city council estates, where they are attracted by the dustbins.

However, they are not by nature scavengers and will always prefer a live baby if they can find one. It looks as if they are beginning to learn. Foxes are also major transmitters of rabies, although not as important in this function as bats. Bats, as I never tire of pointing out, are the only animals which can carry the disease without developing the symptoms. Without bats, the disease would disappear, since death follows rapidly on the development of the symptoms.

Somebody told me that a so-called bat expert, and member of the booming bat conservation industry, is to be heard on the radio denying this simple fact. I am sorry to say it is not a matter of opinion, but established scientific truth, such as may be found in the *Encyclopaedia Britannica* and any textbook on rabies. Even as bats are protected by some of the toughest laws ever passed by a Conservative government, Labour threatens to make foxhunting illegal on government-owned land. What are we to make of the deliberate encouragement of foxes and bats in our society?

Saturday, November 16, 1996

Worth a try?

EVER since Lady Thatcher announced that the chief trouble with her party was that it continued to call itself 'conservative', we have all tended to look at the Conservatives with different eyes. Who are these people, and what do they think they are doing as they restrict our view of the magnificent Barry and Pugin architecture of Westminster?

At the time, we wondered whether this was a prelude to a further announcement by Lady Thatcher that she had decided to join Sir James Goldsmith's disappearing Referendum Party. This at least claims to believe in something – namely a referendum. But no, her conduct towards Mr Major in Bournemouth showed that she clearly intends to remain part of the Conservative Party, which proudly believes in whatever string of platitudes about family values or a free society come to hand.

We may find our way to learning who these people are when we reflect that only 31 out of 325 Conservative members voted against Mr Howard's contemptible Firearms (Amendment) Bill, which removes various rights from all British citizens in response to the Dunblane massacre. It is true that up to 50 Tories also abstained, but they included such as the well-known penologist Terry Dicks, who demands a total ban on the private ownership of handguns and other weapons as a suitable response to Hungerford and Dunblane.

For the rest, we can see the Conservatives as a collection of mindless vulgarians or ruthless opportunists as we choose. Many serious and intelligent people are beginning to ask themselves whether, if they broke the habit of a lifetime and voted Labour at the next election, they could trust pretty Mr Blair to govern the country properly and deliver some of his sensible proposals.

Of course they couldn't. They should not look at Mr Blair's pretty face, but at the hideous mangy old tail which is wagging it from behind. The Labour Party includes some of the most admirable people in Britain, but it also includes all the forces of envy, hatred and social failure, all the civil servants and other public employees who spend most of their time shrieking for more money to spend on their departments and on themselves.

The best we can hope for after a Labour victory is that the International Monetary Fund will take over the general management of the country in a matter of weeks, rather than months. This may be the closest we ever get to the platonic ideal of government by a Committee of Belgian Ticket Inspectors. But at least we will have removed the present collection of unpleasant, ambitious populists. It might be worth a try.

Great choice of careers

FOR several years now I have loyally attempted to ignore the Duchess of York, unostentatiously looking the other way whenever she came into the room, putting my hands in my pockets and whistling nonchalantly whenever people were talking about her.

Now that two pages of this newspaper have been taken up with Elizabeth Grice's sensitive exposition, we can no longer pretend that she does not exist.

It goes without saying that all loyal subjects of the Crown have been following her progress anxiously. Some will have been dismayed by her failure to shine in the various roles she has adopted to date – as a journalist on *Paris Match*, as a television personality, grande horizontale, author, film star.

Now we learn she may be employed at a wage of £620,000 a year as spokesman for a firm which advises young women about their diets.

At one time, people have pointed out, she did not believe in dieting:

'I do not diet. I do not have a problem. I'm just going to be me,' she said defiantly. This seems a sensible attitude for a young person. Some may be unhappy about the disjunctive use of 'me', preferring the more normal 'myself', but I think these people are wrong. Fowler sits on the fence rather.

In any case, hers is a healthier attitude than the normal insistence on slimming. The trouble is there does not seem to be so much money in it.

This leaves the problem of Fergie's future unresolved. No doubt she would like to be a bus driver, but I think it might be better if she tried bus conductress first.

Monday, November 25, 1996

Art and imagination

AFTER seeing a mysterious photograph which appeared on the top of this column on Saturday, I decided that my decision to retire to a health farm in Suffolk for a week had been a wise one. However, these are bad times for watching television.

It is all very well for people like Jack Straw to impose a curfew requiring children to be home by 10pm, but what he is really doing is making them watch more television. I wonder if Straw has watched any recently. It is dreadful. Some of the English people on it are even worse than the Americans.

Last week they were all tremendously worried about the dangers of carbon monoxide poisoning from faulty fires: any excuse to look solemn and talk in affected voices. Why do people watch this rubbish, let alone the endless, incomprehensible American cartoons?

The answer must lie in some form of addiction. Perhaps that is why the Editor of *The Daily Telegraph*, in his wisdom, decided to put a picture at the top of this column* for the first time in 55 years. People will mistake the column for a television set, and be inexorably drawn towards it. Peter Simple, who wrote this column for about 49 years, would be turning in his grave if he

*A myserious photograph appeared without explanation on the top of the **Way of the World** column on Saturday, November 23, 1996. The Editor, Mr Moore, denied all knowledge of it, and people decided it must have been the work of an unknown Planner or Design consultant. See also the entry of November 27, 1997, **Take it away**, on page 205.

had died, which, mercifully, he hasn't.

It was a kind thought to put in a picture, even if it can only show what the people in Canary Wharf think I may look like, as I have never been there. My illustrator, Mr Rushton (who has just been rushed to hospital), thinks it would be tactful to return the compliment and show a portrait of Mr Moore, the Editor of *The Daily Telegraph* (or what people who have never been to Canary Wharf think he may look like). This is the picture which Mr Rushton has sent from his hospital bed in Devonshire Place.

Wednesday, November 27, 1996

Keep them mixed

BROODING in my Turkish bath in Suffolk, I feel how lucky I am to be out of London at the present time while everybody is debating the vexed question of mixed sex wards in National Health Service hospitals. Feelings run very high it appears.

At a dinner party in London recently, Rosa Monckton, wife of Dominic Lawson, sprightly young editor of *The Sunday Telegraph*, nearly came to blows with a young Tory MP who insisted that mixed wards had already been abolished. Lawson, in his 'editor's notebook' on Sunday, characterises it as one of those occasions when 'the convention of polite middle class social discourse is in danger of being broken'.

I could have assured this cocky young MP that mixed wards still survive, having been a patient in one last week. My own experience was an almost entirely pleasant one, if costly to the nation, and my conclusion was that we have nothing to fear from mixed wards as such. Other aspects of dormitory existence, shared with a random collection of sickies, are to blame for the discomfort and embarrassments of hospital, not the gender difference.

The Lawsons will have none of this, and I am rather glad I was not at their dinner party. Lawson explains:

'My wife had only recently been admitted to St Mary's, Paddington, as an emergency casualty, to endure all the indignities of the mixed ward: disgusting night time noises; confused old men in a state of obscene semi-undress, some mistaking her cubicle for their lavatory; young male drug addicts screaming foul abuse at the nurses for refusing to give them their fix.'

I do assure the Lawsons that women patients can make equally disgusting night-time noises, prance semi-naked, relieve

themselves in inappropriate places – and young female drug addicts can be just as abusive. A wardful of men or women would be no different. Yesterday, my deeply loved illustrator, Mr Rushton, came out of hospital, a restored man. It will be interesting to hear about his experiences.

Take it away

OBSERVANT readers point out that the mysterious photograph, which first appeared at the top of this column last Saturday, continues to appear there. What can it mean?

The general opinion in Shrubland Hall Health Clinic, where I am staying at the moment, is that it is a portrait of someone called Martin Bryant, a 29-year-old Tasmanian who shocked many of his compatriots recently by murdering 35 of them. I hope I am not alone in questioning the wisdom of having the portrait of a mass murderer exalted in this way three times a week. Has anybody thought of the possible effect on children and young people?

Senior newspapermen with whom I have discussed the matter suggest that the photograph was probably put there by a design consultant. Charles Moore, the Editor, almost certainly knew nothing about it. In that case I will not reprint Mr Rushton's idealised portrait of the Editor of *The Daily Telegraph* every day until the picture of the Tasmanian mass murderer is removed, as I had intended. Instead, we must think of other ways.

I do not think I have ever met a design consultant, although I have heard about them. A strange sort of consultant, one might suppose, who consults with absolutely no one. They say you can recognise them by the earrings they wear. If the worst comes to the worst, when I leave my health farm, I shall make the journey to Canary Wharf, seek the fellow out and give him a good thrashing. If he is well-mannered and apologises, I will suggest he puts a miniaturised version of the Rushton portrait of Charles Moore at the top of the column, symbolising the Idea of Editorship: wise, concerned, watchful over every little corner of a huge newspaper.*

*The photograph will not appear again.

205

Saturday, November 30, 1996

Life's rich tapestry

THE women's sub-committee of Oxford City Council, which has demanded the removal of certain Old Master paintings from the walls of Oxford town hall, demonstrates how the spirit of Peter Simple's Alderman Foodbotham lives on.

Particular exception was taken to a large picture depicting the Rape of the Sabine Women. Members asked whether it conformed to the council's equal opportunities policies, and suggested it would be offensive to women who have suffered from domestic violence.

A motion before the Labour-run council's public affairs committee asked members to consider 'the possible display of more paintings of women by women, and the possibility of commissioning works by community arts projects'.

We must not for a moment suppose that this moronic philistinism and monomania are typical of women's committees. Any of us could make this sort of mistake if we were foolish enough, or philistine enough, or sufficiently monomaniac. It is all part of life's rich tapestry.

Saturday, December 7, 1996

A taste of old Europe

WHEN I was a young man on the Peterborough column of this newspaper about 35 years ago, I conceived a great hatred for the City livery companies. Junior reporters were expected to dress up in dinner jackets (or sometimes white tie and tails) in the late afternoon to watch elderly businessmen in similar fancy dress proposing toasts to each other and acting out a charade of gracious living which had no relevance to anybody's life at that time.

It was at one such function, sitting next to a distinguished old judge (long since dead), that I learnt what judges wear under their robes. Whatever Mr Justice Hooper of the Queen's Bench division of the High Court will say on BBC2 next week, they mostly wear crotchless ladies' tights, obtainable only in one or two Soho sex shops. That is why you see so many distinguished old gentlemen queuing outside them.

Then and there I decided to go to no more City events, as representing the wrong sort of old England. However, on Wednesday, I found myself in Drapers Hall, Throgmorton Street, for a reception organised by the City wine merchants Corney and Barrow to fete Christian and Cherise Moueix, makers of Châteaux Pétrus, Trotanoy, Latour de Pomerol and half the best wines from the right bank of the Gironde.

The Drapers have an absurdly magnificent hall. Of the 80-odd guests, all the men were in dinner jacket, and many were probably businessmen. We drank '82 Trotanoy and Latour de Pomerol, '79 Pétrus. Monsieur Moueix turned out to be witty, clever, well informed, modest and unbelievably amiable, his wife a vision of loveliness. I even met some pleasant lawyers.

Elsewhere, no doubt, English and French fishermen were squabbling about fishing rights. In Drapers Hall, we celebrated the liberal, humane, bourgeois European culture which still survives, somehow, in our wretched proletarian society. Even the judges in their crotchless tights are our only protection against Mr Howard. I shall never be rude about these people again.

Say not the struggle

IS IT my imagination, or have there been fewer warnings and threats than usual this year from police and government ministers about the dangers of taking a glass of wine in the house of a friend over Christmas?

The original idea of this annual Festival of Abstinence and Immobility was that everyone should be required to stay at home and cultivate family values. In time, Christmas became an anti-police festival of fear and loathing, as everybody sat at home watching whatever sickening rubbish the authorities had decided to show us on television and a few policemen drove around or strutted threateningly out of doors, generally thought to be earning about £40 an hour in overtime.

Perhaps the Government has simply run out of money to pay police the necessary overtime. In Russia, the government has run out of money to the extent that it cannot afford to pay its soldiers, let alone its war pensioners. Only eight per cent of Russians now believe that life is worth living, while 42.6 per cent agree with the statement: 'I cannot stand this disastrous situation any longer.'

No doubt a number of British housewives and Conservative voters would agree with that last statement, but things really are much worse in Russia, as is borne out by the fact that they

have started eating each other. I always argued that the switch from a controlled or socialist economy, where nearly everybody is employed by the state, to a free economy would involve wholesale starvation or cannibalism, or both.

In a particularly distressing case reported from Manturovo, north-east of Moscow, two friends who decided to kill and eat their drinking companion found that the unaccustomed smell of cooking meat brought a crowd to the feast, including the dead man's brother.

I wonder if these poor people realise that capitalism – or at any rate the American version – now requires its workers to eat nothing but salad and drink nothing but water. Will the struggle have been worth it?

Saturday, December 14, 1996

All guns blazing

IT WAS when William Rushton asked to be excused from *Literary Review*'s monthly captions conference on December 3 that I felt the first twinge of alarm. In anyone else, it would have been inconceivable to expect an appearance between two visits to hospital and a dash north to entertain the masses, but for 10 years he had nearly always attended them.

The normal form was for one of the younger members of staff to hold a picture in front of Willie's face. There followed a stream-of-consciousness session: puns, *malentendus*, twisted quotations from Shakespeare, obscenities, clever, oblique references to popular songs and famous television advertisements which were completely unknown to me. All this was delivered in his perfect enunciation, the product of a clever, well-focused mind working at full speed. From this burble of sound the perfect caption was born.

I think he must have quite enjoyed these occasions, although it seemed strange for anyone to take so much trouble for a small magazine. He already illustrated the covers, never missing a deadline in 10 years, and always for a pittance. You could call it professionalism, although his attendance was unpaid. In fact, he needed a serious reason to miss one.

Then, just before he went into hospital last Monday, he expressed doubts about whether he would be up to illustrating today's Way of the World and did an extra drawing, which I hope to use next Monday*. Otherwise, the shock was complete. It was a rascally way to go – even if, in time, his friends will learn to be grateful that he went down with all guns blazing.

A bad time

THE days between a man's death and his funeral are not the moment to celebrate his life, to tell Willie stories and remember the good times. Eventually, as I say, we may be thankful that he decided to leave us at the height of his powers, with a suddenness which took everybody's breath away, but not yet. These days are a time of bitterness and loss, a time for anger, even, as we contemplate the cruelty and horror of death. The one comfort is to discover quite how widespread is the affection in which Willie was held.

The reason he was universally loved was not because he was so funny. In fact, there is often something disconcerting about people who are as funny as that. The real reason everybody loved him was for a basic warmth of character, a total benevolence which no amount of mocking buffoonery could ever disguise.

*See the cover of the book. This last drawing appeared on Monday, December 16, 1996, five days after William Rushton's death in hospital on December 11, 1996, after a heart operation.

I have described how he detested *The Times* newspaper, but there was no malice behind his hatreds, only amazement. His jokes and drawings could appear merciless. It is only when you study them at length that you realise how the driving force behind his work is simple enjoyment. He loved the human race, not despite its aesthetic, moral or social failings, but because of them. And the human race loved him back.